PRAISE FOR
N.A. ROSSI'S WORK

Nicola's work is highly original, macabre and very funny. I am delighted that she has developed her idea into a novel in the tradition of my father George Orwell, the author of *Nineteen Eighty-Four*, who wanted 'to make political writing into an art'.

**Richard Blair, son of George Orwell
and Patron of The Orwell Society**

It's a rollercoaster of a novel with a fabulous playlist soundtrack and a new dawn heroine. This is speculative fiction at its very best, thrilling and fearless. We can't wait to bring this fantastic set of novels to life.

**David Walton, Free@LastTV, developing the
Rockstar Ending series for television**

Rossi's dark, perceptive wit and the industry insights gleaned from her previous career in communications management make this gripping yarn an all-too-persuasive vision of the future.

Cathi Unsworth, The Idler

This is how to make a smashing debut into dystopian fiction; an authentic world building on present-day technology, an eerily plausible solution to the wealth gap, and an exploration of the disturbing moral paradoxes it creates when the public wakes up to the sinister consequences. N.A (Nicola) Rossi's first novel is a just-around-the-corner future thriller with a brain. If her predictions come true, we're all in deep trouble.

Christopher Fowler

Nicola has created a beautifully stark and brilliantly entertaining juxtaposition of the 'what ifs' about science, life, choices, euthanasia and eugenics and raises hugely important questions about who we are and where we are going.

Barry Ryan, Free@LastTV, developing the Rockstar Ending series for television

ALSO BY N.A. ROSSI

For Those About to Rock

Rockstar Ending

Rock On

ROCKAWAY

N.A. ROSSI

resista press

For everyone who has paid the price
for doing the right thing.

CHARACTERS

The Corporation – the firm delivering the Government's Endings program

    Mason, chief executive

    Ricky, Mason's chauffeur

    Tom, chief of staff

    Lola, senior IT manager

    Channelle, corporate affairs director

    Bob, IT security specialist, partner of *Lexi*

    Vini, employee in the Preston Kindness Center

    Sylvia, employee in the Corporation Robotics and Aviation Center

Charlton Green School

    Lexi, teacher and partner to *Bob*

    Ardua, head teacher

    Tyson, former pupil

Brytely – The Corporation's marketing agency

    Stella, chief executive

Portia and Sonny, Endings campaign creative team. Portia's mother is *Karen.* Sonny's sister is *Amina.*

Lars, Endings user experience developer and member of Yuthentic

Yuthentic

Jason, Party leader

Holly, Member of Parliament

Amina , student supporter, Sonny's sister

Willow, celebrity speaker

Activists

Ayesha, retired entrepreneur, Sonny and Amina's grandmother, married to *Ajay*

Jennifer , mother of Bob's school friend *Trevor,* married to *Andy*

Jess, disability rights campaigner and researcher for *Nicky Hartt MP*

Father Aloysius, priest

Henry, human rights lawyer

Fakesy, street artist

Endings escapees

Meg, whose twin adult children are *Alice* and *Adam*

Bryn, George, Mavis and *Liz*

Mabel (deceased)

CHAPTER ONE

PORTIA HAD HOPED THE FEELING of dread would lift by the time she emerged into the pale evening at North Greenwich station. There was a chill in the air. Maybe it was just the change of seasons, knowing that soon the light would be gone, and she would be spending more time in the darkness.

Her journey across town had been unsettling. As the underground train edged closer to the O2 arena, more young people had piled into the carriages and filled the air with exuberant chatter. They proudly displayed their Yuthentic credentials – badges, T-shirts, tattoos and even the odd home-made placard showing their simple sigil – the crossed circle stolen from the 'give way' sign – and their hashtag #ourtime.

How could they be so jolly, she wondered, unless they did not understand that they were promoting a death cult? The atmosphere was not what she had expected from a political rally. It felt more like they were all on their way to see their favorite band perform.

Ten years previously, almost to the day, Portia had followed the same route to see Kylie Minogue in concert at the massive 20,000-seater venue. Her mother, Karen, had arranged the trip from Liverpool as a surprise for her 16th birthday. She was only allowed to open the envelope containing the tickets after the train was south of Milton Keynes. The whole carriage had applauded when the musical greetings card started to play 'Can't Get You Out of my Head' and Portia let out an uncontrollable gasp when she saw the tickets. It turned out half of their travelling companions were on their way down to see Kylie, too.

"I thought it was the princess of pop herself on the train," one wit had piped up. "You look a bit like her, you know?" Times were more innocent then.

Portia headed for the spot outside McDonald's where she had arranged to meet Sonny. They had VIP tickets courtesy of their colleague Lars whose relationship with Yuthentic went right to the top.

"The party would like to reward the two of you for making the Endings campaign a runaway success," Lars had told them a few weeks earlier, during one of their many meetings to plan the marketing for Phase Two of the Rockstar Ending program. True to his word, he immediately followed up with their invitation to the private box.

These days Lars was spending a lot of time with his friend Holly, the Yuthentic Member of Parliament who had given him the inside track on Phase Two. His privileged information had enabled Portia and Sonny to craft a bullseye pitch for promoting the next instalment which was counting down to launch in Spring 2029. They had only six months to go.

Portia had a lot of reservations about their Endings work but designing the campaign had given her and Sonny rockstar employee status in Brytely, the agency where they worked. Her first proper job since university was playing out beyond her wildest dreams. In just three years her salary had doubled. Although her relationship with Sonny was complicated, they worked well together. Lars had christened them the dream team after the Endings campaign drove more than 10,000 old people to choose assisted suicide in its first year of operation. That meant champagne all round at the agency summer party. It was all paid for by their client, The Corporation, who had the government contract to discreetly deliver death on demand.

Even though she was a few minutes late, Portia got to their meeting point first. McDonald's had not been there when she came to see Kylie in 2018. Lots of the old familiar food places had gone. There was no message from Sonny, so she assumed he must be on his way. She was on the verge of texting when she finally spotted him walking from the direction of the car drop-off point. He must have come in an auto.

"What the hell's that?" Portia said, pointing at the gunmetal Yuthentic sigil pinned to Sonny's burgundy camouflage hoodie.

"Nice to see you, too!" he smiled pushing his sleek dark hair back from his face. "Thought I should show willing. I've got one for you as well. There's a tout selling them round the corner."

He held out a rose gold version of the pin in the palm of his hand. "Well, do you want it? I just thought we should join in. It's only a badge."

Of all the gifts he might have given her, he had to choose this.

"Let me see."

He tipped it into her hand without touching. It was warm from the heat of his body. They both knew that there was no such thing as 'only' a badge. Everything was loaded with meaning in their profession. But now was not the time to discuss semiotics.

"Hmm." Portia turned it over, unclipped the back, and pushed the pin through the delicate top she was wearing under her leather jacket. It was just about visible. The pin protruded at the back and scratched her collarbone. She would have to put up with it. "Right, shall we go in?"

As they approached the entrance, they saw a small group of protesters being moved away by security. One of them was a blonde woman whose motorized wheelchair was being carried away with her still seated on it. She was furious and shouting, "I have a right to protest, you murderous bastards!"

"Not on private property you don't," a heavily built woman in a security uniform retorted smugly as she lifted one side of the chair, her colleague taking the other. "Come on Addy, let's get her round the back."

"But they want to kill us!" The protester screamed as they took her in a side door, refusing to be silenced as the motorized wheels spun in the air. More security hemmed in the remaining handful of activists to stop them blocking the entrance to the arena.

"Stop the Endings! Our lives matter!" they chanted in ragged harmony.

"I know her," Sonny said. "The one they just carried off. She was at the HELP Select Committee."

"Yes, it's Jess, Nicky Hartt's researcher. She was in with the People Against Coercive Euthanasia lot. Looks like she still is. It seems the resistance might be stepping up a gear."

Sonny rolled his eyes. "What? Six people with disabilities chanting slogans? You can't even hear what half of them are saying. That's hardly going to make the headlines, is it? They'll have them cleared away in no time." He began to march towards the fast-track entrance. "Come on. Let's get inside."

Lars had bagged them the best seats in the house. Their box had an unrestricted view of the stage. Sonny pointed out various celebrities with Yuthie connections in the audience. He had been researching social media influencers in the planning for Phase Two – along with a parallel brand defense project designed to pre-empt and minimize resistance to the broadened proposals. They ordered some free drinks on the Yuthie app, which Sonny had also downloaded. Two chilled Rockstar cocktails arrived in a glittering robotic cube on wheels. "Well, it seemed appropriate," Sonny said as they clinked their plastic glasses. The noise they made sounded cheap.

"You seem rather taken with all this," Portia ventured, clutching her glass and eyeing the stage where a massive Yuthie hologram was rotating. The sigil was now a silvery three-dimensional globe, which started to float around the massive auditorium prompting a Mexican wave. Sonny stood and waved his arms as it rippled through their box. Portia rose awkwardly alongside him. She took a large gulp. That was going to be the only way to get through the night.

"Just immersing myself for a few hours," Sonny said, "To get the feel of it. The Yuthies are very close to our client. It's a sell-out, you know. My little sister Amina wanted to come."

"You should have given her my ticket."

"They're not transferable. Anti-touting."

"What? You mean there's a secondary market in tickets for political rallies now? How did that happen?"

"There are some interesting rumors about surprise guests. Plus, a lot of young people love what they're doing. Look how much we've benefitted for a start. Your bijou flat. I might even get one soon. They're building more, you know, on some of the decommissioned shopping center sites. I could get a unit on Oxford Street! Seriously. Bang in the heart of the West End. How brilliant is that?"

The house lights were starting to dim while the hologram sigil was spinning faster and brighter. It was so much safer and more spectacular than a real floating ball would have been. The mirage completed its final circuit skimming the heads of the mesmerized audience who seemed to be batting it around into the air. Finally, the globe bounced back onto the stage where, with a loud rumble, it exploded just like the most extraordinary firework. Trust the Yuthies to start with a bang.

As the final fragments of rainbow light floated away, a warm-up showreel began to run on the huge screen hanging at the back of the stage. To the opening bars of 'You're Gonna Go Far, Kid' by The Offspring, a welcome message faded in before giving way to a video montage showing all

Yuthentic's achievements since their first taste of power in the 2022 election.

There were stylized black and white photos of the leaders with their name, age, and a witty one liner designed to tickle the audience's dopamine levels with a wry smile. Every time an image of one of their politicians appeared, they drew a cheer. And with each consecutive picture the roar became louder. Sonny nudged Portia when Holly, Lars' new best friend, flashed on the screen, aged 26, with the caption: 'They'll never get away with it'.

In between the portraits, film clips showed the Yuthie election promises becoming a reality. There were old people living happily in the gleaming dorms that had replaced the care homes, waited on by smiling, germ-free robots, insulated from the squalid troubles that were fast becoming a distant memory. Then came Sonny's award-winning Rockstar Ending campaign. It set off a train of wolf-whistles from the audience as a smiling older woman with shapely legs stepped elegantly into the limo for her final trip. Portia nudged him with her elbow, and he reciprocated with a sideways glance. Finally, the cool graduates, free of debt, gave grateful vox pops. They looked so happy, able to start out on independent lives in their own affordable homes. A generation that had almost given up hope had been saved by Yuthentic's radical plan. And they didn't need to worry about granny either, because she, too, was getting a grand finale.

As the last Yuthie portrait faded from the screen, the place erupted. Jasper, their charismatic leader, appeared. His age was given as 28 and he was described simply as 'The Dude'. The song ended and the crowd went wild.

"Jasper, Jasper, Jasper!" they chanted.

The lights over the audience dimmed and their hero walked on stage. The cheering became deafening. Portia wondered whether she was the only person in the cavernous arena who found the level of adulation nauseating. As if he had heard her, Jasper raised his hands and signaled to the crowd to settle down. It took a minute or two for them to rein in their excitement.

"Friends," Jasper began. They roared again. He lifted his hand, nodding, "Thank you, this is very humbling."

Portia had to admit that Jasper was handsome – especially compared to the average politician. The days when politics could be described as showbusiness for ugly people were fading fast. He was muscular and trim, having rowed for his school and university, and kept up the fitness discipline that he had learned from his coaches, even though he could not get onto the water so often now he was a high-ranking political leader. Looking somewhat younger than his 28 years, his dark brown hair fell in a short skater-boy cut that framed his striking olive eyes. Although not particularly tall, he had the uncanny ability to charm that worked even on those who were determined not to like him.

"We've had something of a year, haven't we?" he began. The audience gave another pulse of approval. "The best so far, mate!" someone from the front shouted. Jasper raised his eyebrows and gazed warmly around the massive space before breaking into a grin in the direction of the fan and showing his approval with the devil's horns hand signal.

"He thinks he's so frigging rock'n'roll," Portia muttered.

"And I'd like to say a special hello to those of you who couldn't get a ticket to Yuthfest '28 watching on the live stream." He looked directly at one of the cameras trained on the stage. "Thank you for tuning in today. It means a lot to me.

"As you know, I'm not one for long speeches. I'm going to keep it brief. You already know how much we've done to improve the lives of people in our country. And I don't just mean the young people – although of course it was us, the youth, who came up with the brilliant ideas that have revitalized our nation. No surprises there. Who else was going to do it? We're the party behind the party."

A whoop of approval ran through the arena. Jasper knew exactly how long to wait before continuing.

"The happiness index has never been higher. Across all demographics. Our nation is officially the happiest it has been for decades." Another cheer rippled around the hall.

"And it's all down to you. To everyone in this room who's shared our ideas. Who's knocked on doors. Who's shared our memes on Splutter. Who's convinced their friends, colleagues, and family that Yuthentic stands for a fairer future, a more equal society, choice and freedom. Not just for young people, but for everybody.

"But we can't afford to be complacent. We're only two years away from the next general election. If we are to sustain our program of investment, we will have to make some tough decisions.

"Let me tell you, we're not afraid of making those decisions. We're not afraid, because choice is at the heart of everything we Yuthies stand for." He paused, looking into the camera that carried his face onto the internet and projected it onto the huge screen behind him.

"Choosing to die? You're murderers!" a lone voice interrupted from the standing area by the stage. Before anyone realized what was happening someone else yelled "Stop the Endings, stop the Endings!"

"It's coercion!" shouted another.

By now, Jasper and the rest of the crowd had worked out what was going on. A tsunami of angry counterargument soon drowned out the sound of the protesters. Security waded in, grabbed the infiltrators, and carried them swiftly away to the exits. They were enthusiastically jeered and abused by the people surrounding them as they passed.

On the stage, Jasper raised his hands to calm the indignant crowd. "You know, my friends, I'm glad that happened.

"I'm glad that happened because we all need to know what we're up against. It's easy to surround ourselves with people who agree with us. But there are still thousands out there who don't see things the way we do. Not yet. And that's all the more reason to keep pushing forward our progressive agenda.

"And that progressive agenda is evolving, thanks to those of you who have taken part in our research program, to make sure that we reflect your priorities in whatever happens next.

"Some of it won't surprise you. More of the same courageous initiatives we have already delivered to help rebalance society. Better housing. Free higher education.

But there was something new. There's another opportunity. Something else you have told us that you don't think is fair. And it's a matter of life and death."

He paused for effect. This time the vast arena was perfectly silent.

"And you have come up with a brilliant idea. A way to build a country that is even happier. What you're telling me, is that we should open up our world-leading Endings provision. That the right to live – and the right to die – should be seen as a basic human right. It makes perfect sense, doesn't it? It's the most important choice of all.

"And what you've said, is that it should not just be the old who get the privilege of a dignified death. I speak for the entire Yuthentic Executive when I say that we have been deeply touched by your incredible compassion. We've been listening very carefully. And you've convinced us. So, I'm pleased to announce today that choice – the ultimate choice – may soon be extended to a few more sections of society."

A gasp filled the auditorium, followed by weak applause. Maybe he hasn't judged this one so well, Portia thought.

"Now, I'd like to welcome to the stage a very brave young person who has been spearheading the campaign for just that right. Join me in welcoming Willow..."

As they played 'Wannabe' by The Spice Girls, a petite woman with long blond hair, wearing dark blue jeans and a white tailored jacket walked onto the stage where she was warmly embraced by Jasper. Portia recognized Willow as one of the top 100 Splutter influencers. There was a murmur of approval and the applause seemed to get stronger again. It filled the arena.

"You wouldn't think there was anything wrong with me, would you?" she began, "But just because you can't see my pain, it doesn't mean it's not real."

The crowd was hushed as Willow told how her two older sisters and her mother, who all suffered from a painful degenerative illness, had ended their lives to avoid prolonged agony.

Whereas their mother had been able to book a Rockstar Ending, and leave the world in comfort, her sisters were too young to qualify for the service. It was only available to the over 70s. The suicide methods her siblings had used had left the rest of the family distraught.

Recently diagnosed with the same medical condition, Willow was now campaigning for humane assisted dying to be available to younger people so that she could die with dignity when her own time came.

It was a harrowing account, and Portia could not take any more. She turned to Sonny and whispered, "I've heard enough of this. Can we please go somewhere else for a drink? If I don't get out of here soon, I'll be the next one to get carted off by the heavy squad."

Sonny knew how anxious Portia felt about Phase Two. Until Jasper had spoken, it had seemed like an abstract creative concept they were working on back at their trendy offices. But now he had announced to the world the Yuthies' intention to further democratize death it had become glaringly real. Phase Two was on course to be rolled out within six months.

"We passed a bar on the way in," he said.

"My round." Portia slowly tipped onto her feet and stretched her legs. "Come on."

CHAPTER TWO

"Is this really what all the fuss is about?" Lexi gazed across a vast rust-colored beach that stretched far into the distance. Under the bright blue sky, she thought she could discern a flat ribbon of green-grey sea just below the horizon, although it could have been a mirage. A curved slither of water snaked in a channel across the damp expanse, feeding the steely pool that lapped rhythmically in the dark shadow way below their feet. They were at the end of Southport pier.

"I told you the sea went out a long way out," Bob said.

"I know, but I was under the crazy misapprehension that I might actually be able to see it." On Lexi's first visit to Southport, the town where her partner Bob had grown up, she was struggling to find something positive to say.

"You can. It's down there, look! You can see it through the gaps in the boards."

"That's not the sea! It's a puddle!" When she saw the disappointment flicker across Bob's face, Lexi immediately wished she had been kinder. He had fond memories of his childhood here, in this odd bleak place.

"It's pleasingly bracing, though, the sea breeze," she quickly added. "And you're right – it will be a great place for my run tomorrow morning. Not a hill in sight!"

"Actually, there are the sandhills," Bob said gesturing back inland to the south. "You can't see them properly from here. But they'll be heavy under foot, and spikey with Marram grass."

"What about the statues? Where are they?"

"Even further that way. Towards Liverpool."

She knew about the hundred humanoid Antony Gormley statues because their pictures were printed on the labels of a trendy bottled beer named after the installation, Another Place. Bob told anyone he saw drinking it the story behind the haunting branding, bursting with vicarious pride that the figures were sited just a few miles from where he grew up. As she gazed into the expanse that surrounded them, Lexi sensed a melancholy in Bob she had never seen anywhere else.

"You miss them, don't you?" she said, quietly.

"Mum and Dad? Yes. When I'm in London I don't think about them very much. But when I'm here, of course I do." He looked out into the distance. "So much of what I used to love about this place has faded away. You've nothing to worry about, Lex. Moving back wouldn't help. I missed Southport's real heyday. My parents had an amazing time here. Even when I was a teenager it felt more alive than it does now."

Lexi did not want Bob to feel down. It was supposed to be a mini break after all, a bit of fun before they both went back to work. "The hotel's lovely," she ventured. They had dropped off their bags in their cozy, dark-walled room before heading out for a walk. Trying to make Lexi feel special, Bob had booked the town's most exclusive place to stay, paying extra for a window that overlooked Lord Street, once the pinnacle of sophistication, with its faded Victorian colonnades. "It's got a funny name, though. I mean, who would call a hotel Boney's? What's that about?"

"The boulevards of Paris were modelled on Southport, you know," Bob's face brightened a little.

"Surely it must have been the other way round?"

"No. Napoleon III stopped here. You can check the dates. Didn't you see his bust in reception?"

"The one with the goatee? I thought it was Charles Dickens."

Bob was clearly uncomfortable in such a fancy establishment, where the clientele was generally younger, slimmer and more fashionably dressed than either of them. That didn't stop the staff making an effort to help them feel at home.

He sighed. "They're better off where they are now."

"You mean your parents? You can say that again."

Right now, she would prefer to be visiting Bob's parents in their retirement community in Thailand. In Southport, even though it was summer, it was twenty degrees cooler than Koh Samui, the beach left a lot to be desired, and there was no sign of a green chicken curry. How Bob was warm enough in just a T-shirt and fleece she had no idea.

Their trip had been arranged at the last minute, when Bob found out he would be taking up a new assignment on the same day that Lexi would start the school year.

They had stayed close to home over the summer. Lexi had been struggling with her mental health. There was no formal diagnosis, but Bob feared she had developed PTSD. His gentle efforts to persuade her to think about herself for once, rather than focusing on her newfound activism, had failed. He thought it was a positive sign, however, when she agreed to the break. Maybe getting her away from London would help her to get things in perspective.

Although the town was a little tatty, some attractions were open. In any case, Lexi was curious to meet one of Bob's old school friends who still lived there. Ever since he had popped back on a flying visit the summer before, Bob had been quietly worrying about Trev and his dad, Andy, who was ill and in a fragile state.

"That's Blackpool Tower, isn't it?" she said, looking northwest across the Ribble estuary, "Over there?"

"It's a clear day, but it's not clear enough to see Paris," Bob quipped.

"You're getting into the pantomime humor, then. Have you ever been up it?"

"Ooh, Missus! Of course I have! All the way! If you think it's windy now, this is nothing like up there! Mum and Dad used to take me to the Tower Circus. Their clown, Charlie Cairoli was legendary. And his sidekick Paul, the whiteface Pierrot. You know, I've often wondered whether Bowie ever came here as a child."

Lexi had come to expect a David Bowie reference from Bob at least every other day. However, this one seemed far-fetched, even for him.

"It's a long way from Brixton, Bob. What made you say that? I mean, why would he?"

"Bowie's clown in 'Ashes to Ashes'…well, he was a bit like Paul."

Lexi shrugged. It was pointless to argue. There was nothing the man wouldn't credit to his idol.

"Why don't we go over there? It's less than an hour away." Bob said.

"To Blackpool?" What fresh horror was this? She had been looking forward to a quiet evening in followed by an early night, ever since she had spotted Morecambe Bay potted shrimps on the hotel's dinner menu.

"The lights are on – Blackpool Illuminations. They had the big switch on last night. Did I tell you The Corporation have sponsored them this year?"

Lexi turned away. It was difficult for her to reconcile herself to Bob being enthusiastic about his employers when they both knew what The Corporation had done. He carried on.

"The Corporation does loads of community investment. They're not all bad, you know. Blackpool comes under their Northern Outreach Board (NOB). Regeneration. Reducing the North/South divide. Levelling up. A bit like you and me!"

She didn't react.

"No community left behind. Anyway, Blackpool has got a ton of their NOB money. Can you see that big building, over on the right?"

She squinted seaward. "The one in the shape of a wave?"

"You've got it. That's the new conference center. We, I mean The Corporation, built that as well. I've got some discount codes somewhere…" On a mission to over-ride

Lexi's reticence, Bob had already pulled out his phone and started scrolling.

When Lexi finally said, "I'm really not sure, Bob," he pretended not to hear. All she could imagine was trailing up and down a shabby, windswept promenade in the dark. She said it again.

"Oh, come on Lexi. It'll be fun!" He was not going to give up.

While Bob absorbed himself in research, Lexi turned back to face the land and looked down the pier. There must have been fifty or so people scattered along its length, mainly older folks in comfortable slacks and lightweight jackets, some with small backpacks, and with the occasional family pushing someone in a wheelchair. Everything moved in slow motion.

She had faced back to look at the sea when she heard a faint buzzing noise. It was like the motor for a small boat, but the open water was too far off. Turning round slowly, Lexi cast her eye to work out where the annoying sound was coming from.

Then she saw it. A small, sturdy drone zooming over the sand on a straight trajectory parallel with the deck of the pier. It was coming towards the furthest point, where the two of them stood being gently buffeted by the wind.

"Oh, for goodness' sake," she grumbled, "Those bloody things are everywhere."

Bob glanced up. "What?"

"The drone. Look. Crikey, it's getting a bit close for comfort."

Bob put his arm round Lexi's shoulder as the machine rose above their heads and paused facing them from a vantage point at the other side of the railing that encircled the structure. She snuggled into his comfortable body. "It's creeping me out," she said, reluctant to turn away in case it made a more threatening move.

"Looks like it's programmed not to cross the threshold of the pier," Bob observed matter-of-factly.

There was a rattle. Lexi jumped.

"Calm down! It won't come any closer, and it's not going to be armed, is it? This is hardly a combat zone." Bob whispered.

A lightweight banner dropped from a slender roller at the base of the drone. There was a cascade of flimsy indigo fabric, the height of a tall person, which unfurled and rippled a little in the breeze. It was printed with the message:

VISIT BLACKPOOL
AND LIGHT UP YOUR LIFE

To the side of the text there was a picture of an illuminated Blackpool Tower, in the style of a vintage tourism poster.

"In other circumstances that would be quite pretty. Please don't tell me the arrival of this pest is a coincidence." Lexi flapped her hand over the railing as if to shoo it away, but the little Unmanned Aerial Vehicle (UAV) just hung there, out of reach, taunting her with its soft whirring as the banner rippled below. She squeezed in a little closer to Bob, knowing that she trusted his judgment on all things technological. He had been reading up on drones recently for the new job.

Still, she was keen to get away from the damned thing. "Can we go inside? I don't want to come back out until it's gone."

The prism-shaped glass pavilion at the end of the pier housed a small amusement arcade and a café selling drinks and snacks. You could buy old coins to operate the vintage machines, sterilized between uses. Smells of metal, disinfectant and coffee came in clashing waves as they walked around jangling small amounts of change in their hands. All around them, a series of electronic noises competed for their attention. Periodically the taped sound of copper tinkling against steel suggested that a jackpot could be within easy reach, even though they never actually saw a machine pay out more than a couple of pennies.

They fed a few coins into slots to kill time. Lexi kept glancing through the glass wall that fronted onto the beach, looking South, only to discover the drone was still stalking them.

"Oh, buzz off!" she said louder that she had planned, her frustration growing.

"They're annoying aren't they, love?" A woman who was wiping down the machines with spray disinfectant had overheard her. "Don't worry, they don't hang around for too long."

Her badge said 'Karen, here to help'. Her shoulder length blond hair was blow dried into a flattering style and her khaki green overall was a perfect fit. She had flawless nails and makeup. Lexi thought she looked way too smart for a job in an amusement arcade. Karen's Scouse accent suggested she lived towards the south of the town – or further out. Bob had explained that there were two distinct accents that converged in Southport, Liverpool at one end and Lancashire at the other.

"She's right. It'll go soon," Bob caught Karen's eye, and smiled. "There'll soon be someone else in the area for it to torment."

"I just need to ignore it." Lexi screwed her eyes shut for a few seconds, then span round, irritated, and turned her back to the window. When she spotted the pinball machines everything changed. Three vintage tables stood side by side, each with its own theme: Guns 'n' Roses, The Ramones and The Who's Tommy.

"Whoa," she said. "What change do we need for these babies?"

Karen helped them work it out, gave the tables a quick spray and left them to it. Without wasting a second Lexi was in position. The Who's 'Pinball Wizard' began to play as she shot the first ball around the table inspired by their rock musical, Tommy. Bob started the Guns 'n' Roses 'Not In This Lifetime' game but had used up all his shots in no time. At least he got it to play 'Sweet Child O' Mine'. He watched Lexi as she frantically hit the flippers to keep her ball in play, her score rising with each move. She was in her element and oblivious to everything else around them. This was a side to Lexi that Bob had never seen before. He would never have guessed.

"I'm out of practice," she said when the final ball disappeared down the hole. "Now, let's try this one." She moved to The Ramones table, "How many more tokens have we got?"

While Lexi played on, Bob wandered back to the window and stood facing the drone. It was still there, taunting him with its banner. There was only one way to make it go away.

"OK, you win," he said, swiping to buy the cheapest tickets he could find to enter the Tower complex. A few seconds after he made the purchase the drone had gone. "Good riddance," he murmured to himself before trotting back to see how Lexi was doing.

Karen was cheering Lexi on while giving Guns 'n' Roses a polish. The two women were of similar build, their hair the same length – though Lexi's was brown and ruffled by the wind. "It's a collectors' item," Karen confided to Bob above the rattling of the flippers. When Lexi's final ball tumbled into the depths, all three of them let out a yell of disappointment as the machine blurted the bars from the chorus of 'Glad to See You Go'.

"I'll tell you what," Karen said, "How about a couple of free replays?" With a mischievous wink, she took a bunch of keys out of her pocket and unlocked the front, reaching inside to adjust something. It immediately sprang back into life, retaining the points Lexi had already scored and inviting her to play on.

"There you go," Karen said. "Enjoy! I'm normally at one of the arcades in Liverpool. We don't have any pinball there. Or any windows, either. This place is sound."

"Wow!" Lexi glanced up for a split second to say thank you before becoming transfixed, once more, by the gameplay.

By the time she had used up all her free credit, Lexi had managed to produce tinny renditions of 'Suzy Is a Headbanger' and, with her highest score, 'Rockaway Beach'. She had no idea what she was listening to, but

Bob could not help enlightening her.

"How do you know about all this stuff?" Lexi said. "I mean, I know you are obsessed with The Thin White Duke, but – this lot as well?"

"Mum and Dad saw The Ramones live, you know," he said. "In Liverpool. They're in the collection." When Bob had moved into Lexi's house, he had brought with him hundreds of vinyl records that his parents had left for safekeeping when they moved abroad. He pointed out the individual band members whose faces had been drawn onto the illuminated cabinet display.

"At Eric's?" she asked. He had talked about that club before, a punk haven which stood opposite the place where, a decade previously, The Cavern had showcased The Beatles.

"Funnily enough, no. Romeo and Juliet's. It was a pretty unlikely venue for them. At the top of a shopping center. They played very fast, apparently."

"Yeah?" Lexi was zoning out. "Has our little friend gone yet?" She glanced over to the window.

"I am pleased to inform you that the coast is clear."

"What a relief. Can we go back to the hotel now?"

Bob nodded. As they wandered back towards the open air, Lexi was turning over in her hand their last remaining vintage coins. They predated the pinball slots.

"Look at this, Bob!" Lexi pointed to a Zorro machine, a glass cabinet containing an unsophisticated, creepy animatronic torso, dressed in what someone in the previous century thought a fortune-telling gypsy should wear. It was hideous. "Let's dump the last of our change in here."

She fed the coins in the slot and instantly regretted it. Lights feebly blinked on and off and a scrap of paper was extruded from a slot at the front. It said:

One life. Live it.

"Well, thank you for that." Lexi said. handing the motto to Bob to read. "Now tell me something I don't already know."

CHAPTER THREE

"CAN'T YOU SEE HOW CREEPY this thing is?" Portia said quietly as she handed Sonny a bottle of Another Place beer, leaving her own on the bar. She rubbed her hand on her jeans to get rid of the condensation from the cold glass.

"Kind of." He raised his eyebrows. "But it's where the power is. And the Yuthies are gaining popularity all the time. Even old people are voting for them now."

"I don't see many of them here. Do you? You'll be telling me they are bringing the generations together next!"

"Relax Porsh." Sonny touched her shoulder. She drew back sharply. "Come on. This is all about understanding what drives our client. You've got to get your head into work mode."

"First they came for the grannies, and I did not speak out because I wasn't a granny." Portia sighed and looked around the Indigo, another venue in the O2 complex reserved exclusively for Yuthfest. They had only been able to get in by flashing their VIP passes.

She fidgeted with the plastic wristband they had been given to guarantee access to all areas. It was printed with the words 'Freedom. Choice. Independence'. In any other circumstances she would have been happy to be associated with the language of liberation, but the ideals had fallen into the wrong hands. The place was almost empty. The Yuthie leaders, who would be hosting the afterparty, were still playing to the crowd over in the main arena. She and Sonny had been bickering ever since they left their box.

He took a sharp intake of breath. "Give it a rest, Portia! You're getting everything out of proportion. I know 10,000 sounds like a lot of deaths but compared to the numbers that would be passing away anyway, it's not all that many."

"They're people, not numbers."

"Who knew? Yes. They are people making a free choice that lots of other demographics would like the chance to make."

Portia folder her arms across her chest. She pressed her lips together.

"Look, if you want to go home, Porsh, get out now before the others arrive. You can't be like this in front of the Yuthies. If you want to leave, I'll cover for you. But I refuse to fuck this up. We're in the inner circle here. It's gold dust for growing the account."

Before she could formulate a response, Portia saw someone familiar arriving at the entrance. There was no way out now. The woman was picking up a cocktail from a lithe humanoid robot that did a gyroscopic dance while, at the same time, keeping the tray perfectly level. She snatched the glass, clearly irritated by the palaver.

"Look, it's Stella! I didn't know she was coming?" Portia said. "She's seen us. I think I've missed my departure window."

"Best behavior," Sonny whispered, scarcely moving his lips. "Come on, you got this!"

Portia and Sonny switched on their best smiles and walked towards their boss, Brytely's chief executive. Stella had chosen a more casual look than usual, a shiny, navy satin jacket decorated with a large Yuthie diamante brooch, dark jeans and towering patent ankle boots.

"What have I missed?" were Stella's first words.

"They put on a great show," Sonny told her. "That Jasper's very charismatic. I mean, like, wow!"

"Now tell me something I don't know." Stella scanned the room just in case she could spot someone more important to talk to.

Portia carried on, ignoring Stella's indifference. "They've publicly committed to Phase Two. Well, pretty much."

"Hmm. Excellent! So, all systems are go. Anything else I should be aware of? Any negatives we need to counter?"

Someone needed to tell Stella about the crowd's mixed response to the news about Phase Two, but Portia did not trust herself to sound dispassionate. She nodded at Sonny, "Why don't you…"

He was happy to oblige. "I don't see any mainstream reporting of it, but there were a couple of scuffles with some protesters. Nothing serious."

"Oh, please! Not the fancy-dress brigade again?" Stella had been dismissive of a previous protest in which activists had momentarily dominated the headlines. Their chilling piece of street theatre outside a Corporation Disposal Center, with the added attraction of a guerrilla mural from globally renowned street artist Fakesy, had caused their client some problems. Catastrophic PR had only been averted when a quick-thinking employee had diverted that morning's cohort of euthanasia candidates to another location.

"I don't think so. They were only people with disabilities. Security got them out. No one was injured or anything," Sonny explained dismissively.

"Well, not as far as we know," Portia felt compelled to add.

"What do you mean, Portia?" Much though Stella hated being presented with bad news, she would rather hear it from one of her own team than be wrong-footed by a client.

"Well, we don't actually know if anyone was hurt or not. We haven't asked, have we Sonny?"

He pulled a dismissive face. "And if they were, who would care?"

"Let's not go there," Stella said. "If Jasper's as smart as they say he is, I am confident it will all have been handled discreetly."

The pulsating music that was playing in the background was slowly getting louder as the club began to fill up. Rank and file Yuthentic members from every demographic group – well, under 30 at least – swarmed in sycophantic huddles around the members of the executive who were now meeting and greeting. Sonny's phone rang.

"It's Lars. I need to take this," he said.

While Sonny chatted on the phone a few steps away, Portia cast around for something career-enhancing to say to Stella.

"I like your jacket," she ventured. They had bonded over clothes once before. Stella had been hugely impressed by Portia's Kylie look at the agency summer party. That bright, clear evening on a superyacht was a world away from this lackluster nightspot.

"Harvey Nicks," Stella spoke half-heartedly, looking over Portia's shoulder for a few seconds before slipping her device out of her pocket and starting to scroll. Portia abandoned the idea of trying to talk and decided to mirror her boss instead. It was less stressful. She scanned numerous news channels, hoping that the protesters had been noticed. There was nothing.

"So, ladies," Sonny said, slipping his phone back into his pocket. "If I could interrupt for a second? Lars has got us in to see the big man!"

When Lars had said, earlier in the week, he might be able to swing a meeting with Jasper, neither she nor Sonny had believed he would pull it off. That explained why Stella had turned up.

"What? All of us?" Portia asked.

"Yep. He wants to thank Brytely – and I quote, according to Lars – for their 'drop dead gorgeous' Rockstar Ending campaign. They are waiting for us right now. Come on! We need to get up to the balcony."

Stella had met Jasper once before, when she had been invited to an exclusive party in a Chinook helicopter. Her invitation had come courtesy of Mason, the chief executive of The Corporation. He had treated a handful of his most important contacts to an unforgettable New Year's Eve experience. They had hovered over London watching The Corporation's midnight drone display from a unique, if rather noisy, viewing platform.

"Stand by to be charisma-bombed," she whispered, as they reached an area that overlooked the main floor, cordoned off with rope.

Behind the impromptu barrier was a circular table that snugly fitted six chairs. Jasper was on his feet waiting to greet them, although he appeared slightly taken aback when Stella lunged at him with a couple of inaccurately targeted air kisses.

"Don't worry you creep, our jabs are all up to date," Portia wanted to say.

Instead, she held out a hand and smiled directly into Jasper's face. He wore a subtle grey eyeliner, and his hair was cut to just the right length to give him a tousled look while allowing his penetrating eyes to shine through. "I'm Portia," she said in her most neutral accent. "Pleased to meet you." He held her hand for just long enough to suggest he might not want to let go, before going on to welcome Sonny.

Lars lurked behind Jasper, smugger than ever, wearing a T-shirt from his Slayer collection, as always. His straggly black hair tucked behind his ears. Stella gave him a little wave. He nodded at his colleagues before introducing Holly, his close friend and a Yuthentic Member of Parliament.

Holly's heavy-handed questioning at the Heath, Euthanasia and Legacy Planning (HELP) Select Committee, where the Rockstar Endings program had been subject to intense scrutiny, had not endeared her to the Brytely crew, but they knew that they needed her on their side. She looked the same as she had on Parliament TV, with her wild red hair, black trousers and a black silk shirt flowing over the top to cover her full physique.

Next to her, Jasper looked exceptionally well-sculpted. Fat friend, Portia thought to herself, oldest trick in the book. And freak friend, too, if you count Lars.

Jasper indicated that they should all take a seat. "Thank you, Stella, Sonny, Portia for stopping by today. You beautiful people must all have competing demands for your time at the weekend. So, I am especially grateful for you dropping in on our little show.

"There are two things I want to say. The first one is thank you. When we committed to fulfilling the potential of the 2020 Euthanasia Act, frankly, we knew it was a gamble. Dicing with death. Well, we pulled it off! You, us, and our fearless delivery partners The Corporation. It is only as a result of your – shall we say 'sweetening the pill' – that we are now in a position to move on to Phase Two. So, thank you, my friends.

"Secondly, I want to listen. The success of Yuthentic has been built on listening. Here is your chance to air any issues you may have, to talk about any stumbling blocks that might get in our way over the coming months. There is no doubt that Phase Two will be a bumpier ride. Helping people over 70 to die, well, it's a no-brainer, isn't it? We learned that from COVID. People are less sentimental about mortality when the person sadly dying is – shall we say – already much nearer their end than their beginning.

"This next phase is going to be different. Wider access could be more sensitive. And I wanted you to know that I appreciate your agency taking this reputational risk with us. We don't want to lose the gains we have already in getting our ideas...what's the word I'm looking for... normalized, yes. Is that clear?"

"Absolutely Jasper, we're with you 100 per cent of the way," Stella gushed enthusiastically.

He could have said anything, Portia thought. and her response would have been the same. He can see right through her.

"That's reassuring, Stella." Jasper smirked. "Now any questions? Portia? Sonny? Lars has told us all about you. Quite the stars."

Sonny shook his head, graciously, "It's all clear boss," he said.

"Erm...I have a question, if that's all right?" Portia was determined to sound confident. Sonny had frozen into a studied neutral expression by her side. He was trying to seem unconcerned. Stella looked surprised that she might have something to say but nodded her to go ahead.

"Please, tell me what's on your mind, Portia." Jasper fixed her with a penetrating gaze.

She felt a flush of adrenaline and cleared her throat.

"I was wondering if, well, you had any thoughts about the protesters. You handled the interruption today brilliantly, by the way, but do you have any guidance on how you might want us to pre-empt any such problems in future. When you have to bring in the heavies the optics are never very good. And I was wondering whether you, yourself, actually have any reservations about what we might be starting here? Like, erm... morally."

Portia could feel her colleagues distancing themselves from her. Their silence was almost palpable. But someone had to ask, didn't they?

"Those are intriguing questions, Portia," Jasper said, glancing sideways at his fellow Yuthies. Lars and Holly were staring incredulously, but the party leader remained calm. "Let me deal with the bigger issue first. The most determined advocates for extending our world-leading Endings work are its potential beneficiaries. People who choose to take the ultimate autonomous action, in a civilized and dignified manner. Like our friend Willow, for instance."

Lars was now nodding furiously in agreement. Portia looked blank.

"Willow," Jasper looked surprised she had not recognized the name, "Who spoke today. People like her. Surely their arguments stand up for themselves?"

"I wasn't sure how to take it." The last thing Portia wanted was for Jasper to realize that she and Sonny had skipped off to the bar before Willow had finished speaking. "Maybe we could take a recording of what she said to some focus groups?" she suggested, feeling for a graceful way out.

"Excellent idea. But do you have a view? What is your emotional response to such a moving story?"

"It's hard to put into words…" Portia ventured.

"Seriously?" Jasper's tone was becoming sharp. "For the creative genius behind one of the best marketing campaigns of the decade? I can't believe that." Jasper said. "How could you fail to be convinced?"

"Absolutely!" Lars snorted.

Stella, realizing something wasn't right, stepped in. "Jasper, darling, whatever Willow said it would have been impossible for her to be as memorable as you."

There was an awkward silence.

"Well, you don't need to worry your pretty little head about the protesters," Jasper continued, now bored of Portia's halting excuses. "They have been dealt with. The matter is closed."

The arrival of Jasper's next appointment saved them from further embarrassment.

"We should never have walked out, you know," Sonny said as soon as he and Portia were alone again. "That was a really bad decision. I should never have let you talk me into it. The dude had given us the best seats in the house. No wonder he was pissed off."

Portia was unrepentant. "And what kind of show was that supposed to be, exactly? Suddenly we're all obliged to watch some poor soul who has been manipulated into having suicidal thoughts giving a talk on why they think it's all such a great idea. Whatever happened to trigger warnings?"

"And while we're at it," Sonny went on, "I learned when I was on secondment at The Corporation that sociopathic leaders don't mean it when they ask for honest feedback. Surely you knew that?"

"Is there anything else you'd like to explain to me?" She snapped, although she was more annoyed with herself than she was with Sonny. He was right, she could have handled the situation better. "I can't stand it here any longer. I've got some thinking to do. Say goodbye to Lars for me, will you?"

"Don't be like that. Come on, have another drink."

"No. I'll see you on Monday."

Portia was relieved to escape the claustrophobic darkness of the club. She emerged blinking into the bright indoor mall that encircled the O2 arena. Her eyes gradually stopped smarting as they adjusted to the synthetic light.

She passed rows of overflowing chain restaurants and bars as she walked briskly to the main entrance. What the hell was she doing here? She believed she heard the Radiohead song 'Creep' playing, and then wondered whether she had just imagined it. They're making me lose my sanity, she thought, picking up her pace to get out into the air.

There was a long queue for the official merchandise shop. She was glad she had not paid for anything that evening. While she might be working for them, indirectly, she drew the line at giving the Yuthies any of her own hard-earned cash.

As Portia crossed the wide pavement, she felt her device buzz. She was annoyed at herself for hoping it might be Sonny. Maybe he had decided to leave, too, and wanted to meet her for a drink. She could certainly do with one. The message was puzzling at first:

"Appreciate your frankness, Portia. Rare quality. Hope we meet again, feisty one. J"

So much for Sonny's assertion that sociopaths didn't want honest feedback. Nevertheless, she would not contemplate meeting the leader of a death cult for a drink, or anything else for that matter. She gave a silent huff. Portia must have been the only person in the vicinity who would turn Jasper down. Without a second thought, she deleted the message and the contact number knowing that if she spoke to him, she could not trust herself to keep things civilized.

The train back to her tiny apartment was heaving with Yuthies again. They all seemed so happy and excited. It just made her feel worse. She tried moving down the train, but every carriage was filled with optimistic chatter about what a great day it had been punctuated with speculation about Jasper's relationship status. His charisma was undeniable, and he had scored a direct hit with his promise of freedom, choice and independence to a generation which, until Yuthentic arrived, felt trapped and forgotten.

It all sounded so reasonable, so why didn't she like what was going on? Maybe Sonny was right. Maybe she was just having a bad day.

Portia flicked on the screen in her tiny living room and perched on the edge of her cheap foam sofa. After the hubbub of the train, she felt lonely. She could have been at a club having free drinks and chatting to Sonny. But she had stormed off and left him in preference for a night in on her own in the world's smallest flat. What was wrong with her?

All she had wanted was a job that paid the rent. Brytely gave her that and more. They had even pulled some strings to find her this bijou place to live. Her bottle of champagne from the work summer party was still on the shelf under the TV, gathering dust, with the thankyou card propped up against it. She had wanted to give it to her mother, Karen, but they did not see each other very often. The longer she was in this city, the more she missed her family's unconditional love.

There was only one thing for it. Her mum was the sole person who might be able to lift her out of this pity party.

"Hiya our kid," Karen said. "How are you doing?"

"Oh, OK. Where are you?" She could hear a low, rhythmic clatter in the background.

"I'm not bad love. Sorry about the noise. I'm on the train."

"What? Have you had a day out with the kids?"

"I wish. No. They've shut the arcade for a few weeks. Too many gambling addicts in the area. It's having a negative impact on the borough's position in the State Happiness Index Table. Not that it was that good to begin with. Anyway, they've closed us down for a cooling off period while they work on getting the poor sods in check. Marcus has been allocated to an outreach program and I've been redeployed to an amusement arcade in Southport until we reopen."

"That's a long way to travel." She worried about her mum alone on that train, at night.

"It's only an hour. Manageable provided the Merseyrail keeps running. And so far, so good. Bernie next door is helping out with the kids. I don't know what we'd do without her. Honest to God. Anyway, how's things with you?"

"Same really. I thought about you tonight. I had to go to a work thing at the O2. Remember when you took me to see Kylie? That was such a brilliant day out, Mum."

"It was great fun. So, who was on tonight then?"

"Nothing special. Just had to go to a client meeting."

"Sounds a much better job than doling out change for vintage penny arcades, which is what I've been doing all day. Was that boy there?" She had told her mother about Sonny when she had come to stay six months previously.

"Yeah."

"How's that going?"

"I really don't know how I feel about him. Sometimes I think it would be worth it, other times he just drives me mad. A bit like the job, to be honest."

The train went under a bridge and the background noise surged for a few moments. Portia waited for her mum to get clear of the din. "I thought you were doing really well at work?"

"Yes, we are. I mean, I am. It's just there are some things about what I have to do that I'm not sure about."

"What sort of things?"

"Like, ethical things."

Her mother laughed softly. "Welcome to my world, love!"

"What do you mean?"

"Do you think I like working in an arcade? Some of the things I see. The problems. People making a right mess of their lives. It's shocking. Really brings you down sometimes."

Portia knew Karen's employer had paid for private medical treatment for depression, but she had assumed her problems were down to the pressures of being a mum trying to make ends meet rather than her having existential doubts about working in the gambling industry. How could she not have realized?

"Does it bother you that much, Mum?"

"Of course it does! Seeing misery every day and pretending it's all just a game? But there's nothing else for me round here. Even the care work's being done by robots now."

"What about your dressmaking? You could do that."

"It's fine for now, really."

"But that dress you made for me, for the summer party, it was beautiful. So many people commented."

"It was only as beautiful as the young woman wearing it. Like I said, the arcade suits me for the time being. We just need to wait a few weeks for everything to get back to normal."

"How do you cope with it, Mum?"

"I need the money. Three little kids to support. I've tried going on benefits but it's more depressing than working in Winners, believe me."

Portia was silent. She had known her mum for a quarter of a century, and yet had not known her at all.

"Look, if you're feeling low why don't you come home to Liverpool for a weekend? You could meet me in Southport on a day I'm on an early shift, bring the kids over, make a day of it?"

"I'd love to, but things are going mad in the office. I don't think I can take the time off. There's a massive launch coming up, and I'm sure I'll end up working weekends again."

"How about if I come down there? It was a laugh last time, wasn't it? I don't even mind if you need to pop into the office. At least we could have dinner together, maybe more if we're lucky. What do you think?"

Portia glanced at her shelf again. Next to the bottle of champagne was the little 3D-printed statue from the 'Pete Burns – Freak or Fashion Icon?' exhibition she had been to with Karen.

"I would love that."

"OK. I'll work out some dates and send them over."

"That would be amazing. We had such a brilliant time."

"Good. I'll be down before Christmas. You hang on in there, pet. You're a clever girl, but you've got to understand. People like us, we just have to do what it takes to survive. I don't know what you're worried about. You've got a good life down there. Don't be too precious. Principles are all very well, for those who can afford them."

CHAPTER FOUR

L EXI WAS FLICKING THROUGH A room service menu on the wall screen. She had kicked off her shoes and lay, half propped up on pillows, on the inviting king size bed.

"I could get used to this, Bob," she said. "Look – they do a bacon cheeseburger. We could order a couple of them in, catch up on a boxed set. Run a bath…" She shot him a look that was the nearest she ever got to seductive. Bob turned away and stood by the window, fidgeting with the tulle curtains.

"It's broad daylight, Lexi! We can do all that at home! Where's your sense of fun?"

"Where's yours? I had fun at the arcade." She carried on scrolling, avoiding his gaze.

Bob glanced back across the room. "The burgers do look nice, but you don't know what you're turning down. If you've never been to the Blackpool Illuminations, it would be a crime to miss them. Anyway, you like your fish and chips, don't you? It's Harry Ramsden's centenary this year."

"I've been to the one in Gatwick airport. How can their place in Blackpool be any different? It'll just be some mediocre franchise, stuffed full of riff raff, won't it?"

Bob slowly took a seat on the bed facing her. "I know what all this is about. You're being difficult because of the drone."

It had not occurred to her until then, but Lexi had to admit he had a point. "Maybe. A bit. I'm not going to be bullied by a buzzing bit of plastic with an ulterior motive."

"Resistance is futile!" Bob joked in a robotic voice. She mellowed a little.

He shifted onto the edge of the bed and put his hand on hers. "No one is telling you what to do, Lex. But I am asking you to come with me to see the lights and maybe – don't panic – to get out of the car for a wander about. It's one evening out of your life. I'm in your town all the time. It wouldn't kill you to show a bit of interest. Anyway, the sea air will help you sleep."

When she realized how disappointed Bob was at her reluctance to let him give her a tour of the high spots, Lexi gave in. He was right, she was being churlish. And they could still snatch a couple of hours in the room.

By six o'clock they were cruising out of town in the van. The air had become warmer. Lexi opened the window and Bob put on the local radio station. He started humming along to a tune that seemed familiar, but which neither of them could name.

"I thought we could park at the Pleasure Beach," Bob said. "Have a mooch round there and then drive along the prom to see the lights, once it's dark."

"Sure." She had decided to be gracious and to say yes to whatever Bob suggested. He knew the lie of the land.

On the outskirts of Preston, a large, beige, rectangular industrial building appeared ahead of them at the side of the road. It was impossible to miss. "What's that monstrosity?" Lexi asked. At the back of it there was a metal chimney reaching high into the sky releasing a faint wisp of smoke. "How on earth did they get away with siting that here? What an eyesore!"

Bob shrugged. "I haven't seen it before, but then it's a few years since I came out this way. They can throw up those things in weeks now."

As they drew closer, Lexi saw that someone had cut a hole in the razor wire fence that marked the perimeter between the industrial site and the flat, green land that surrounded it. A robotic unit was methodically painting over some graffiti that had been sprayed along the wall facing the road. It looked like the kind of machine you would find on a car assembly line, its base heavy but the spray arm moving up and down at speed as if it were expertly coloring something in on an enormous scale.

"You wouldn't want to get in the way of that metal arm," Lexi said.

"No need to worry. Asimov's first law. It will have all sorts of built-in safety features. A dead man's handle for the robotic age."

She did not like the sound of anything with a dead man in it. As they sped past the site of the damage, Lexi craned her neck to try to see what was being painted out.

"Hey, has your friend Fakesy been up here?" she joked. The robot had almost finished obliterating it. All that remained, at the very end, were a few letters: TRATE

"Trate?"

"What? Do you mean traitor?" Bob said, his eyes fixed on the road. He had only been able to give the operation a cursory glance as he was still refusing to surrender to automatic steering.

"No. It's a different spelling." You could take the teacher out of the school, but you couldn't take the school out of the teacher.

"So, what rides do you fancy, then?" Lexi said. She had been looking at the long list of rollercoasters and attractions on the Pleasure Beach app. They would have a few hours to kill before dark. The clear skies guaranteed that the daylight would last late into the evening.

"Whatever would be most fun, love."

As they sped on, an advertisement came on the radio from The Corporation. It was talking about how pleased they were to be sponsoring the illuminations and promising everyone a 'Reet rocking good time'.

Lexi reached forward and turned it off. The silence was intense.

"I still work for them," Bob said. Something about being on his home turf had made him a little less wary than usual of fighting his corner. Lexi's disapproval of his employer, The Corporation, was verging on contempt. "The new job and all…". His eyes were fixed on the road.

Lexi sniffed sharply. "I know. And if you hadn't been with them back when…"

Almost losing control of the steering, Bob cleared his throat loudly, pointing to their phones which were side by side on the dashboard.

"Sorry," Lexi said, sharing her partner's conviction that their phones were listening to them all the time. As they drove the last half hour in silence, she leaned forward to pull down the eye shade at the top of the windscreen. They were driving directly into the sun. She returned to her device, occasionally suggesting rides she thought they might both enjoy.

"How about the Log Flume?" Bob piped up out of the blue. "I used to love that."

"It's not here," Lexi said, "But there are some other water rides."

"Can we give one of them a go? I've got the kagoules in the back."

It was easy to find a parking space among the other visitors, many of whom, Bob noticed with a hint of pride, were driving their own old cars rather than using the boring autonomous cabs that had taken over in London. "It's like all the second-hand bangers have come here to die!" Lexi said, scanning the car park. "That old Merc must be 25 years old."

"And still running. Built to last!" For someone who was immersed in new technology, Bob had an incongruous sentimentality for vintage vehicles. "Who cares if the paintwork is a bit flaky?"

"A bit? It's got terminal dermatitis!" Lexi could not see why Bob thought a rusting heap of metal, its bonnet crusted with flaking lacquer, was so special. She felt weary.

"What's wrong?" Bob said.

"Nothing. It's just – I don't know – it's not quite what I expected." She made a big effort to smile. "Come on, let's go into the fun park. Quite apart from anything else,

I could murder a donut."

Once inside, Lexi was on more familiar ground.

The Pleasure Beach was just like the attractions she had visited before. While queuing for the rollercoasters she told Bob about a trip to Disneyland Paris with her best friends, the twins Alice and Adam, whose dad, Paul, had taken them there for a long weekend when they were all 13. The site had only been open for a few years and it seemed like the most exotic treat possible at the time, even though it was the last week in October and it had rained continuously. The twins' mother, Meg, who Bob had met in troubling circumstances, had missed out by being away on business at the time.

"The weather's much nicer tonight," she said, "I'm warm enough in a hoodie."

Around them, other visitors were scantily dressed in shorts and summer tops. Lexi listened to the voices of the people around her – an array of Northern dialects, some of which were so broad she found it hard to understand what they were saying. She had forgotten people really spoke like that.

Bob rummaged in his bag and brought out their two waterproofs. "Valhalla it is, then!" He handed one to Lexi and slipped the other over his head. "The Vikings were big news up here, you know."

"Maybe I'll get some ideas for things I could use in class," Lexi said, for the first time conscious of her long, southern 'ah' sounds. She zipped up the jacket, pulled the hood over her head and tied the drawstring in a bow.

"This calls for a selfie!" she said, holding out her phone and steering Bob into position so they could grab a picture in front of the 20-foot, fire-breathing dragon that marked the entrance to the ride. "Hang on a sec. I've got to send this to the twins! Blackpool is giving Disney a run for their money tonight."

They took a seat at the front of the Norse longboat, complete with its garish dragon figurehead, and already awash with water. She felt her flat canvas shoes become sodden. As water lapped around her feet, their boat edged forward into the dark.

After five minutes of being buffeted, drenched, frozen, and observing a series of schlock horror tableaux, she was relieved to return to what was left of the daylight outside. Bob brushed the water from the surface of his jacket, pulled back his hood and checked up on the sky.

"Come on," he said, "I've got something else to show you."

"Where are we going?" she was chilly after the drenching in Valhalla. "I'm not up to another ride. Can't we just find a pub?"

He led her through the walkways. People circled above them, suspended in a serene vintage rocket ride. Rollercoasters rattled at speed, the clanking metal gears ratcheting them to the top of each slope before the carriages were released, dragging screaming passengers to their next thrill.

"Hang on here a sec." Bob disappeared into a champagne and oyster bar, returning with two large paper cups. "Classy or what?" he beamed, handing one to Lexi. She would rather have had a cup of tea to warm her up, but she took it from him and did her best to look grateful. "Cheers!" She gave an enthusiastic swig.

"Hey! Don't drink it all yet," Bob said. "We're going down the front to watch the sunset."

For all her expectations about the evening, Lexi had never dreamed that the sky would be so stunning. A massive yellow orb rested on the horizon. Around it blazed a fluctuating, iridescent spectrum of orange and violet. Lines of propellers in the wind farm, far out at sea, spun silently in tribute to the spectacle as the couple stood in awe, watching the changes in the light.

"Don't say I never take you anywhere romantic," Bob said, finally.

"Wow," she said hanging onto his arm as the warm light flattered his comfortable face, turning it a pinkish gold. "I can't argue with you about that." They stood still, huddled together until the final sliver of the sun disappeared.

On the way back to the van, they picked up a Tex Mex meal to eat in the front seat as they waited for the dark. Bob fished out one of his Faraday bags and they put their phones in it so they could talk freely.

"I'm sorry I've not been the best company," Lexi said.

"Don't apologize, Lex. You've had a tough year. It'll get better from now on, though, won't it?" He rested his hand on her leg. "You'll be OK."

"I hope so. It's just hard to forget what I saw in those places. I'd never even seen one dead body until this year. Then they all came along at once. Like London buses." She gave an unconvincing laugh.

"Oh, Lexi. I worry about you. The night terrors scare me more than you," Bob said.

"It's only every so often. And it's getting less frequent. I worry more about The Corporation expecting you to do something terrible. I mean, what if you had to program killer robots?"

"That's not going to happen!"

Lexi tried to be positive. "I'm sure there are other nice places to work out there. Honestly. What about sustainable energy? That's ethical."

Bob looked uncomfortable. "Please, Lex, can you just leave it? I'm starting in the new place on Monday. It's not a controversial part of the business. I mean, delivery drones. What is there to object to with that? You're the first one to appreciate a pizza."

Lexi had just scooped up a large taco chip smothered in guacamole, salsa and melted cheese. The first bite had fractured its precarious structure so badly that the only solution was to stuff the entire thing into her mouth. All she could do was nod.

Ten minutes later they were pulling out of the car park and driving north. Bob skirted the back of the town. He was insistent that they should begin their drive at the far north end following the promenade south towards the funfair. It was the direction they had always taken when his parents took him to the lights.

"Now, let's see how they've spent that NOB money," Bob muttered, still warmed by his nostalgia. "They should be coming up soon. Grab one of the phones and open the app, would you? They've recorded a soundtrack that syncs with your location."

To their right, on the side where the beach and the sea lay obscured by the night, they could not miss a glowing hologram of The Corporation's logo which dominated the sky. That point marked the beginning of a multimedia tribute to the pop music heritage of the North West. At first came Northern Soul, and then a homage to 1960s Liverpool with stylized portraits of The Beatles and Cilla Black. Lexi blinked as she watched the images and listened to the medley. It all seemed a bit obvious.

"Finally, something worth listening to!" she exclaimed as the cover of the Soft Cell album, Non-Stop Erotic Cabaret, loomed ahead and their hit 'Tainted Love' began to play. No sooner had Lexi and Bob started singing along with the words, however, than it faded down and switched to the next artist. "I wish we could have heard all of that one," Lexi laughed as they crawled on with the flow of the traffic, remembering Bob's pride that Marc Almond, the lead singer in the band, had once been a pupil at his school.

"This app's getting on my nerves," she said, as it jumped again. They were on to 80s Liverpool now, and Frankie Goes to Hollywood's 'Relax'. "The stupid thing won't let me pause."

"Turn it off if it's annoying you."

"Yep." She flicked the button, and they coasted on in silence. 'Madchester – RAVE ON!' flashed overhead, and a jittery neon outline performed a boisterous dance. "That's Bez from The Happy Mondays. What a character!" Bob chuckled as the figure spun tirelessly through its mesmerizing routine.

The Tower was lit up ahead. Streaks of color sketched out its unmistakable structure, piercing the night sky. Lasers projected from the top, now and again splashing flickering holographic images of various rock stars into void.

Lanterns and configurations of other lights were strung across the road, with a whole section celebrating the music Bob and Lexi knew only too well from their brush with the Rockstar Ending playlist. Bob was excited by the Bowie section but tried not to show it too much in case Lexi accused him of being obsessed again.

When they drew up closer to the Tower, they could see a stage built on the wide walkway facing the iconic building.

"I've heard about this," Bob said, pleased for once that the traffic had slowed to a snail's pace so they could take in what was going on.

Lexi leant forward to get a better look and gasped. On the platform, five lithe humanoid robots were demonstrating phenomenal dancing prowess. Unfortunately, Lexi was terrified of robots. Since she had witnessed one suffocate Mabel, one of the Endings escapees, she could never see the machines as benign or entertaining.

A few months previously, on arriving in the state-of-the-art facility for elder care, Lexi had found Mabel alone and unresponsive. She had frantically begun CPR and called for help. The medical robots that came to her assistance sealed Mabel into an airtight resuscitation device, then shamelessly turned it off, depriving her of oxygen and wiping out any chance of recovery.

At the memory, Lexi's mouth went dry and she felt dizzy. With trembling hands, she rummaged for a half-drunk bottle of water in the van door and took a long swig, telling herself not to over-react and silently counting to ten to calm her breathing.

This is Lancashire, girl, not the Death Star. Pull yourself together.

Oblivious to the fear that Lexi was working hard to suppress, Bob was looking on in wonder at the robot display. He had heard that the machines had been programmed to do everything from hardcore headbanging to a full Wigan Casino floor show. But seeing it live was something else.

Light-sculpted flames shot high into the night. Music pumped into the street. Take That's 'Relight My Fire' blasted out as the five robots gyrated suggestively, just like the boys in the band – some of whom hailed from Manchester – had done back in the 1990s. The music immediately triggered happier memories. This had been the soundtrack for the couple's childhood parties. Lexi knew all the words and started humming along in a concerted effort to overcome her fear, and Bob joined in.

"That's incredible," Lexi said. "How on earth do they do that?"

"Motion capture," Bob said, sparing her the full details. "Though not from the lads. I doubt they could move like that now. Stand-ins following their old routines."

The robots dropped to the floor in unison, then sprang up from their backs onto their feet, striding around the stage in a neat formation, their robotic arms waving in the air. Some serious thrusting action took place where, if they had been human, their pelvis would have been.

Pedestrians clustered around the stage, laughing and joining in with the moves where they could. Occasionally one of the figures would somersault, drawing a gasp and a cheer from the crowd. Lexi was grateful that she and Bob were further away.

"What's that, now?"

She had turned from the dancing display and was looking at the base of the Tower on her side of the promenade. More illusions of flames licked at the edges of the wide, pale building in sync with the spectacle that was facing it.

In the middle of the blank canvas the hashtag #BetterTogether was spelled out, as if spray painted black against the reflected light. A couple of security guards made phone calls and looked up into the sky as if they were trying to work out where the slogan was coming from. It could only mean one thing. Lexi followed their gaze into the darkness.

"Bob! Look!" She felt her face flush and tried to point out the graffiti, but a tram lit up like a neon spaceship trundled past and ground to a halt right in front of the writing.

"That's something else I remember," Bob said, turning to look at the tram, "They're good, aren't they?"

As Bob steered the van steadily away from the Tower Lexi twisted round but the tram blocked her view. Something stopped her from saying any more about the familiar hashtag, which gave her a feeling of hope. Bob had tried so hard to make it a fun evening. Still, she was certain that she had not imagined it. Her friends in People Against Coercive Euthanasia (PACE) must be stepping up the pressure here in Blackpool, too.

"It's amazing, isn't it?" Bob chirped on, "Those thrusters are something else!"

"Way to go!" Lexi clenched her lips and nodded enthusiastically, feeling excited that activism was alive and kicking in the North West.

Reprising their car karaoke of 'Relight My Fire', they passed through the Golden Mile, the area directly south of the Tower, where crowds milled around the amusement arcades chatting, smoking, buying food. A massive drone display buzzed overhead, forming stars and hearts around the message:

WISHING YOU A REET ROCKING
NIGHT FROM THE CORPORATION

Lexi settled back into her seat for the ride back as they left town. It was pleasantly warm. The windows were closed, and the glass of champagne and Tex Mex feast had made her sleepy. When Bob saw her eyes were closed, he clicked the radio on low to keep him company for the hour's drive back.

"The organizers of the Blackpool Illuminations are under pressure tonight from their sponsor, The Corporation, after a group of activists hijacked the light show in front of the Tower that is the focal point for the 2028 illuminations. Hackers used a drone to project the hashtag #BetterTogether onto the building where it could be seen for almost an hour until it was finally shot down by security.

"A spokesperson for the North West branch of People Against Coercive Euthanasia has claimed responsibility for the disruption: 'We are merely using non-violent means to draw public attention to the growing intergenerational resistance to The Corporation's shady death business.' The

Corporation claims to have completely revised its controversial end of life service following 'teething problems' which were exposed at a meeting of the HELP Select Committee earlier this year.

"The Corporation has been spearheading an investment program in the North. No-one from the company was available for comment, although it is believed that they are angry about this disruption as their sponsorship of the lights has reputedly cost them in excess of £3 million.

"We asked PACE if they were also responsible for damage that had been done to the Corporation's new state-of-the-art Kindness Centre, built on the outskirts of Preston, and which has been subjected to physical attacks. We understand from an insider that, only this morning, one of their exterior walls was defaced with a phrase from Dante's Inferno.

"They told us that, while they would never encourage their members to break the law, they have a degree of admiration for the artists who had carried out the work and whose aims are clearly in sympathy with their own."

Bob looked to see whether Lexi had heard the news report. He wanted to protect her from all those worries. She had let her eyes close, and her head had fallen to one side. It took him back to the rides home from Blackpool in his parents' car. At no time in his life had he felt more secure, dozing in the back seat, listening to his mum and dad whispering. "I think he's nodded off, bless him."

Only tonight, Lexi was the one pretending to be asleep.

CHAPTER FIVE

W HY DIDN'T THEY INVITE TREV, Bob's old school friend, and his parents to join them for lunch in the hotel? Lexi thought it would be nice to splash out on their last day.

When Bob phoned to ask, however, they said they would rather meet at the café in Hesketh Park. Trev's father, Andy, was not keen on fancy restaurants these days. If he was having a bad time with his tremors he would not want to eat in public. Nevertheless, Andy was enthusiastic about seeing Bob and wanted to meet Lexi as they had heard so much about her the previous summer.

After parking the van on the road, they easily found the place where Trev, Jennifer and Andy had already grabbed some seats. The café was little more than a prefabricated shed with picture windows and a cluster of tables outside. Fluffy clumps of cloud were scuttling across the sky, but the sun was surprisingly warm when it shone through.

"How do you like it up here, then?" Andy asked Lexi as Bob and Trev disappeared inside the unremarkable building. He stooped a little in his seat, a tall, wiry man whose clothes looked too big.

"I've been enjoying the fresh air," Lexi said. "Bob marched me up the pier pretty much the minute we arrived."

"It's a tradition, taking people to look at the place where the sea should be. This must all seem rather boring in comparison to your hometown. It's not what it was, Southport, but we've always liked it here, haven't we Jen?"

His wife nodded. Lexi warmed to her immediately. Jennifer was the epitome of a sprightly, petite older woman, with greying well-cut curls and a lively twinkle in her eyes. She wore nicely fitting jeans and a long-sleeved tunic in an acid green ethnic print. Matching toenails peeped through her flat gold-studded sandals. Even though she was well over 70 she dressed like someone thirty years younger. "Did Bob say he'd taken you to the lights last night?" she said.

"Yes. It was quite a show." Lexi was trying not to sound underwhelmed but feared she may be failing. "The robotic dancers were something else. They freaked me out a bit at first. I fell asleep on the way back."

"They were on the local telly last week," Jennifer went on. "Goodness knows how much it cost to coax all the members of Take That up here to do the switch-on. I thought we might go ourselves this year. We don't usually bother but it sounds like they've done something a bit different. Was the drive alright?"

Before she could answer, the boys came back with the goods. They were chatting like they had never been apart. Trev was just as Bob had described him – a similar height to his friend, average build, but with far less hair, dark and cropped close. He looked tidier, slimmer and fitter than Bob. Lexi wondered why he was still single. Bob had done better at keeping his curly brown hair even if it was always a bit on the messy side.

Lexi and Jennifer had both opted for a small yoghurt ice pop, Trev had a chocolate covered ice cream on a stick, and Andy didn't want anything. Bob was delighted with his Fab ice lolly, pink and white striped with one end dipped in chocolate and coated in sugar strands. Lexi pushed to the back of her mind the inevitable consequence, a cascade of confectionery adorning the front of his shirt. What did it matter? They were on holiday.

During the run-down of what the visitors had got up to the previous day, Bob's revelation that Lexi had turned out to be a whizz at pinball made everyone smile. "Good for you," Jennifer said, reaching across and giving Lexi's arm a squeeze.

"You're looking stronger than last time I saw you, Andy," Bob ventured cautiously. He had visited the family the previous summer. It was not long after Iris, one of their in-laws, had succumbed to the Corporation's marketing and secretly booked herself an Ending, leaving a legacy of distress and anxiety.

"Sorry about all that," Andy said, "I was on a bit of a downer last time you were up, but we're much better now, aren't we, love?"

"We've been keeping our screen time down," Jennifer volunteered. "And helping Esme and Steve out with the kids. Andy's even come out on the golf course with me. That's been a bit of a turn-up for the books!"

"I can only ride around in the daft buggy, but it's still nice to be out," Andy nodded. Trev put an arm round his father's shoulder, "That's the spirit, Pops!"

"Very pleased to hear it," Bob said. "What did you think of the presents I sent up?"

"The little bags? Fantastic. We've always been big Led Zep fans." Andy smiled, "And giving me one with all those runes – well, that was inspired! And the lady's rune for Jen, of course."

Bob's sideline in designing and selling music-themed Faraday pouches was going from strength to strength.

"We're all using them right now, as it happens." Jennifer opened her handbag to show their phones, side by side, each one snug in their signal-proof casing. "In fact, I wanted to ask if you did commissions!"

"Anything legal considered! What did you have in mind?" Bob was always looking for ways to get his precious bags, which enabled people to stop their phones being tracked or listened to, into the hands of as many people as possible.

"I'm involved in a couple of things locally. I thought they might be good fundraising merchandise."

"She never stops, you know!" Andy said.

Lexi approved. "I'm a big fan of keeping busy. What do you get up to, then, Jennifer?"

"When I turned 70, I thought it would be good for me to work on a language, you know to keep my brain working. I go to an Italian class. Then I decided to start something creative."

"Wait 'til you hear this," Trevor said shaking his head in disbelief. Lexi imagined that Jennifer might have taken up embroidery or – the latest comeback craft that was all the rage – raffia mat making.

"What? Do you think I'm too old to do street art?" Jennifer retorted.

"Good for you!" Lexi said, silently scolding herself for having had such conservative expectations of Jennifer, just because she was old.

Bob smiled encouragingly. "Sounds fun. You should be proud of your mother, Trev!"

"Did you know that Bob's friendly with Fakesy, Jennifer?" Lexi said, giving him a gentle nudge with her elbow.

Bob shook his head, awkwardly. "Hardly friendly. Just Christmas cards, really. His designs are much better than mine. I'm sure you can imagine. We met through work a few years ago."

Jennifer's eyes opened wide. "No! You're joking? He's my idol!"

"He's certainly very clever," Bob said, matter-of-factly. "I arranged access when he came in to do a surprise mural at the school where I was working. The one where Lexi still teaches, actually."

"We're not supposed to be political at the street art group," Jennifer sighed. "Some nonsense to do with the funding from the council. But I have to tell you, I'm starting to lean in that direction. I'd love to see something like that Fakesy mural round here. The one he did to have a go at The Corporation. Very clever," she chuckled admiringly. "Sadly, I don't yet have the talent myself. It's a work in progress."

Trevor became stern for a moment. "You can forget that Mum! It was you who told me a bunch of disabled protesters at the Yuthie conference got beaten up. That's not happening to you! In any case, we've all got to look after Dad, haven't we?"

"Have you already forgotten what happened to Iris?" Jennifer snapped, "And all the worry that effing Corporation has put your father through? Believe me, Trevor, it would be well worth the risk."

"One life, live it!" Lexi said, enthusiastically, remembering Zorro's advice. Bob looked away.

There was an awkward silence.

Hesitantly, Lexi continued, "How did you hear about the protesters being hurt, Jen? It's not been reported anywhere. Was it through PACE by any chance?" Bob gave her a gentle kick under the table. She knew he wanted her to drop it. But now Jennifer had invoked the specter of The Corporation she could not let it go.

"Not now, Lex, please!" Bob sighed.

Jennifer wagged a finger at Bob to indicate that she was more than happy to carry on the discussion. "This is important. Yes, Lexi. It was. In fact, I'm a member. They've given us quite a bit of practical help with all we've been up against as a family."

"Hey Mum," Trevor was more conciliatory this time. "Let's not bring all that up now. Please? This isn't the time or the place. Why don't you tell Bob and Lexi about your new art project? It's a cheerier topic of conversation for a sunny Sunday afternoon, don't you think?"

Jennifer could see that Trevor was getting agitated, and that Andy, too was uncomfortable with the way the discussion was going.

"Go on Jen. Tell us about your art," Bob grinned encouragingly. "It sounds intriguing. I'd love to know more about that. I'm sure Lexi would, too."

"Well, we got funding from some foundation or other that's giving money out to help 'improve the North', whatever that's supposed to mean. Anyway we put in a proposal to paint a set of murals commemorating the famous faces of Southport. They seemed to like it."

"Not Red Rum again!" Bob interjected. "This place has more than enough tributes to that old nag as it is!" He had told Lexi about the statue of the famous local horse, a three-times Grand National winner, which in his opinion looked more like a Dartmoor pony, cast in bronze, than the thoroughbred steeplechaser that had galloped to victory.

"Oh Bob, you've reminded me – can we have a look at it?" Lexi wanted to see for herself whether the work of art was as underwhelming as Bob had claimed.

"It must still be in the Wayfarers Arcade." Jennifer explained. "Used to be so elegant. It's been turned into a dorm now, though. The space isn't open to the public anymore."

Lexi suddenly felt cold, reminded once more of that terrible final visit to Mabel. She realized Bob was trying to catch her eye to see if she was OK. He quickly changed the subject.

"So, who's been up for the star treatment then, Jen? With your paintings?"

"Well, I wanted to do Marc Almond or Miranda Richardson, but I was over-ruled. We settled on Jean Alexander in the end. But she's just the first one. There's no shortage of empty walls. I've been telling them we should have a big party next summer. You know, invite the people in the pictures – well, the ones who are still alive. If we can make it happen, you'll both have to come! You can even bring your mate Fakesy, Bob!"

"No harm in asking him," Bob said, "But as his identity is a closely guarded secret, how would you even know if he's there?"

"They're spending a lot of money up here now," Andy said. "Shame we don't seem to be able to kickstart the shops, though. Lord Street's still terrible. Those beautiful colonnades are only good for providing shelter to the tramps nowadays."

"Who's investing? The government?" Lexi asked.

Andy nodded. "Yes. Them and The Corporation."

Jennifer rolled her eyes.

"Hard to tell where one ends and the other begins," Andy went on. "We've got it all. Dorms. Drone hubs. Kindness Centers. You must have driven past their new depot out on the Blackpool road. It's massive. Shame it's robotic everything, though. They give them all that money, but I can't see where any jobs are coming from. You've reminded me, though, Jen. I got a little brochure in the post from them about the Wayfarers dorm. It looks very comfortable. I have to say, I was quite interested in popping in for one of the short stays. Might come in handy to give you a break when the inevitable happens."

"Oh, stop it," Jen said. "You are not going anywhere near one of those places. Honestly, you block them from intruding onto your screens with their insidious propaganda, and then the devious beggars sneak in through the letterbox when your back is turned!"

Lexi felt a deep wave of nausea. "Too right! I'd keep out of there if I were you," she said seriously. "I visited one recently. Can't say I was impressed. Those places are not as safe as they make out."

Andy was undeterred. "Well, you can't stop me having a look at it. I can't believe they'd let you come to any harm. One of the things I like about The Corporation is the way they let you make your own choices. It's a free country, isn't it?"

"By and large." Even Bob wanted to deter Andy from setting foot inside the dorm, now. But he didn't want to fuel an argument. All he could think about was The Eagles song 'Desperado' which considered the concept of freedom to be badly over-rated.

"So, Jen," Bob said, "Back to the matter in hand. What is it you'd like on your pouches?"

"I've been thinking about a line from Dante's Inferno. *Lasciate ogne speranza, voi ch'intrate.* Do you know what it means?"

CHAPTER SIX

W HEN BOB'S BOSS, LOLA, TOLD him his next
assignment would be at the Corporation Robotics
and Aviation Plant (CRAP) he had been intrigued.

She had already made it clear that his first choice –
returning to work at Charlton Green School, where he
had first met Lexi – was not an option. That job had been
the sweetest gig of his life, but his role had been given to
someone else when Lola took him away on a secondment
to head office.

Up at HQ he was supposed to be helping The Corporation get to the bottom of a security breach. Lola had not
worked out that Bob knew a lot more about the incident
than he was letting on. From his desk, a stone's throw
from the chief executive's grand corner office, he had been
in the perfect position to cover his tracks. If only it had
stopped there. He had not been able to resist pulling off a
few more covert tricks to support PACE.

Mason, the chief executive of The Corporation, had
got so angry about the embarrassing series of security
bungles compromising the Disposal Centers, that he had
fired his head of security, Marco. He had got rid of the

wrong person, as it happened. But Mason didn't care. He just needed a senior enough head on a plate to show to his client, the Minister for Health, Euthanasia and Legacy Planning (HELP), that he was taking the issue seriously. While Mason's firing Marco had deflected any suspicion from Bob, he was still relieved to put some distance between himself and the project he had secretly undermined.

In any case, at a new workplace he would be able to sell his sideline in Faraday bags to a new set of faces. Assuming, of course, that they were not all robots. He already had an idea for one featuring the Tubeway Army single 'Are 'Friends' Electric?'. Once he was settled in, he was sure he would be able to come up with a few more options.

Even though there was free parking onsite, Bob could not risk taking the van. Instead, he had walked ten minutes to the P12 bus stop. He shuddered a little when he climbed aboard, having loathed driverless buses ever since one had run over his precious cat, Wotsit, on a day that had turned out to be momentous for both him and Lexi.

The bus dropped him a few streets from the industrial estate where CRAP was situated. The Corporation had bought up vast swathes of Bermondsey when it had built Brookwood, its Disposal Center, the ultimate destination for thousands of assisted suicide customers. That was before the rebranding as a Kindness Center. Brookwood's discreet location away from the main road had helped the Corporation to keep their gruesome secret under wraps until Lexi and her activist friends, with Fakesy's assistance, had exposed it to the world's media.

It had turned out that Bob's new office was just across the road from the very place where he and Lexi had rescued five old people from death only eight months previously. He was so proud of her. It was Lexi who had physically infiltrated the facility and got them out, with him providing technical backup from the van. Still, the last thing he needed today was a security camera matching the mystery infiltrators' getaway vehicle to their newest employee. It could get things off to a difficult start if he were arrested for industrial espionage on his first day.

Ironically, Lola was sending him to CRAP because of his security expertise.

"These things are going to be everywhere," she had explained during a walking meeting with him, a few weeks before, as they wandered along the Thames embankment. "Soon they'll be as common as cars. In the air and on the ground."

He had taken the train to London Bridge station and met her by Southwark Cathedral. Together they had skirted the bustle and enticing aromas of the foodie destination Borough Market and headed for the river. Bankside was busier than they had hoped it would be, with tourists and runners competing for space at wildly differing speeds.

"They're not here, though," Bob observed glancing around. "The machines."

"No – it's too busy. Once the footfall gets too dense the insurance becomes prohibitively expensive. But small-town Britain is going to be heaving with them very soon."

Bob remembered the pizza that arrived in a delivery droid during last year's visit to his friend Trev's. The insulated mobile box had played some Italian-sounding song while proffering a large Quattro Stagioni. "I've seen one up North. Shame, though. They could do with giving the jobs to actual people."

"Our role is not to reason why. We're here to keep things running smoothly. The plant you'll be going to is all new build, state-of-the-art manufacturing. Robot begets robot. You get the idea? They've also got the control center there. It's where they track everything. Only someone like you, with top level clearance, would be allowed in."

They had walked past Shakespeare's Globe with its half-timbered walls and thatched roof. The pavement widened right out into a square in front of the Tate Modern, a monolithic, red brick former power station turned art gallery which towered to their left, casting a cool shadow that reached across to the water. The flow of the wide, grey river was paused on a high slack tide. A mime artist resembling a Cyberman, from Dr Who, jerked about on a box painted silver to match his spacesuit.

Lola continued, "There's no problem getting the things built. That's the easy part. Even the exoskeletons. You're going to love those. But we are always worried about security. Remember what happened with that drone?" She shook her head in disbelief. "No one outside has picked up on it yet, but we've lost a few more of them. It's a reputational catastrophe waiting to happen."

How could he forget? During Bob's secondment to HQ, he and his young colleague Sonny, seconded in from the marketing agency, had been surprised how easy it was for them to take over the controls of one of The Corporation's drug delivery drones for a bit of impromptu surveillance. They were lucky no one was injured when it unexpectedly crashed to the ground.

"I need someone I can trust to assess vulnerabilities. You know what it's like. The people who develop new tech never want to admit to there being any flaws. Let's face it, we both know first-hand this stuff isn't as un-hackable as they claim."

"Nothing ever is." Bob broke from Lola's direct gaze. Occasionally, he wondered whether she suspected his involvement in the break-in that had caused The Corporation such a headache.

He looked for a prompt to steer her away from talking about hacking. Someone had set up a van selling churros. The smell of sweet batter, cinnamon, melting chocolate and dulce de leche was overpowering. "Wow, they smell good," he said.

"You want one, don't you?"

Lola had worked with Bob long enough to know how much he loved food, and how hard he struggled to resist eating too much of it. Although tempted, on this occasion he said no. The risk of dribbling cinnamon sugar and hot sticky sauce down his chin – in what was ostensibly a business meeting – was too great. "Maybe on my way back."

By the time they reached the Millennium footbridge, he had accepted the job, and Lola headed across the river towards the dome of St Paul's Cathedral to make her next appointment in the City. A busker with a badly applied Aladdin Sane stripe sang David Bowie's 'God Knows I'm Good' strumming an acoustic guitar connected to a tinny amplifier. Bob hummed along and turned to head back home, only stopping when his phone connected with Lexi's.

"I'm off the bench, love," he said as soon as she picked up.

They had suspected his period of enforced gardening leave would be coming to an end when Lola had asked for a meeting. Lexi was quiet, and then asked:

"So, where are they sending you?" Bob's contract allowed The Corporation to move him anywhere in the country, but they had both been hoping Lola would let him stay close to home. "I've been keeping all my fingers and toes crossed for you."

"It's good news. I'll still be in London. Plus, I've managed to swing a few weeks off before I start at the beginning of September. I'll be back in harness about the time you go back to school."

"What a relief! You can tell me about it when you get home. I'm just in the changing room at the gym." Lexi rang off, and Bob started to think about how they could make the most of their last few weeks off work. He had convinced her to travel with him up to Southport, but it had not gone as well as he had hoped. She just could not let go of her obsession with saving everyone. A bigger problem was that she was finding it harder all the time to disguise her loathing for his employer, but she had stopped short of demanding that he quit.

It seemed like no time at all until the day came to start his new job.

The building could not have been more anonymous. Another huge, beige rectangular box which took up an entire block. There was no logo or company name on the outside. It could have been any data center or distribution hub hidden in plain sight.

A person-sized entrance opened on to the pavement at one end. Round the side, a series of different sized roller shutters periodically slid upwards to release a delivery robot which would trundle out onto either the pavement or the road, depending on its size. Higher up, there were hatches for the unmanned aerial vehicles, just like the one he and Sonny had hijacked earlier in the summer. As Bob looked up, one of the high doors opened to release a white drone with a body the size of a shoebox. It elegantly cleared the building, rose above it, and buzzed away in the direction of the Old Kent Road.

As he approached, the electronic fob in his pocket told the building that Bob had arrived. He heard a series of clangs from an array of heavy-duty bolts just before the door sprang open and an automated voice said, "Welcome to The Corporation, Bob. Please follow the blue lights on the floor to your workstation."

Floor LEDs always reminded him of being in an airplane. That was where he had first seen them. The idea was that they could signpost the exits in case of emergency. Now they used them everywhere to guide people around unfamiliar buildings. It saved sending junior members of staff down to collect visitors and shepherd them around. With cameras everywhere no one was going to dodge off course.

He arrived at an industrial steel lift where the same disembodied voice told him to stand clear of the door and exit when it stopped. "You have arrived at the CRAP Operation Center. Have an awesome first day, Bob," it said as the door slid back.

Bob felt his heart rate quicken. The room he had entered bore an uncanny resemblance to one in the Disposal Center, only a few blocks away. He had hacked into the CCTV there to help shield Lexi, back in January, when she had penetrated their defenses. It made perfect sense that The Corporation would re-purpose the architect's design for a panopticon, the point from which a small team of human beings could observe everything going on in the building.

A dozen colleagues, each at their own workstation arranged in a nest of circles facing outwards, were surrounded by a vertical cylinder of floor-to-ceiling glass suspended above the factory floor.

The ground area below them was divided into concentric sections, with the outer third serving as the dispatch area Beside roller shutters that opened out onto the street, delivery robots of various sizes and shapes were lining up to be loaded and released in batches. Directly opposite the exits, on the other side of the building, the robots returned to be unpacked and passed through a sterilizing chamber before being loaded up for their next job.

The heavy manufacturing took place in the center of the ground floor. Large robotic arms surrounded by cages swiveled at breakneck speed, assembling components. A couple of humanoid-shaped bots walked the floor. Bob quickly worked out that they were being controlled by two operatives who wore VR headsets, lightweight motion capture suits and haptic gloves, each wandering around their individual glass-enclosed side cubicles situated either side of the lift. The intelligent floor, moving like a multidimensional magic carpet beneath them, guaranteed that they would never crash into a wall.

Transfixed for a moment by their absurd dance, Bob did not notice the woman approaching him. "You're Bob, right? Hi, I'm Sylvia, one of the supervisors," she extended a dry hand with a firm grip. "Shall I show you around? Your workstation is just there. I've put you in the seat with the clearest view."

Bob could not help smiling. Her choice of words was straight out of David Bowie's 'Life on Mars'. That had to be a good sign.

"Sounds ideal – at least while I get to know the place."

She led him to the edge and together they scanned the mass of activity around them. "It's all been designed logically. Ground floor, dispatch round the walls, heavy manufacturing in the middle. The first floor – it runs round like a gallery, see? That's where we do lighter-weight build, component design and testing. And finally, the top floor where the aerial drones are loaded and dispatched. You'll hear colleagues talking about 'up in the gods'. They mean up there. The units launch from the hatches cut into the right-hand exterior shell and come back for re-loading on the left. All the cargo is lightweight for the UAVs. It's taken up there from the basement. The only floors you can't see from up here are the underground parking and storage levels, but the monitors pick all that up. We have lifts in all four corners running the goods for dispatch up and down, and conveyer belts linking each corner."

"Impressive."

Sylvia nodded. "When it's running properly it's slick. To be fair that's most of the time. In here, at least. So, head office said you're a security specialist, right?" Sylvia said.

"Yes. It's one of the things I do."

"Between you and me, we really need one."

He was careful not to give away too much about what he already knew and was keen to say something encouraging. "There are breaches all the time, in every company in every sector. You just don't hear about them very often." Bob said. "How long have you been here?"

"I have a few years on the firm. I was at another Corporation site for a while just over the road. The Kindness Center. It wasn't called that then. Took a bit of time out. Then they put me in here."

"I've had a few different assignments with them over the years myself," he said.

A slow, soft beeping noise interrupted their conversation.

"Sorry, I need to check this out," Sylvia sighed. "It's only a level three, but we should have a look anyway."

"Sounds like a good idea," he smiled and nodded. "Level three?"

"One is the most serious. The alarm tones get louder and faster the more threatening the issue might be to the reputation of The Corporation. A level one is deafening. Flashing red lights. The whole caboodle. It freezes the plant. Brings it to a complete standstill. If you weren't panicking before you will be when that siren goes off. As supervisor, I get ten minutes to log an interest in the L3 or it automatically begins to escalate."

Now they were standing at workstations facing out towards the clear surrounding wall. With a few keystrokes

Sylvia linked up with one of the large screens suspended from a web of metal cables above the work area. White letters flashed up on a black background.

'L3 alert. Drone incident. Supervisor login required.'

Bob watched Sylvia place a finger on the back of her personal device and enter a series of characters through the keyboard on the workstation. Her nails were badly bitten, and her hands looked 20 years older than the rest of her, marred with patches of eczema and torn cuticles. After a few more commands she had managed to silence the acoustic alarm and called up the live video feed from the drone in question. He could not work out why the screen was dark grey.

"Where is it?" Bob asked.

"Well, visual feed's no use," Sylvia said. "Let's see if we can get the location data on the display." She focused on the smaller monitor in front of her keyboard and entered a few commands while she carried on explaining more details. "Our patch runs up to the river, Vauxhall to Greenwich, and then down to Kennington, Camberwell and Peckham. It shouldn't be outside the geofence."

"Does that happen?"

"Not very often. It's usually down to the wind. We had one get stuck on an open top bus over by London Bridge. It did three laps of the city with no battery power. Took us a while to work out what was happening. Seems like this one's in Peckham."

The grey blur was replaced with a colorful map. Bob recognized its style from his own recent tricky brush with drone control. A paper plane, representing the unit, sat squarely in the middle of the screen.

"That's quite high," Sylvia said, running her eyes over more stats. "Do you know, I think it's on the roof of Peckham Levels. They won't be open yet. Too early for cocktails, thank goodness. I'm going to assume no one's hurt. I'll send out one of the new Motherships to pick it up."

"Motherships?"

"They're our recovery vehicles. Heavy duty drones fully equipped with cameras and claws. You can imagine what we call them when we're down the pub."

"Give me a clue."

"It's the title of a song by Robbie Williams. And it's not 'Angels'."

CHAPTER SEVEN

C HARLTON GREEN SCHOOL HAD GONE from strength to strength since Ardua had arrived. The head teacher was so proud of what they had achieved that she made the students wear the school's 'outstanding' rating like a badge of honor. It was emblazoned on the back of every child's hoodie, so they would never forget the high standard they were expected to maintain.

Their academic achievements were strong enough, but it was their scores on the School Happiness Index Table that attracted the most praise. At a time when mental health problems among school-age children were escalating to the highest ever recorded levels, Charlton Green was the exception, devoid of despair.

It was not widely known, however, that much of their success had been down to Bob.

During his secondment to the school, he had come up with the idea of using the surveillance system he installed for The Corporation's education division to spot early signs of anxiety, depression and suicidal ideation. There was nowhere for the children to hide from the ubiquitous cameras tracking every nuance of their facial expression.

If an unhappy child did not respond to their treatment plan quickly enough, Ardua would find a place for them at another school in the federation. Those most at risk would be transferred to the Pupils' Intensive Special Support Offsite Federation Facility (PISSOFF). Most parents pulled out all the stops to keep their offspring at Charlton Green. They wanted their children to have 'outstanding' on their back, not the stigma of a referral unit.

It helped Ardua's cause that May, a 14-year-old Charlton Green pupil, had taken her own life a few years previously. After that, the headmistress became ruthless, knowing that her school's exemplary reputation was only as good as the last news story. When a school governor dared to question her methods, she was quick to point out that being high on the SHIT tables was in everyone's best interests. Quite apart from anything else, it would keep the school well-funded for the foreseeable future. She simply could not risk any child dragging down their average, however needy.

Lexi knew that Ardua had made some bad decisions. She missed her friend the music teacher, Francis, in particular. There had been no option for him to stay after they sold off all the instruments and put the money into surveillance cameras. However, Ardua had created a new job for Lexi when all the mathematics teaching was given to the AIs. And with the cameras came Bob. She still enjoyed teaching Creative and Interpersonal Skills, even if at times she felt like the only person left who cared about the students.

As she waited in the corridor outside the head's suite Lexi could hear muffled voices. She checked her phone to see if there was anything from Bob about his first day in the new job. Nothing yet. He would probably tell her about it later. They had not spent much time together in the morning. Tired from the long drive back from the North, they had got up later than planned, and Bob had shot out of the door to catch the bus before they had any time to talk. She missed the days when they worked together at the school. Everything was so much simpler back when they first met.

A young man who she immediately recognized, came out of Ardua's office. "Hello Miss!" he said with a warm grin and firm handshake.

"Tyson! What are you doing back here?"

One of her favorite former pupils, Tyson had won a scholarship to a prestigious music school and was about to enter his second year. After Francis left, he had trained for his audition at a local music project run by volunteers. He was a gifted pianist who Lexi had helped through a difficult time when his friend May had been found dead. It had been a distressing period for everyone.

"I'm doing some talks for the music school," he said enthusiastically. "They want to attract students from more diverse backgrounds to apply. I get paid to be an outreach ambassador and I thought it would be nice to come back here. My folks still live around the corner, so I called by to see Miss and she's invited me to speak at the careers event. Like you taught us, meeting in person creates so many more possibilities. I'm so pleased I've seen you. Is Bob around?"

"No, he's not here anymore. They moved him on to another assignment a while ago, I'm afraid."

Ardua appeared at the door. "Ah Lexi, I can see you now," she said, ignoring Tyson. "Come in."

Lexi could not resist giving him a quick hug goodbye. "Stay in touch. I'll tell Bob you were asking after him," she said, "and I'll look out for your talk. I'm so proud of you."

"What a lovely young man he's grown into," she said as she entered the head's suite and clicked the door carefully shut behind her.

Ardua barely looked up. Tyson's success had nothing to do with the way she liked to run things. "Indeed. Now, how can I help you?" Perfunctory to the last.

Lexi spoke slowly. "I'm worried about something, Ardua. A few of the older kids have been telling me they went to the Yuthie convention at the weekend."

"You're normally all for them getting involved in politics, Lexi. Let's face it, most of the sixth form have got the vote now. What's the problem?" She was irritated.

"It's some of the ideas they're coming back with. They're… well… worrying." Lexi was feeling for words that did not make her seem to be over-reacting.

"You didn't have a problem when the pupils were taking all those days off for environmental protests, did you? If I remember correctly, one might say you even encouraged them." Ardua grunted. She had not agreed with Lexi's liberal stance on attendance at the time. The head had only backed down from issuing her with a formal warning when Lexi started to do unpaid remedial teaching for those whose commitment to the protests put them in danger of falling behind at school.

"This is different." She was annoyed at Ardua's dismissive attitude. "You haven't heard what they've been saying."

"Oh please! The Yuthies are mainstream. Whether you agree with them or not, Yuthentic is the new establishment. They are driving a progressive social agenda. They have a substantial cohort of elected Members of Parliament. They have more seats now than your friends the Greens ever had."

"This isn't about my political beliefs!" Lexi was indignant. "It never has been."

Ardua waved her hand, dismissively. "And I'm sure I don't need to tell you that national profiling shows that they are having an unprecedented positive effect on the under-18s Happiness Index."

"How do you know that?" Lexi had not expected Ardua, who was normally doggedly apolitical, to be a Yuthie fan. What was her angle?

"I've been doing some research." Ardua peered at Lexi over her spectacles. "As it happens the board is thinking of appointing one of the Yuthentic politicians to be a school governor. It never harms to have friends in high places, does it? I can't imagine they'll do badly at the next election."

The prospect of Yuthentic being invited into the school where she had invested so much love over the years made Lexi afraid. She was at a loss how to convince Ardua of the dangers involved without revealing how she knew so much.

"They have some frightening ideas, you know," Lexi said, slowly.

"Freedom? Choice? Independence? It all sounds rather good to me," Ardua retaliated. "Aren't those things you want the children to have? I certainly do."

Please, Lexi thought, don't put those words on the hoodies. "Theoretically, yes. But there's more to Yuthentic than that."

"They're all the same, politicians. Whoever's in or whoever's out, I just need to put the interests of our school first."

"No, Ardua. We need to put the interests of the children first." Her words had slipped out in a more confrontational tone than Lexi had planned.

"It's the same thing, my dear." Ardua's smile was patronizing.

Lexi took a deep breath. "Aren't you concerned about the Yuthies' attitude to... well... to suicide? You must have seen the coverage over the summer. That Disposal Center horror. Gruesome. It would never have happened if they hadn't driven it through."

"Some of the nuances were unfortunate, but it's all been sorted out now, hasn't it? In any case, our pupils are hardly in their target group. We don't have many 70-year-olds in our classrooms, do we?" She was talking down to Lexi in full flow now.

"No, but..."

Ardua stood up and began to pace the room. Lexi had worked for her long enough to know that this was the signal to leave. She stood to go. There was no point in saying anything else.

"Lexi. You're a great teacher. But you overthink things sometimes. You need to let this go. You won't change my mind. Therefore, I suggest you stop worrying about the things you cannot change and concentrate on what you do best. Teaching."

CHAPTER EIGHT

W HEN SCHOOL FINISHED AT FOUR o'clock Lexi was still thinking about the things the teenagers had said. Her pointless meeting with the head had only made things worse. The kids had rolled into her lessons proudly brandishing their Yuthie wristbands, sigil badges and jewelry. When she had tentatively asked where they had come from the kids' eyes lit up, and they could not stop talking.

"Oh, Miss, you should have seen him. That Jasper – he's incredible," one had said. "My big brother has got his own flat thanks to the dude." She had heard one or two kids singing their praises before, but this was more sinister. One boy, Ronan, even mentioned Phase Two, but when she asked for more details, he was mercifully vague.

"The choice thing, Miss. I don't know why you look so worried about it. Anyone would think you don't trust us. We're not stupid, you know. What they say – it's exactly the same as what you tell us. To be confident, to trust our own judgment. You should join the Yuthies, Miss. You don't have to be under 30 or anything. Their values are exactly the same as your values."

"No."

Lexi was uncharacteristically short with Ronan. She softened, "Sorry. They're not for me. Maybe you will convince me otherwise one day." With a forced smile she sent him on his way.

All day, she was anxious about the prospect of Yuthentic contaminating her precious school. It was impossible to put it out of her mind. There was still nothing from Bob. It would be another couple of hours until he got home. She had to talk to someone about what had happened, and although Bob was usually the one she would offload on, she had been pushing it with him recently. Her going on about The Corporation all the time was tough for him, and she even wondered whether he had deliberately avoided her that morning so as not to hear any more. She would have to find somebody else to talk to.

Lexi's friend Ayesha lived close by and was often around during the day as she was semi-retired. When Lexi messaged her, Ayesha immediately invited her to pop round. They had not seen each other for a few months, as Ayesha had spent much of the summer on an extended yoga retreat and walking holiday in the Cevennes with her husband, Ajay.

"Lovely to see you! How was your summer break? Teachers are so lucky! All that time off."

On seeing a friendly face, Lexi could not hold it together a moment longer. Despite her determination not to cry, she was overwhelmed and collapsed into sobs the moment she set foot inside.

"Whatever's the matter? Bad first day at school? Oh, come in and sit down. You can tell me all about it. This calls for cake." Ayesha steered her friend into her sleek modern kitchen, which was filled with warm afternoon light. She poured her a glass of water and presented her with a big box of tissues.

"You can cry as much as you like. Ajay's gone to do some shopping. He won't be back for a while. I had a shift this afternoon."

Ayesha volunteered at a local charity shop connected with People Against Coercive Euthanasia. What had started out as a retirement project, sorting and selling second-hand clothes and ornaments for a few hours a week, had turned into something she had never expected. Lexi knew that Ayesha had quietly saved several lives. When old people brought in unusually large quantities of their possessions, it could be a sign that they were preparing in secret for a planned death. Simply by chatting to the customers, making them aware of the manipulation to which they had often been subjected, and offering them the services of PACE's legal team, she had helped several of them stay alive.

As a fellow activist, Lexi knew she could trust Ayesha completely. Together, they had already done some daring things to counter the geriatric death program, conceived by Yuthentic and delivered by The Corporation, that was sweeping the country. The public outcry they had provoked earlier in the summer, however, had now faded, and Lexi found herself wondering whether they had actually achieved anything.

"How was your vacation?" Lexi ventured, as she took a third tissue from the box.

"It was amazing. I'll tell you all about it. But first, what on earth has upset you so much?"

"I thought I was all right 'til I got here. But it's everything, Ayesha. Everything."

As Lexi was engulfed by another wave of tears, Ayesha brought out an elegant white bone china teapot. It had a long spout and slender gold handles. She sliced coffee and walnut cake onto delicate plates and filled matching mugs with strong tea for each of them.

"This is a lovely set," Lexi said, relieved to have something nice to say about a household object rather than having to go on about killing people all the time. Even she was bored with talking about it. "Not fussy but still special."

"A little beauty every day makes life worth living," Ayesha said grabbing two gold cake forks from a drawer. "There's more if you want it."

They sat quietly at the breakfast bar for a few minutes sipping tea and eating forkfuls of sweet cake. Ayesha resisted the temptation to fill the silence. She could see it was hard for Lexi to know where to start, but after a second slice and a refilled mug, she was finally ready to talk.

"I can't stop thinking about what those monsters did to Mabel."

"It must have been terrible for you, being there when it happened. Do you want to talk about it?"

"She never knew anybody cared about her. I was too late."

"I'm so sorry."

"We went to all that trouble to save her life, but it wasn't enough, was it? The damage was already done. I even started CPR. Then the machine took over. I thought the cavalry had arrived, but I should have known better. Everything stopped. The silence was devastating. They said she had been gone too long. I couldn't get the damn thing off her. I've been in touch with The Corporation. I'm not family so they don't have to tell me anything." She started crying again.

"I'm sure you did everything you could," Ayesha said softly.

"You can't fight them. Once they've got you in there, it's all over. They have complete control." It was the first time Ayesha had seen Lexi look scared. "They make it seem so humane, so clinical. Kindness Centers? What a joke! I've been having nightmares, but Bob says I can't tell anyone. He made me refuse the counselling they offered me because I was there when it happened. Bob said they will mess with my mind, and I have to move on. I know I need help but Bob's dead against it." Until she had spoken to Ayesha, Lexi had not realized how angry she was.

"I'm sure he has your best interests at heart, Lexi. After all he knows how these things work. And you can always come here."

"I can't even get medication without telling an outsider why I feel like this," Lexi said. "Bob has been trying to cheer me up in his own way. We even went away for the weekend."

"How lovely. Anywhere nice?"

"It didn't really work. Well, it was OK. He took me back to his hometown, up north. It's supposed to be the seaside, but there wasn't any sea. The best thing was the pinball machines. And Jennifer – his friend Trevor's mother. She was lovely. She's one of us."

"That's an exclusive club!" Ayesha laughed, "I'm honored to be a member, Lexi."

"You know what I mean. She thinks about stuff. Does things. She's involved with PACE. Her husband had been targeted. It's obvious. But she's fighting them off. All over the country people are waking up to what's going on. For the first time, I understood that I am part of a national movement, not just some mad old teacher in South London with a delusional fixation on saving people. She even mentioned our Fakesy. I couldn't believe it."

Ayesha's eyes were wide. "You didn't give anything away, did you?"

"No, not really. But you should have seen Bob's face when he thought I might. It was a picture." Lexi chuckled, but Ayesha didn't laugh.

"All that stuff he's done to help us, Lexi. It could land him in a very difficult position. Don't be too hard on him."

Lexi took another gulp of tea. "I'm not ungrateful. Goodness knows I was on my own long enough. But you've got to admit he's an odd bod. Plus, he actually works for them, Ayesha. The deathmongers. Can I really forgive him for that? He doesn't actually kill anyone, well, not as far as I know, but it's the same firm. I can't help asking myself, how can he do that? Especially after everything I've been through. And when I wanted to have a proper chat with Jennifer, to try to help her, he steered me right off. He was embarrassed."

"He has risked everything. You would never have got the five out of the Disposal Center without his help. Not a snowball in hell's chance. And who knows how that could have ended?"

Lexi nodded. "I know. I can't help thinking I was lucky to get out of the dorm alive, too. The robot threatened to sedate me, you know, if I didn't stop making a fuss about Mabel. And you're right. Bob is a good man. I don't want to spend the rest of my life without him."

Ayesha wondered whether she had heard her correctly. "What? Surely you haven't been thinking about splitting up?"

"I keep asking myself what I'm doing with someone who works for The Corporation. It could become a deal breaker. I don't want it to, but I'm not sure how much I can trust him."

"You've been under enormous stress, Lexi."

"Tell me about it."

"For goodness' sake, don't do anything rash. You need to talk to Bob."

Lexi nodded. "I've tried. I'll try again. There was a moment in the van when I should have said something, but I just pretended to be asleep."

"Choose your moment. A time when you're not too angry would be best, you know."

"I don't think there can ever be at time when I'm not angry." It was hard to believe this calm bright room was only a few miles away from all the horror she had seen so recently.

"You know what? I didn't even come here to talk about Bob!" She blew her nose.

"We need more tea, I think." Ayesha tipped the tea-leaves into a built-in bin somewhere behind the breakfast bar, swilled out the pot and filled the kettle. "Go on, keep going. I'm multitasking."

"Today at school, a whole load of the kids turned up looking all pleased with themselves because they'd got tickets to the Yuthie conference at the weekend. I felt sick."

"At the O2?" Ayesha said. "My grandson was there as well. His sister was furious she didn't give her his plus one."

"Oh no. I'm so sorry to hear that. Is he a member?"

"No, a friend from work invited him. Sunil won't do anything stupid. Mark my words. What did they say that worried you so much?"

"The kids told me that they completely filled the main arena. Every single seat was taken at £100 a ticket. Who knows where they get the money from. The ones who couldn't attend in person had seen the livestream. They were buzzing about it. Do you know what it is? Mass hysteria. I haven't seen a group of teenagers this worked up since Take That split up in 1996. My friend Adam, at school, was obsessed with them. Today's kids always seem more worldly than we were back then. They're born cynical, and maybe that's not such a bad thing. Most of the time they are aware they are being manipulated. They've grown up with it. But this time it's different. And what's worrying me most is that they've gone public with Phase Two. Not one of the kids had a bad word to say about it. It's really going to happen, Ayesha. I don't know whether I have the strength to fight them anymore. And if I had to choose between fighting The Corporation and keeping Bob…" Lexi was lost for words.

"Bless you, Lexi. You don't have to choose. Look how far we have come!"

"I'm exhausted. I've never felt this conflicted about anything. And I really want it to work with Bob. He's everything to me. The reason I haven't been able to talk to him about it properly is that I'm terrified of driving him away."

CHAPTER NINE

"**Y**OU ALREADY HOME?" LEXI SHOUTED. The shower was running, and she could hear loud music playing. Bob did not reply.

She dropped her backpack at the bottom of the stairs and ran up to knock gently on the bathroom door. Inside, Bob was singing along loudly to the chorus of David Bowie's 'Queen Bitch'.

"I hope that's not about me!" she shouted cheerily through the din.

"Can't hear you. I'll be out in a minute," he yelled back.

Lexi felt frustrated. She had psyched herself for a calm discussion with Bob about the mountain of things that were preying on her mind. However, she knew it would be unreasonable to expect him to get into all that on an empty stomach. Even though she was stuffed full of coffee and walnut cake, she set about half-heartedly browsing the fridge for dinner ideas. After various indulgences during their weekend away they both needed to get back onto a healthy eating plan.

"Is Niçoise salad alright?" she said when Bob eventually joined her. He had got changed into long grey shorts and his black 'Heroes' T-shirt. "We haven't got much in."

"Sounds good. Shall I make the dressing?" He reached into a cupboard and started assembling ingredients while Lexi put two eggs on to boil.

They moved around the kitchen, each effortlessly allowing the other just the right amount of space to complete their next task. As always, each dropped their phones into the Faraday box that stood on the side.

"How was your first day?" she asked, surprising herself with how convincingly she avoided sounding like someone who disapproved of what her partner did for a living.

"Nothing controversial."

She wondered whether that was meant to be some kind of dig, but she could not believe it would have been deliberate.

"That sounds promising," she said.

"People seem alright. There were more actual human beings there than I had been expecting. That could be a good thing, I suppose. I'm guessing there must be around fifty on shift at any one time. It's a massive place. Busy. Lots for me to do."

"That's good. You hate being bored, don't you?"

"True."

"Are they involved in any of the, you know…" She was annoyed with herself. Why had she even asked? And why could she not bring herself to say it, the Endings work? She did not have to spell it out. Bob knew immediately what she meant.

"Oh, no. None of that. It's only the newer builds that are 'integrated'. Like that one we drove past in Preston. At my place it's mainly manufacturing and delivery ops. They told me they are working on doing more with the exoskeletons, but I haven't been across to that floor yet – only glimpsed it on the CCTV. Looks interesting, though."

"What are they?"

"Erm. The best way to describe them would be wearable robots. A bit like the dancers we saw at the weekend, only with people inside."

"Goodness. I'd be seasick if I were inside a robot that moved that fast!"

"I have to say, I'm happy to be in the control room for the time being. But it might be fun to have a go in one if I ever get the chance."

"What do they use them for, Bob? Sounds like something for military application to me. I thought you said you'd opted out of that." All the tech firms were involved with weapons in one way or another. However, The Corporation was among a handful that gave their staff the option to minimize their involvement with combat technologies. It helped them to get their shares included in ethical investment portfolios. A kicker for the stock price.

"Yes, I have. But it can never be a hundred percent. There's inevitably cross-over. That said, the robots in our place are all intended for civilian operation. Lifting heavy loads, construction, medical applications. That kind of thing. Unless they're going to start smothering people with sourdough pizzas."

"Very good." She was only partly convinced. "What did you do for lunch?"

"Just what I took with me. The box is in the dishwasher. I might get a delivery tomorrow. Perk of the job! We have staff discount on loads of food places because they use our droids."

"Are there any healthy options?"

"Um, I haven't really checked."

Before she could stop him, Bob had taken a garlic baguette out of the freezer and popped it in the oven. "Do we really need that?" she ventured. "I do," Bob said, "You don't need to have any if you don't want to."

The tempting smell of garlic butter soon filled the kitchen. By the time it came out, the soft bread was impossible to resist – even for someone who had just eaten two substantial slabs of cake. They perched at their small kitchen table with the salad plated and the baguette in the middle. Day was turning to evening. Bob was quiet for a while. He was hungrier than Lexi and focused intently on his food before eventually looking up and asking her how her first day back at school had gone.

"A bit tricky, to be honest."

"Why's that, then?"

She fidgeted with a piece of bread. "Oh, Bob. I don't want to have an argument."

"Don't be silly. Why would that happen?"

"I've been trying not to keep going on about, well, you know, all the stuff that's happened. PACE and everything. But I don't seem to be able to get away from it. Not even at school. I'm sorry." She looked worn.

Bob put down his cutlery and laid his hand over hers. "We said no secrets. Remember what happened last time? Come on. Tell me."

"Promise you won't be cross?"

"I want to help you, Lex."

"But at the weekend you tried to stop me talking about it."

"I'm sorry. I should have explained on the way home, but you slept most of the journey, and when we got back it was late. To be honest, I was worried about Andy. He's fragile. Going on about the Endings – well, it's for them to sort out, isn't it? As a family. I just wanted us to have a nice break without bringing all that up, again. Do you see where I'm coming from?"

"Yes. Now you put it like that I can see why you tried to shut me up."

"That's a bit brutal."

"But it's how it felt. We live in this nice, safe world where no one talks about what's going on under the surface. The taboos around death work in their favor, don't they? Not to mention the threat of being accused of believing conspiracy theories. But they are killing real people. Real lives. Real deaths. I've seen too many of them, now."

"I get it." Bob tried to show he was listening even if he had no idea what they could ever do about it. "How could anything have happened at school, though? They're just kids. I've heard of starting them young, but that seems ridiculous!" Bob's ill-judged attempt at humor fell flat. She looked dejected.

"Bob, they're joining the Yuthies in droves. The kids. I can't stop them."

"It's not your job to stop them."

"You're starting to sound like Ardua now. You'll be saying 'Freedom. Choice. Independence' next."

"What? Have you talked to your boss about it?" Bob looked concerned. "What did you say?"

"Nothing compromising. Anyway, it was pointless."

"You two have never exactly been on the same wavelength."

"But at least she's normally keen on protecting the children." She shrugged. "This time, she just doesn't see the danger."

"Why would she? Most people haven't seen what we have."

"Yep. And you still work for them." She could not keep it in any longer.

"That's what this is really about, isn't it?"

"Not entirely. But of course it bothers me, yes."

Bob started to clear the plates and began making tea. The kettle started to hiss, and he moved closer to her so she would be able to hear him above the noise without having to raise his voice. "Let's get back to the kids for a minute. What did they say?"

"They are all head over heels in love with that Jasper. I hate to say it, but I can see why. He gives them hope. Our generation has failed them, and we're not even boomers! One kid even suggested it would be a good idea for me to join. He thought he was being nice. I was really snappy with him. I'm starting to turn into someone I don't like very much. I'm really worried I'll lose it in class."

"So, do you want to leave?" Bob asked, not sure what else he could suggest.

"No! How can you say that? You know I love my job."

"Same for me," Bob said quietly. "On balance we both like what we do."

"Yes, but my workplace – the school, well, any school actually – is not managing industrialized death."

"Of course not. But then neither is CRAP. We're doing nice, helpful things that simply take some of the tiresome old friction out of life. Bringing people food and medicines. Helping those who have had injuries to build up the strength to walk again. Seriously, Lex, on the 'do no evil' index, I think my job has a better score than most."

For the first time she detected something in his body language that suggested he might soon begin to count down the number of times he was prepared to have this same argument. It made her feel sick. He changed the subject.

"You were back later than I'd expected."

"I'm glad you reminded me." She grabbed her backpack and reached inside. "Ah. It may not have travelled so well." From the depths she retrieved a nest of gold and white checked napkins which she peeled back to reveal a piece of badly bashed coffee and walnut cake. The inside layers were greasy but it had just about held together. "Ayesha sent this for you. She's very kind."

"I don't always say the right thing, Lex, but I do try to be a good listener." He reached across for the package and used his dressing-smeared salad fork to break off a chunk.

"You are. But I think I need professional help. I may have PTSD. The factory was bad enough, but being there when they suffocated Mabel. I feel such a failure." She thought she was going to cry again.

"Oh dear. What did Ayesha say?" His mouth was half full of cake, and his words muffled.

"I am worried for her. Her grandson Sunil went to Yuthfest. She seems to think he's immune. But you never know."

"Don't say that. I'm sure nothing bad will happen to him."

Lexi took a deep breath. "You're probably right. Maybe I should spend a bit more time worrying about myself for a change. What choice do I have? Carry on going to work. Listen to the kids. Give them a safe space to talk. And stay involved with PACE."

"Hang on a minute, Lex." Bob put down his fork and shook his head. "You just said you think you've got PTSD? Surely it's time to take a break from being an activist?"

Sitting back in her chair, she folded her arms tightly. "We've already established I can't risk using the Corporation counselling service. You're absolutely right – there will be triggers in the algorithm. If there's a sniff of me having done anything illegal the tapes could end up anywhere. It would be too risky for both of us. But I have to keep fighting. If I walk away I will never forgive myself. In fact, I will feel a hundred times worse. As if it weren't bad enough already, Phase Two is coming and the world needs to know that youth is no longer a guarantee of safety. Any one of us could be next."

"So…?"

"So I will keep on going to work. Just like you. It's what I love. It's all I know. And it's the best hope for keeping me sane."

Bob looked hurt. Why didn't she see ever say that he was part of the solution? He would have to spell it out.

"Well, you know you can always talk to me. Quite apart from the fact that I love you unconditionally, there's the small matter that what you know about me could result in a prison sentence." Another attempt to lighten the mood with dark humor that fell flat.

"But Bob, I need more than that. I need to know that you are prepared to take action." She looked him in the eye.

He held her gaze. "You know that already."

"Still prepared, then."

"I'm disappointed you thought you even needed to ask. Of course I am." He one final question for her. "So, you don't want me to leave my job at The Corporation? I thought that might be the only answer."

"It's not ideal, but no. I won't ask you to do that. It's who you are."

"Thanks, Lex," Bob said. "I'm glad to hear that, finally."

Lexi looked at him directly. "And anyway, why would I want you to leave? Having an insider could come in handy again."

CHAPTER TEN

H UNDREDS OF METALLIC, SUGAR-COATED ALMONDS glittered in a delicate frosted bowl under the Brytely office lights. They had become the confectionery of the moment since an influencer on Splutter had served them up at their wedding. Their fans had gone on to construct thousands of stories around the otherworldly pebbles which seemed almost too gorgeous to eat.

Recognizing the aspirational treats immediately, Portia told herself that something with a nut inside had nutritional benefits. A handful would go perfectly with the coffee she was about to make. She reached out to help herself, but stopped in her tracks when she saw the tiny words printed on them. Freedom. Choice. Independence. Ugh. She had not even licked one yet, but she was getting a nasty taste in her mouth.

"They were in the Yuthie goodie bag," Sonny said cheerily. He had crept up behind her in the open plan work kitchen. Portia flicked some switches on an appliance to kick off the coffee making process, selecting medium roasted Ethiopian beans which came with good enough sustainability credentials.

"More like a small backpack, to be honest. It was one of the best hauls of freebies I've seen. They had seaside rock as well, but that's for a lower demographic, obviously. So I gave it to my sister." She winced at his choice of words but did not pull him up on his careless snobbery. He didn't know her mother was working at the end of the pier, after all. In her rush to get out of the arena, Portia had not stopped to collect her mementos, but it looked like Sonny had picked up enough swag for the whole office.

"They've tried to copyright the sigil, but I've told them they're wasting their time," he went on, "I mean, a circle with a line through it? Do me a favor! They stole it in the first place." She noticed that some of the almonds had been embossed with the Yuthie symbol, too.

"So now you're the go-to source for the Yuthie inside track? Please tell me that means we don't need to talk to Lars anymore?"

"I'm afraid not. He is still the Yuthentic supremo. Even if he did introduce me to a few more of the Executive on Saturday." He stopped short of saying 'after you left'.

"Who was that then?" Portia was grateful he didn't dwell on her having run off. Perhaps she had been a bit rash. She was all too aware that they had the Phase Two planning workshop coming up that week and she could not afford to let her doubts derail it.

"Lars took me to meet Holly. Big old bird. She was a bit scary to be honest."

"She's a Yuthie! Of course she was scary!"

"I mean, aggressive. Beyond the usual off-the-scale creep-o-meter reading."

"Yeah, well, if you believe Lars the woman's got a lot going on. Anyway, would you say she was aggressive if she were a man?"

"Yes, I would."

Portia arched her eyebrows in disbelief as he went on. "Oh, come on! You saw her at the Select Committee. She was a total bitch."

Softening a little, Portia replied. "Fair enough. I wasn't sure whether she was simply rising to the occasion. So, what was she like then, this Holly? Apart from frightening you." Was she flirting, now, in some inept way? Neither she nor Sonny could be certain.

Whatever was going on, he seemed to like it. He laughed, anyway. "She's a complete devotee. A true believer in the wealth distribution agenda, as we know, and as a result a huge fan of our Endings work. She couldn't stop going on about it. Lars had obviously told her about both of us. Seems rather keen on the old Slaytanist. She was sorry to have missed you, actually."

The thought of a Yuthie MP knowing her name made Portia squirm but she tried not to show it. "Wow. I'm... honored. Maybe next time I'll allow her a few more moments in my presence."

Although she had a mountain of work, Portia didn't want to move away from Sonny. No matter how much she tried to tell herself she should restrict contact and keep their relationship purely on a professional footing, she could not escape the fact that he was the closest thing she had to a friend in a city she found alien and full of contradictions. The entry level office flirting lifted her days. It was a consolation, too, that she knew more about him than any of her other work colleagues. Enough to lose him his job. She even knew his real name, Sunil, although he did not know hers. Plus, he had nearly kissed her once and she had spent the last nine months kicking herself for backing away. The coffee machine grinded and whirred.

"Did you get up to much at the weekend?" she asked, keeping it casual.

"I saw my grandparents on Sunday. They are just back from some big walking and yoga holiday thing. Away for months. You know what they're like."

She had met them only once, but Sonny's grandparents, Ayesha and Ajay, were unforgettable. Kind, welcoming and generous. He had taken her to a New Year's Eve party at their house which had turned out to be full of surprises.

"Nan's still asking after you," Sonny said while the noise of the coffee machine provided acoustic camouflage.

"She's lovely. Both of them." Portia could never imagine introducing anyone from her family to Sonny. The idea of taking him up to their tiny, overcrowded house out by Liverpool airport was absurd. Having seen how at home he was in his grandparents' mini mansion she was certain that Sonny would be alienated forever – and probably also repulsed – if he saw the place she came from. That was another reason her crazy idea of a relationship with him had to be a non-starter.

"I'm lucky, I know," he said, graciously. "They've done so much for me."

Portia shot him a wry look. His grandparents had inadvertently launched his meteoric advertising career when they inspired the Rockstar Ending campaign. The concept had been born from the insight Sonny had gleaned from them into what made rich old people tick – in their case an addiction to luxury travel and strong penchant for rock music. They ticked all the boxes for their target group. The three As. Affluent, Aging and Alive.

She could not help saying, with a little exasperation: "Honestly? I'm not convinced you have any idea how lucky you are."

"Maybe," Sonny said nonchalantly. He was getting used to Portia's edges. "Anyway, I'm glad you reminded me. Nan's invited you over again. They're having a party. You should come."

"I'd love to." She faltered a little. "Provided I'm free, of course." What a joke. They both knew that, apart from when she was at work, Portia was nearly always free.

Talking about Ayesha reminded them both of their shared secrets.

When Brytely and The Corporation had been called to give evidence to the Health, Euthanasia and Legacy Planning Select Committee, Ayesha had surprised them both by appearing in the public gallery. At first, Sonny had denied that Ayesha was there, but Portia would not let it go. His reticence was all the confirmation Portia needed to believe that his grandmother was somehow involved in the lobby against the Endings program. Why else would she have turned up?

"Anything else to report from Saturday?" She needed to stop thinking about the night of the near-miss.

Sonny nodded playfully. "Ah, I get it now. You're worried you might have missed something? Don't fret, I won't tell anyone you bunked off. I suppose there were a few bits and pieces. I've written some notes. Actually, I came over to ask whether you'd have a look at them for me. I'd value your opinion. I want to make sure I get the tone right. We have to remain objective in all this, after all, don't we?"

She rattled the sugared almonds and turned them over in her warm, sticky hand. She had been clutching them for so long that the words were beginning to smudge. The word 'modeerF' – had somehow been transferred onto her palm. She thought about how popular 'Stairway to Heaven' had been on their playlist and how she and Sonny had spent an afternoon sending each other witty messages when they stumbled across allegations of backmasking. Researching the music for the campaign had been one of the best bits of the job. It was just a pity about what they were selling. Maybe 'freedom' backwards was some sort of satanic spell? She hoped not. It was now imprinted along her lifeline.

"Objective, Sonny? Really? I'm not sure I believe that's possible. But I appreciate we are obliged to make it look that way. Sure. Send it across."

Checking each other's work was nothing new. Even though their relationship could be awkward, most of the time it was rewarding when they worked together. That was part of the problem.

As she read through what Sonny had written, she was struck by how normal he had made their Saturday night sound. All they had witnessed was a happy crowd of ordinary young people heading out to see a superstar. When she saw the words 'twenty thousand' describing the capacity of the O2, the Pulp song 'Sorted For E's and Wizz' popped into her head.

She thought ruefully of the time before she was born when young people did other things. A time that seemed freer, edgier, riskier. Best of all, unpredictable. Her mother and her grandad had told her so many stories about the music scene when they had been younger.

It was her grandad's memories that interested her most. Nights out in Liverpool at Eric's, hanging round Probe Records. How he and Nan used to get a babysitter so they could go over to Manchester when The Hacienda was at its glorious height. It had all helped when The Corporation had asked Portia and Sonny to join a brainstorm on their sponsorship of the Blackpool Illuminations. There was a hint that someone at the top thought Madchester would provide some inspiration.

Drifting off into the past at her desk would not get Portia's work done. She bit into one of the sugared almonds, hoping it would not live up to its promise. However, it was delicious. The sugar hit instantly helped her focus, and there were quite a few more of them lined up on a piece of tissue. Resistance was futile.

This was what she had to do for a living. Check the homework of some guy on whom she had a ludicrously complex and futile crush. She began to make notes on her second screen and was about to put her thoughts into a message when a chat window popped up.

Sonny: Hey. I've got the date of Nan's party. Saturday 28th October. 1970s theme. Lots of scope for you to dress up again!

Portia: Ah.

Sonny: What?

Portia: Mum's going to be down that weekend. I do want to come, though. Could you ask them to move it? Ha.

Sonny: I'm sure they would do anything for you, but the venue is really special, and they booked it ages ago. I've got a better idea. Why don't you bring your mum? Nan would love it. The more the merrier. And you can get her to make you another one of those retro outfits to die for.

Portia: Can I let you know?

Sonny: Sure. Anyway, what do you think about my jottings?

Portia. Did you leave out the riots on purpose?

Sonny: They were hardly riots. More of a minor tussle. Do you think we should mention them?

Portia: Hell, yes! It was the most authentic part of the evening. And we can't ignore the anecdotal reports about the activists being beaten up. Well, we can't say it quite like that, obvs.

Sonny: OK, can you pop something suitable in there?

Portia: Sure. We can check it together later. And I'll get on to Mum. Where is this party going to be, anyway?

Sonny: Somewhere unforgettable.

CHAPTER ELEVEN

"WHAT HAPPENS IN BLACKPOOL STAYS in Blackpool," A humanoid robot whispered eerily before it pulled away and made some unconvincing movements with what was supposed to be its face. It took Jess a few moments to realize it was supposed to be winking.

"This place is more like uncanny valley," she retorted, swiping a glass of wine from the tray it was holding as quickly as she could. The machine replied in a hurt tone, "There's no need to be nasty, is there Jess?"

Before Jess could engage in any more robotic banter her boss, Nicky Hartt, beckoned her away, saying "Save your energy for the real people."

"It even knew my name!"

"Of course it did. That's just basic facial recognition. We only need to stay until I've had a few words with Mason. Then we can go on somewhere else."

It was the first time the Member of Parliament and her researcher had ventured so far from London on official business. After an absence of almost 30 years, the Labour Party had decided to return to Blackpool for their annual conference. All the other political factions were making a big fuss about regenerating the North, and they needed to jump on the bandwagon.

The town had fallen out of fashion in the late 70s. Their event trade had been lost to places with better train connections, modern and accessible venues and accommodation with ensuite bathrooms. Back then, Blackpool could only offer one or two faded grand hotels, forcing other delegates to lodge in a maze of one-star B&B accommodation. Tiny bedrooms were packed tightly into crumbling Victorian buildings served by 19th-century plumbing, stained hardboard furniture, and clashing décor that failed even to qualify as ironic.

Recently, however, things had started to get better for the town. The Corporation had fought off some serious competition to win the contract to build a new tourism and conference hub, quickly smoothing away a slight whiff of controversy that surrounded the bidding process.

What resulted was a lavish, Vegas-style complex overlooking the sea, itself built in the shape of a wave, with a maze of interconnecting spacious halls that could be used for events. The façade was lit at night, all year round, in thousands of mesmerizing pulses of color designed to reflect changes in the expanse of water it faced.

On the fringes of the site, The Corporation had also, true to their promise, built more than a thousand units of affordable housing which had blown away any final fragments of resistance to their plans from the local council. They were so used to throwing up the accommodation around the country it cost them nothing in architectural fees, and the flats were ready within six months of the proposals being approved.

Another big factor in the resort's rebirth was The Corporation's provision of comfortable autonomous road transport. Visitors were no longer forced to freeze on windswept platforms, waiting for erratic trains. The Corporation's customers could be whisked to the North West in safe, clean, soft yet supportive autos featuring an onboard menu of top-class entertainment and a variety of nutritional options. Now, the holiday began at your front door.

"Trust them to entertain us in the room with the best view." Jess could not hide her deep suspicion of The Corporation.

"Yep. We're in The Cairoli Room. Right on the crest of the wave. I bet the sunset's amazing on a clear night." Nicky followed Jess's gaze out to sea. They were surrounded by an expanse of darkening sky that flung a fine, relentless drizzle against the sheer glass walls and ceiling. "Thank goodness we don't need to go out there." An airplane entered their field of vision on the left, climbing steeply over the water before banking across the sea and disappearing into the thick mist.

"When can we get out?" Jess fiddled with the controls for her chair, itching to escape.

"Can you just stop moaning for five minutes? You know I've got to speak to Mason. He knows I'm coming. Amber said she would introduce him when they get here."

When the pandemic stopped travel, the party conferences had been through a couple of virtual years, where debates were held online, and pundits had speculated that real life events would die out. They said that the party conferences were a relic of a bygone age, useful only to lobbyists. However, the reverse had happened. People craved in-person contact. Corporate event budgets, which had been dwindling for years under pressures to cut costs, had been replenished. Nowhere was the sociability boom more conspicuous than among those companies that depended on political goodwill to maintain their income stream from the public sector.

"They've lucked in bigtime this year," Jess said, "Actually owning the conference venue. I'm sure that gives them an unfair advantage. Not that anyone would have bothered to object."

"There's no point going on about it now." Nicky did not want to discuss talk about how they felt about The Corporation in a place she suspected would be equipped with their listening technology. She made a 'zip-it' gesture to Jess, as if sealing her own lips. "I'm not being rude, just need to be careful, OK?"

Jess sniffed and took out her phone. "At least there's no problems getting around here with my chair," she observed coldly while she scrolled.

CHAPTER TWELVE

"I'M SORRY WE CAN'T ARRANGE for you to visit our Kindness Center while you're up here," Mason said to Amber, Labour's shadow minister for robotics, who would soon be accompanying him to the reception as guest of honor.

They were in a private suite directly below the Cairoli Room. The open space was dotted with classic mid-20th Century furniture that gave it the feel of a museum. It looked stylish but nobody ever wanted to sit in it.

Amber had become curious about The Corporation's plant on the road that linked Preston to Blackpool, after she had seen a story the night before on the local TV news. She had flicked on the screen, in a much smaller room in the same complex, while she hung up her clothes, and heard how the new building was being subjected to attacks.

A high-pitched whistle came from a hairline gap in the sliding doors that led out to a balcony. It annoyed Mason that they were unable to properly shut out the foul night. This was supposed to be the best room in his showcase building. He glanced at Channelle, his corporate affairs director. She knew him well enough to realize what was bothering him and nodded. As soon as the meeting was over, she would message the building maintenance team.

Through the rain, Mason eyed the lights on the horizon that marked out the banks of wind turbines. Trying to recreate the Dubai experience on the Lancashire coast might have been over-ambitious. On the other side of the glass, steam rose in erratic swirls from a hot tub that was exposed to the squall. Maybe they could synthesize a more soothing vista in future?

"We could arrange for you to join us at another facility when we are back in London." Mason suggested.

"I don't see why not," Amber said.

Their proximity to the jacuzzi was making her uncomfortable. She loved a spa, and in other circumstances she would have been the first one to slip into a bikini. But this was neither a hen weekend nor a romantic getaway. It was work, and she was under orders from the party leader to be extra nice to Mason.

The Corporation was openly giving money to all the political parties to help cover their running costs. Provided they declared it, the practice was legal. Labour needed the cash more than ever. Their funding base had taken a hit when many of their young supporters had defected to the Yuthies. Even their merchandise looked dated. They just couldn't seem to get it right.

Furthermore, Mason was fast becoming a global celebrity despite his reluctance to court the media. There had been a few tussles with journalists, but he had ridden them out and emerged unscathed. The Corporation's operations fell smack in the middle of Amber's portfolio as they were a recognized leader in robotics.

"You're not taking me to Brookwood, I hope?" She could not resist mentioning The Corporation's automated euthanasia center which had been subject to a headline-grabbing attack from PACE activists and the legendary street artist, Fakesy.

"We've made a lot of changes," Mason continued calmly. "Now, however, I believe we need to go and meet our guests."

The Mayor of Blackpool, complete with chain of office, was all over Mason the moment he came in the door. Someone said 'housing delivery targets' and there was a warm hum of approval. Amber was by Mason's side, and when she saw Nicky's blond bob in the crowd, true to her word she beckoned her over.

"We meet in person. At last," Nicky said, taken aback by the warmth of his firm, smooth handshake. No matter how much she wanted to hate Mason she couldn't. He had helped her to save the lives of several of her constituents, intervening personally to cancel their Endings plans. That was in the days when signing up meant an inescapable contract. Mason had seen to it that other people could change their minds in future. It wasn't his fault that Yuthentic had forced through such a terrible process when the assisted suicide laws had been first relaxed.

She had heard from others that there was something mesmerizing about being in Mason's physical presence and now she was experiencing it full-on. Penetrating grey eyes, silver hair, a lightly suntanned, just wrinkled-enough complexion and rock hard, trim physique. He was the full package.

"Delighted. I will always be grateful for the information you gave me," he said. "We're over the teething problems now."

After all, Mason had reassured everyone that he was in control by publicly firing his head of security. Nicky found herself smiling conspiratorially. "I appreciate the help you have given to my constituents, and I have to say it's wonderful we can be in touch in person."

From the start, he had been so genuinely concerned about the anomalies Nicky had exposed that he had taken the unusual step of giving her his phone number. Smiling again, he looked directly into her eyes.

Unsettled, Nicky nevertheless managed to carry on. "I'm sorry to be the bringer of bad news again, Mason..."

Channelle interrupted. "I'm afraid Mason needs to get ready for his talk. Can you pick this up later? We need to go to the backstage area, right now."

Mason still looked relaxed. "Well. if Nicky doesn't mind huddling behind the side panels with us, we might be able to clear this up." He cut Channelle dead and gestured that Nicky should follow him. Nicky glanced at Jess who nodded, "Go on. I'll meet you back here in a minute."

As the technician brought out a small battery pack and started to fix it to the belt of Mason's trousers, they talked. "Could you just make sure the sound is off, please," Mason said.

"Sorted boss." The technician showed him the switch.

"The thing is, I wanted to let you know I'll be asking a question about Phase Two in the House. A number of people I represent are anxious about the provisions of the

Euthanasia Act being extended."

"That's a political decision," Mason said, turning awkwardly in the confined space as the tiny microphone was clipped to his lapel. He glanced at Channelle who was just in earshot.

She stepped forward on his cue to join the conversation. "We were under the impression that the final approval for Phase Two would be a formality. According to our legal team, under the Euthanasia Act the Secretary of State has the right to extend the scope without going before Parliament."

"That's true," Nicky said. "But I'm still trying to get it discussed. After what happened last time, it's in your best interests as well as mine that this does not just go through on the nod. The reputational impact for you could be severe. Personally, I'm more worried about the emotional consequences for the vulnerable people being targeted and their relatives."

"No one is targeted. They are simply invited to use the service," Channelle said brusquely.

Nicky shot her a dismissive look and focused her response back at her boss. "You're not stupid, Mason. You can see how it looks. People are saying you're way too close to Jasper, by the way. He's not someone you want to get close to. You must have heard about his henchmen attacking disabled protesters at Yuthfest? I'm sure you don't want to be hauled up before another committee."

"Is that a threat?" Channelle said, now looking more rattled. She refused to be sidelined. Mason did not flinch. He came back with a calming smile.

"There's no need to overreact. As Channelle said, the green light for Phase Two is a political decision. It was courteous of you, however, to let me know your concerns. Maybe we can pick up on this again when I'm not about to go on stage. Can we switch the mic on now, please?"

With a final firm handshake, Mason stepped effortlessly up onto the podium. Nicky moved in the opposite direction and saw Jess waiting for her by the exit. If she moved quickly, they would be able to escape before the speeches began.

"I don't know what he said to you, but don't fall for it," Jess hissed, as the heavy door closed softly behind them. "He'll wrap you round his little finger if you let him."

CHAPTER THIRTEEN

I T WAS DARK OUTSIDE WHEN Mason met his chauffeur, Ricky, as arranged, on the ground floor. She was never late, always smiling and elegant in an informal, sporty kind of a way. A little shorter than Mason, she had a slim, boyish build and tidy brown hair cropped short at the sides and longer on top.

In sharp contrast, a bored night porter yawned and scratched his head, gazing absentmindedly at a screen behind the reception desk, unaware that the shapely cyclist looking at him was his chief executive. On the other side of the reinforced glass that encased the palatial entrance, five armed private security guards were spaced out in a line. Mason was pleased to see that they, at least, looked alert. With so many politicians onsite, The Corporation could not take any chances.

Mason's cycling shoes clacked and skidded as he tripped across the highly polished stone floor.

"I've checked her out. Everything seems to be running smoothly after the journey," Ricky said as Mason took his cycle helmet from her, and checked the adjustment, while she steadied the featherlight light carbon fiber bike upright with one hand. There was not a single scratch on it. The lubricated gunmetal chain sparkled under the lights. "I know you don't want to hear this boss, but security says you should have one of them follow you. The board will go mad if anything happens."

"Oh, please," Mason said, "I'll be fine. I've got the tracker on it."

"It's not the bike they're worried about."

He rolled his eyes.

"If they must."

Mason had woken feeling more tired than usual. Having carted the bike all this way, though, he was determined to get outdoors. They had driven up in the top-of-the-range pickup truck, with its enclosed box that doubled as a bike workshop, just so he could bring it. It looked more like an armored car than an SUV. He knew he would be fine once his legs started spinning.

His morning ride had become something of a ritual, even when he was travelling on business. It was more complicated overseas as he never wanted to put his precious Lois into the hold. Belonging to an international elite cycling group – the Biking Executive Road Killers (BERKs) – had been a godsend. When he was on another continent there was always some other Lycra-clad leader who could lend him a bike from his stable for a few hours.

Today Mason had about half an hour for a solo sprint before being incarcerated in his back-to-back schedule. He was hoping that the exercise would prepare him to negotiate the rest of his day with a clear head.

The night before, he had arranged his cycling shorts, a long-sleeved racing top, socks and gloves on a chair, so he would be able to get out quickly. Poached eggs with black pudding and a peeled kiwifruit were ordered for his room at 7.15am. If he got the timing right, as he usually did, he could catch a glimpse of the dawn outside, take a quick shower, bolt down his food and be on the road back to London ready to join his first call at 7.30am.

The dark, moonless sky had cleared. A light sea breeze ruffled the tufts of spikey grass that sprouted from the low sand dunes hugging the sides of the road.

There was hardly anyone else around as he started making his way into town on the narrow road that ran along the coastline. Although he could not see the water, he could hear the waves breaking on the shore somewhere to his left. It was peaceful as he rode past clusters of low, unremarkable houses and motels where all the sensible people were still asleep.

He wondered how the Corporation sponsorship of the Blackpool Illuminations was being received. It was a pity he had not been able to pop out while the robotic dancers were performing. The brand team had told him that their spectacle was being shortlisted for some big awards. But they always said that.

Unfortunately, he and Channelle had been tied up with local dignitaries the whole evening. The mayor seemed happy enough, and more than one of the guests had remarked on how much they had loved the Take That experience. Those involved in running the local entertainment industry had asked him a lot of questions about further investment. It seemed there was no end to the possibilities for The Corporation.

As Mason rolled onto the Promenade, the streetlights were switching off. The dunes had petered out and he could just about see the flat wet beach on the other side of a wide concrete pavement to his left. Without the shelter of the sandhills, he felt the breeze more keenly. Out at sea, an endless row of tiny lights marked where the vast banks of wind turbines perpetually whirred.

He arrived at the stage opposite the Tower where he knew the robots performed. In the cold dawn it was nothing special. Automated cleaning machines slid along the pavements, hosing away the debris of the night before with powerful, targeted jets. It felt like everyone else in the town was still in bed with a hangover. Mason sailed slowly past skeletal outlines of unlit tableaus and light displays, pale grey frames sketched against a sky that was gradually starting to color. The Manchester music scene tableaux had been his idea. Memories of a time that now felt a world away.

To lift his mood, he would need to get his pulse racing. He turned the bike round and began his return trip, getting a wave from the security officer on a motorbike who had been slowly tailing him. He began to pedal faster.

As he headed back towards the conference center he was pleased to see that the Corporation light show was pulsing gently on into the dawn. He turned inland before reaching the gate to his hotel, and followed the high cream stucco wall until, towards the back of the complex, it was replaced by a mesh fence topped with ribbons of razor wire. Surely the team could find a better way to keep the site safe that didn't make it look like a maximum security prison?

There was a screech of wheels as a car sped past him in the opposite direction. Before he realized what was happening, his outrider had accelerated into a protective position alongside him. As they neared the gate to the complex the motorcyclist waved Mason in and parked the bike across the gap, just in case. Mason was unsettled as he saw two of the other security guards fixing what looked like a sheet over part of the wall. The wind caught an edge.

There were a few spray-painted letters underneath. Not more graffiti? It was a pain, but he knew his guys would get one of the paint bots over from the Kindness Center pretty quickly. They knew the drill. No heavies. That was more the Yuthies' style. He made a mental note to talk to the new head of security about stepping up surveillance. The attacks were an irritation he could do without.

CHAPTER FOURTEEN

"**I** NEED YOU TO REARRANGE MY day, Penny," Mason said, on loudspeaker, as he tore back the Velcro on his shoes, peeled off his socks and cycling shorts, and threw them into his open suitcase. There was no need for pleasantries.

It was past dawn now. The sky was lighter although the dunes and the sea beyond were not yet in full daylight. When Mason returned, he had left the room in semi-darkness so he could take in the vast landscape without it being marred by internal reflections. There was a sharp, triple knock on the door. Breakfast had arrived early. He ignored it. They could wait.

"I want to call into the Kindness Center in Preston first thing, today. See what you can do."

He could trust Penny to restack his appointments. She had to do it most days. The knock came again, only louder this time. Rap-rap-rap and a muffled "Room service". He muttered a low-grade term of abuse under his breath. Hadn't anyone told them who he was?

It would be too much of a struggle to pull back on his damp, tight shorts. He was reaching for a towel to wrap around his waist when the door swung open without warning. Fumbling, he quickly draped it across his lap.

"Do you mind!" Mason blurted.

"Sorry sir," the waiter said, not looking sorry at all. "Where would sir like it?"

He gestured to the low glass table by the sofa, positioned to face the horizon. The man trotted across the room and dropped down the tray, hesitating for a second. It was obvious a tip would be out of the question. With a slight hint of regret at barging in so suddenly, he left. Mason's kiwi fruit was rolling about on a square plate from the impact. No one had bothered to peel it. He put his hand over the plate to see whether his eggs were warm. Only just. It would have to be food first, then shower.

The chauffeur was one of his favorite staff. They had travelled a lot together. Just by being with him, Ricky had learned a lot about Mason and some of the other BERKs, although they knew hardly anything about her. Mason never asked questions about what his employees did outside work. He liked to think that working for The Corporation was the most important thing in their lives.

Human Resources had done an excellent job when they hired Ricky. Aside from having a calming personality, she had worked as a mechanic for a professional cycling team. She took pride in keeping Lois, his favorite bicycle, in tiptop condition. It was a perk of the job that pleased them both.

By the time Mason was dressed and packed, the timing of which he had got down to a fine art, the bike had been meticulously cleaned and stowed for the journey. Not a grain of sand remained. Furthermore, Mason's PA

Penny had sent him a message: 'All sorted, details with Ricky'. As they pulled out onto the coast road, she started talking him through the revised order for his day.

"It's a bit early for a surprise visit, boss. The site manager's off today, but his deputy Vini is expecting us. As of ten minutes ago she was on her way in. We'll be there in half an hour, and right now you have a call with Channelle."

Bang on 7.45am, the scheduled time, her voice filled the car. "How do you think it went last night?" he asked his director of external affairs who was still in Blackpool overseeing their exhibition presence. "You understand these people better than me."

"Yeah, fine. Your speech went down well. That Terminator joke always gets a few laughs. We could have done without Nicky turning up with her sidekick, though. What was she thinking?"

Mason sniffed. "I agree it wasn't the right place to talk about such sensitive matters. Still, I can't help suspecting we're getting something wrong if an MP feels they have to doorstep me at a public event to get their point across. You can't deny she comes to us with useful information, every single time."

He waited to give Channelle the chance to agree with him. There was silence, so he went on.

"Is there anything else you haven't told me?"

"As far as I can tell Phase Two is a done deal, if that's what you mean. You only have to look at the Yuthies' track record of driving things through. We're just down to formalities." There was something hesitant in her tone that made him think she was not convinced.

"I get that. But what about public sentiment? When they find out what it really means. Have we any idea how that might play out for us?"

"I don't know. But I can get some research…"

"So you haven't checked it out already?" Sometimes he could not resist a little verbal slap to push one of his staff onto the back foot. Channelle was used to it and carried on.

"It's a risky set of questions to ask. Controversial at best. But we could do it through a third party if you were worried."

"It's not that I am worried. But the data will be useful. Get it sorted," Mason said. "Get legal to give me a call on how the contract is shaping up, would you?"

"OK."

Long before the onboard information system directed Ricky to turn, Mason had worked out that the big beige unbranded box ahead was the Kindness Center. The double gates recognized their pickup truck instantly. An outer barrier slid back, admitting the vehicle into a large steel cage where a team of four-legged headless robotic dogs crawled over the car's surfaces, checking for explosives, cameras and other forbidden goods. Mason knew that the sniffers weren't terribly effective, but they put on a good show, and until very recently had served as a foolproof deterrent against opportunist intruders. Although the robodogs were benign, keeping them in the cage suggested that they might have a murderous side.

Ricky pulled up alongside one of the many roller shutters that punctuated the walls. A short, curvy woman with long, sleek black hair and a welcoming smile came out and headed briskly towards them, narrowly missing being whacked by the car door, which swung open automatically.

"I'm Vini," she said, recovering her composure, "Delighted to meet you."

She led him inside. There was no natural light as they followed the long, depressing concrete corridor that ran around the perimeter of the ground floor, eventually entering a lift which took them up to the control center. Her brief from Penny had made it clear that Mason had only half an hour, so she needed to get him to the heart of things at once.

"I'm sorry you don't have time for a full tour," she said. "All our stats are excellent. We're meeting or exceeding all our targets. In the manufacturing and drone center we're employing around 200 local people in rotating shifts."

Mason nodded seriously. "How is morale?"

"Our Staff Happiness Index Table score has been consistently high. We are receiving those who have sadly died through a separate entrance, so the less robust staff do not have to see them."

"How well do you think the integration works?" Mason asked.

"No issues." Vini wondered whether she had been smiling too much.

The floor below them was divided into two unequal sections with a high partition wall sealing off one corner. Most of the space was taken up with robotic manufacturing and dispatch. Drones were launched from the floors towards the roof.

Behind the wall was the area where the assisted suicide customers were incinerated. Although the section was encased in a beige coated steel casing, he knew from the floorplans he had glanced at in the car that the furnace would be at the farthest side, surrounded by an array of insulation, cooling and filters to prevent any smoke or smells being expelled into the atmosphere.

Mason looked around the control center. What she said appeared to be true. No one looked like they were about to have a nervous breakdown.

"Our employees don't mind the depot being multi-purpose?"

"We run thorough psych tests in the recruitment process." She replied. "Now we've ironed out the teething problems with consent, and the moment of death happens further upstream – in a dorm, at the customer's home or in one of the designated hotels – there is practically zero chance of anything going wrong here. We're super-robust. Not one of the disposal operatives has even accessed the confidential counselling. We get aggregated figures. Anonymized, of course."

A fat drone flew out from one of the high floors and hovered under the ceiling. A square hatch opened directly overhead, and it quickly rose with a gentle swaying motion that made Mason feel slightly dizzy. Then, it disappeared.

"And drone losses?" he asked.

"None yet," Vini said cheerfully. "It's the biggest drone fleet outside of London serving a radius of 25 miles with subdepots and recharging stations in Blackpool, Southport, Wigan and Blackburn. We're the pilot personalized advertising hub, too."

"It all sounds too good to be true." Mason twinkled his eyes to try to get her to open up. "So what aren't you telling me?" He spoke slowly, trying not to sound too sharp. He almost felt sorry for the poor girl. She was only following the company script, after all.

"Sorry?" she looked confused and a little nervous.

"The vandalism? You're aware of it, surely?" He raised his eyebrows.

"We cleaned it up right away, Mason," Vini said, staying calm.

"But it was still all over the local news, I understand."

One of the other staff, sitting at a nearby workstation, overheard and shot Vini a sly look, questioning her ability to find the right answer. Mason didn't see. He was looking at Vini intently, now. She blushed but still did not speak.

"Could it have been an inside job?" Mason probed.

"Highly unlikely according to the HR AI. The profiling goes very deep."

"How did they get in, then? What happened to the cameras?" he asked.

Her face fell. "There's no footage, I'm afraid. We will have the entire perimeter covered in a couple of weeks. There was a huge push to get everything up and running before the Illuminations were turned on. They brought forward the opening date for the Kindness Center at short notice. We couldn't get all the cameras installed in time. Those we do have are concentrated around the main access points and more sensitive areas. We dealt with the invasion as soon as we found out."

"But we can't let this happen again, can we?"

"No, Mason."

He wondered whether he was being too brusque. It was not Vini's fault the place had been targeted. He allowed his facial muscles to creep into a soft smile, just like his coach had taught him. With 360-degree feedback you never knew who the algorithms would ask to rate you. He needed to leave her feeling positive about their interaction.

"Thank you for making the time to see me. Let's see if we can get this sorted out over the next few weeks, shall we?"

He was distracted momentarily by a screen behind Vini, hanging above her head. It was one of many that encircled the floor of the control center. She saw his eyes flick up and was relieved that his attention had switched to something else. The display showed another ground level hatch in the external fascia opening to admit a pallet. On it lay a stack of nine person-sized boxes, three on each row, being ferried in on an automated fork-lift machine. A ticker ran across the bottom of the screen giving the names of the dead, interspersed with the simple phrase 'rest in peace'.

"We get the names from the barcodes," she said. "It's a sign of respect." Mason nodded and blinked.

After the boss had gone, Vini was distracted. It had been touch and go. She kept asking herself whether there was anything she could have done to make the visit go better. If her mother had not been staying with her, she could never have got in at such short notice. As it was, she had to break off in the middle of the baby's morning feed. All the way through the meeting she had been worried about breast milk leaking through her clothes.

Most of all, though, she was convinced that her mind had gone blank when he was asking her simple questions. She had a chance to impress the CEO and she had blown it. All she could think of was her crying baby and the mysterious words that the vandals had written on the wall. *Lasciate ogne speranza, voi ch'intrate.*

Back in the car, Mason sipped from a flask of chilled water and slowly rolled his shoulders a couple of times. He rotated his ankles and then his head, first clockwise and then back the other way.

"I'm synching with the in-car video," he said to Ricky. "OK."

There was a ringing tone, then Jasper's face appeared on a screen that popped up in front of Mason. The Yuthentic leader looked at him coyly from beneath his tousled hair.

"I know all about you, Mason. You have been sleeping with the enemy, haven't you?" he said facetiously.

Mason had been working with Jasper long enough to understand his humor. Remarks like that only deserved a short reply. "Hardly," he said.

"What was it like?"

Mason was not going to be provoked. "Blackpool is making a comeback. You'd be surprised. It's really rather charming. There's plenty for people of all ages up here. You're too young to remember its heyday. So am I. But there's boundless positive energy. A hunger for reconstruction. You need to bring your show up here, you know. It would play right into your fairness agenda. Not to mention you'd get more recruits."

Jasper sniggered. "Do you ever stop touting for business? You're just annoyed Yuthfest went to one of your competitors, aren't you? All in good time, my man. All in good time."

"So tell me, Jasper, why did you want to talk to me?"

"I just wanted to ask if you had discovered anything I might find useful. From the opposition."

So that was it. "There's an interesting word."

"Meaning?"

"Opposition. You gave me the impression that Phase Two would go through quietly. I'm hearing rumors to the contrary. What do you think of that?"

Jasper was irked that Mason had turned the tables, and now seemed to be questioning him. It was not how he had wanted the call to go. "The public is on our side," he snapped, and ran a delicate hand through his hair, pushing it back from his face.

Mason watched the political mastermind for a moment and wondered whether Jasper's grey eyeliner was permanent. It suited him.

"How can you be so certain? I'm picking up resistance. And the news around Phase Two hasn't even broken through into the mainstream yet."

Jasper was defiant. "We're ahead of you. Seriously, by the time the sad remnants of the media have fumbled for an economy pocket torch to shine onto the issue, public opinion will already be so firmly fixed in favor of Phase Two they won't have the appetite for taking us on."

"That's a rather bold claim," Mason said and took a sip of his water.

Jasper looked a little too quizzically into the camera. "I was under the impression that I could rely on you – and those talented boys and girls at Brytely – to help us persuade people what's good for them. Good for us all." He was taunting him now. Mason knew what was coming next. "Unless you would like us to take our business somewhere else? It's not too late to split the contract, you know."

They both understood that The Corporation had already invested too much for Mason to walk away now. If he lost the business the board would never forgive him. His face was perfectly still.

"We've never let the government down before, Jasper. Don't worry. We're not about to spoil our track record now."

"Good. You focus on the logistics and leave the politics to me."

CHAPTER FIFTEEN

B OB HAD DRIFTED INTO A comfortable routine. The hours at CRAP were civilized. Best of all he got to hang out with the robots. Who needed to play a three-dimensional chess game like 'Go' when you could be thrashing an android at table tennis during your lunch hour?

When he had been there for about a month, Lola dropped in. She arrived bearing gifts. Coffees – a double espresso for her and a hazelnut latte for him; and a couple of croissants sprinkled with almonds and streaked with dark chocolate.

Bob had been expanding his range of Faraday bags and was in two minds whether to give one to his boss.

What if she disapproved of his runaway sideline? Lexi reminded him that Lola did not need to know his lock-up garage was crammed, floor to ceiling, with stock. Not if he was only going to present her with one of them.

He plumped for Aretha Franklin, from his 'Queens of Soul' collection. He remembered her singing along to 'Respect' at a karaoke night, years back, when they had worked together at the bank. Fifteen of them crammed into a tiny room somewhere near Spitalfields market. A corporate hospitality chicken coop. Bob had surprised everyone with his performance of' 'Starman'. They had all joined in the chorus.

That was in the happy times before Lars had arrived and started turning everyone against him. Just as well. The creep would have ruined the evening with his favorite Slayer song, 'Angel of Death'.

It had been a relief when Lola helped Bob to find something new. By some odd quirk of fate, he had recently crossed paths with Lars again. This time, however, his nemesis was working for one of The Corporation's suppliers and represented a less serious threat to Bob's sanity.

"That's lovely. Thank you," Lola said when he dragged out the squashed gift and handed it over. He was a little surprised when she added, "You never know when one of these might come in handy. That was a good night, wasn't it?"

Bob was touched that she remembered. "Long time ago. Must be, what, eight years?"

"Goodness, yes."

They tore into their croissants. Lola had even brought a couple of napkins which she set on the table between them. A small cloud of icing sugar left a film of sweet dust on the table.

"So, how's it going?" she asked.

"No incidents. Well not above level three," he joked. "Seriously, though, I'm enjoying it. Have you got time for a tour?"

"Not really."

"Shame." Bob looked disappointed. "There's some amazing machines here. It's not all mundane pizza delivery droids, you know. Although, admittedly, there are quite a lot of those." He knew she got extra appraisal points for face-to-face meetings with team members, but that could not be the only reason she had taken a whole morning out to see him. Her time was too valuable.

"How are you getting on with the security review?" Lola asked.

Surely, she already knew? "It's all in the reports, boss. I've identified three main vulnerabilities. Two require software patches which I've already requested. There's one hardware issue which will take longer to fix. The drone stability is an ongoing issue. It doesn't go wrong very often, but when it does it's a car crash. One of the aviation specialists has got a team together."

"Yep. I've seen all that. And the people? Any concerns?"

"Sorry?"

"The people."

She did that thing where she left a long silence hoping he would fill it. He refused to play and waited for her to go on.

"We both know security is never just about the technology. There's one person here who was present when another breach took place. I'm not going to say who it is. But if you pick anything up, let me know?"

He knew that she meant Sylvia but was not going to let on. "You're being rather enigmatic, Lola. Where exactly do you want me to focus my attention?"

"Just keep an eye open. OK? Speak to me in person if you see anything suspicious."

Great. Now they were asking him to spy on his colleagues. This had to be the fallout from Project Houdini, his last assignment, which had been closed without a comprehensive resolution. The rest of the business might have consigned it to the area of corporate history they would prefer to forget, but it was obvious that something about the incident at the Disposal Center was still bugging Lola. If she suspected Bob, however, she was not letting on.

"Anything else?"

She seemed hesitant. "Yes. Mason has asked if we can come up with something for his cycling executives' network, the BERKs. To be honest, I'm not sure what he has in mind. But could you scope it for me? Be discreet. We would not want the media to pick up on it, you know? Channelle will go bonkers when she finds out."

"What sort of thing is he looking for?"

She had no idea. "Something memorable that he can show off to his chums. Sorry, I mean, to the global CEO community, all of whom have significant influence on their organizations' purchasing decisions."

"Like what sort of thing? Is he looking for a whole new bike, or a modification? Navigation? Security? Training? A bot to carry their bags?"

"Hold those thoughts. Mason's chauffeur Ricky will be the best person to talk to, if you can get hold of her. She knows loads about bikes. I'm hoping you can come up with something he likes between you."

"Well, I'll give it my best shot, Lola. How long have I got to think about it?"

"A load of his pals are coming to London for a big ride at the end of March. He'd like to have something ready – at least an advanced prototype – by then."

"I'll see what I can do. Is that all?"

"There's one other thing. Your old school, Charlton Green, are having a careers event. I know we don't have a lot of jobs going for actual people, but HR has asked if we can do something for them. They've been a beacon school for The Corporation since you worked your miracle with the kids' suicide prevention program. With all the focus on jobs in robotics at the moment, could you pop down there? Maybe take a demo with you?"

"That I can do. It will be easy. In fact, it will be a pleasure. I know just the thing."

CHAPTER SIXTEEN

"**Y**OU CAN'T WEAR THAT IN public!" Lexi said. "How many times do I have to tell you? You'll get arrested!"

"But it's perfect for a 70s party." Bob said, already exasperated, as he tugged at the fine, embroidered white silk dressing gown in a futile attempt to get it to reach further down his thighs. "No one else will have anything as special as this."

Lexi sat on the end of the bed while Bob paraded in front of the mirrored wardrobe, checking from every angle in the hope of a better result.

She had had a feeling this was going to be an issue from the moment she had told him they were both invited to Ajay and Ayesha's 70th birthday. "I know how much you love it, Bob, but even if you ate nothing for the next three weeks and somehow managed to get it to cross over properly at the front, that kimono would still be too short to go out in."

Bob looked at his reflection longingly. She could not help wondering whether they were both seeing the same thing. "But Bowie wore one almost exactly like this onstage in 1973. He had a cape over the top at first, but then revealed what was underneath. It was a momentous evening, that Hammersmith Odeon show, the night he killed Ziggy, 3rd July…"

"Stop!" Lexi would have to fight hard to compete with what was going on in Bob's imagination. "First of all, there will be no points for historical accuracy. And secondly, it's our friends' birthday party, not a Bowie tribute night."

"Announcing Ziggy's retirement was arguably the most momentous night of his career. Well, apart from the terrible business with the wardrobe…"

Lexi could listen no longer. "And thirdly – not to put too fine a point on it – it's not just your thighs that are different to Bowie's. The Thin White Duke was a different age, shape – and arguably gender – to you, Bob. At least in the 70s. So, no. You're going to have to find something else to wear."

"The Thin White Duke was 75-76," Bob mumbled, indignant.

"Well, you're not going as him either. You're not thin and you're no Duke. And don't even think about Aladdin Sane makeup. You would look ridiculous. Plus, I have no interest whatsoever in going as Angie."

For a second, she thought he might cry. She could not let him make a fool of himself. It was time to dig deep and muster all her very best schoolteacher positivity.

"Bob. I am sure we can come up with something more flattering. For both of us. And something that doesn't give away all your…erm… secrets!"

They were still arguing about it a week later.

Both of them were tired after a busy day at work. Since arriving home, she had plodded through a pile of marking while Bob pulled together what they called a 'bits and bobs' dinner to eat in front of the TV. A warm focaccia, some slices of bresaola and salami, dips and a bowl of olives were arranged on the low table in front of the sofa with two mugs of tea.

A documentary on the life of Greek singer Demis Roussos had popped up in the guide as a viewing suggestion. It was the picture of him in one of his flamboyant robes that had made Lexi think a caftan might work.

"You know what, Bob? I'd be perfectly happy as a generic 70s woman. Why don't I just dig out one of my beach outfits and stick on some beads and a headband. That would do the trick, wouldn't it?"

A week had passed since their failed attempt to reach a decision. Now they were running out of time. After Bob's fashion show they had avoided the subject. They hated arguing and were both nervous about bringing the subject up again.

"I don't think so," Bob was quick to dismiss the idea. "No. That would be too much like the 1960s. And it would not be very flattering. You've got nice legs. You don't want to hide them under a tent."

He lent forward and scooped some hummus onto a piece of bread. Lexi eyed him apprehensively.

"You're not still hoping to go as Bowie, are you?"

"Probably not."

Bob carried on scrolling through the screen while they discounted another dozen ideas.

"Just because we're in our 40s doesn't mean we're only interested in old music and mid-life crisis reality TV, for goodness' sake!" Lexi said as various prompts appeared suggesting what they might like to watch. "And what the hell is that? Helping your parents decide when to die – a whole docuseries? How dare they!"

"There should be an opt-out…" Bob flicked the screen away from the offending page as quickly as he could.

"You can say that again!" Lexi quipped.

"Why don't we just put on some relaxing wallpaper. While we have dinner?"

"Sure. Sorry. I didn't mean to lose the plot."

A cityscape appeared on the screen. Towers of varying shapes and sizes were outlined against a sunless sky that alternated between orange, pink and violet in a loop of permanent artificial dawn. There was a soothing sound of traffic and birdsong. Headlights moved gently along embankments.

"We've only got ten days to work something out." Lexi said separating a thin slice of meat from the pile with a fork.

"I know." Bob was nervous. "Look. I have had an idea. Will you hear me out?"

"Of course. Go on."

"Well, I've been thinking I could go as a Ramone. All I need is a pair of jeans, T-shirt, black leather jacket. It's a classic look. And not entirely undignified, provided I keep the pogoing under control."

Lexi thought for a moment. She was in danger of agreeing with him. "But your leather jacket is brown," she said.

Why did she have to be so literal? "Well, I can splash out on another one. Or get a fake. That's the easy part."

She nodded approvingly.

"And they come in all shapes and sizes so you don't need to worry about anything unexpected popping out." He could not resist one last tease.

"Cheeky!" She giggled. Finally, he seemed to have come up with something she approved of. He felt a little of the built-up tension loosen in his shoulders. All he wanted was to make her happy. Recently it had been getting more difficult to believe that was possible.

"So that's me sorted, then."

Lexi was touched that Bob had put in so much thought. "Yes. I can see that working."

"I've got jeans already so that's easy. I quite fancy a wig though."

He was right. His hair, kind of short and brownish, could not be less rock 'n' roll. Still at least a wig wasn't makeup. She could never see that working on Bob's round face. "OK."

She had hoped that would be the end of it, for tonight at least, but now Bob was on a roll. "And I think you'd make a good Linda, too," he said.

"Who? Linda McCartney? What, turn up in a blond wig carrying a plate of vegetarian sausage rolls? Camera round my neck?"

"No! Don't be silly."

"I thought that could be a good idea. Surely you don't mean Linda Lovelace?"

"No! If I can't go in my kimono you're not going as a porn star. Don't you know anything about music? Linda

Ramone."

Lexi was puzzled. "But there wasn't a female Ramone! I know that much. I've played the pinball machine!"

"Linda was Johnny Ramone's wife. Look, there's bound to be loads of pictures of her online. Here we go."

With a couple of strokes, Bob had extinguished the ambient urban dawn and flipped up an internet search window. "Look. She would be perfect for you. You could zhuzh up your hair, sunglasses, boots. You practically have all that stuff already. You've got to enter into the spirit of it, Lex. We can't let Ajay and Ayesha down. Anyway we don't get out much, and this *is* rock 'n' roll."

He instantly regretted his last few words. They both knew what came next in the introduction to David Bowie's 'Diamond Dogs'. For tonight at least, he hoped that she would not start banging on about genocide.

CHAPTER SEVENTEEN

"THERE'S SOMETHING I NEED TO tell you," Portia said to her mother as the car set out from her Lego-like block of flats and started rolling silently through East London towards the party venue. "I'm afraid it's a bit weird."

"That sounds ominous." Karen had thought there was something not quite right since the moment she arrived. "You're not taking me somewhere dodgy are you? Not in these thigh boots!"

"Of course not! And in any case, you make a stunning Debbie Harry. It won't be long now 'til you find out where we're going. No, it's something else."

"Is this the best time for a serious talk? At the start of a big night out?" Her face froze. "Jeez. You're not pregnant are you love?"

Portia cackled. If only her mum knew how unlikely that would be. "No! It's nothing like that!"

"If it's not that, how bad can it be?"

"The thing is, everyone we're going to meet tonight, well, they don't know my name is Paula."

Karen was thrown. "What?"

Portia had managed to conceal from her mother, for some years, that she had changed her name as part of a bid to reinvent herself. After much angst, she had come up with an explanation designed to avoid any embarrassing confusion when she finally allowed her two worlds to cross over. "It was just one of those things. Someone misheard me on the first day when I was introducing myself at work, and it kind of stuck."

Karen did not look completely convinced but decided at once that she should go along with her daughter's story. It wasn't the first time she had pretended to believe her. There had been numerous occasions when, as a teenager, Paula's account of where she had been and what she had been doing had not quite stacked up. No harm had come of turning a blind eye then. At least, as far as she knew. It was a relief that it was nothing worse.

"Oh, OK love. What do they call you, then?"

"Portia."

"Hmm. It's not that different, I suppose. Could be worse. I can see why they got it mixed up. So, what do you want me to call you?"

"It's not that I mind them knowing my real name. I just didn't want you to be confused."

"OK. Are you sure these boots aren't too much?"

"They're amazing. You look great."

"Hang on a minute!" Karen was sitting up in her seat and wriggling around to try to get her bearings on the city as she peered out of the window. "Why have we stopped here?" She instantly recognized a familiar landmark. "Has the auto broken down? I never trust these blooming things."

A soothing disembodied voice announced, "You have reached your destination." There was a click as the doors unlocked.

Portia was checking the zip on the front of her silver leatherette catsuit to make sure it was in the right place. She looked up and grinned. "Nothing's wrong, Mum. This is our stop."

"It can't be. We're in the middle of Tower Bridge!"

"I know we are. We're going up. Just like in the Pink song. It's time to 'Get the Party Started'!"

Karen still looked puzzled. Pink was not an artist from the 1970s. How could that have anything to do with tonight? "Sorry to sound thick, but up what exactly?"

"Up that." She followed her daughter's gaze through the cab window, and onto the magnificent twin structure that stretched above them.

"Oh my God! Up there?"

"They've hired it for the party."

Portia clambered out of the vehicle and reached back to grab Karen's hand. The two women stood on the pavement and looked around as the car slid away to collect its next set of passengers. There was something reassuring about the disinfectant mist that clouded the capsule between fares, provided you didn't have a terror of being trapped inside. Now they had perfected the process there wasn't even any residue to taint your clothes. The faint whiff of Jeyes Fluid when you got in was fake, as the sterilizing chemicals were actually odorless. They had added the smell as an afterthought to improve public confidence in the service.

The twin gothic turrets that marked the middle of Tower Bridge seemed almost unreal, defined by illuminated beige stone and blue ironwork against the starless black sky. Looking back towards the West, the river reflected the lights that marked the next crossing upstream, London Bridge. The occasional party boat motored past carrying passengers on an inescapable loop.

"You can't get the full impact when you're actually on the bridge, can you?" Karen said, craning her neck to gaze upwards at the intricate construction directly above them.

"Sorry about that," Portia joked, "Shall we blow out the party and just go for a walk along the Embankment instead?"

"Oh, give over!"

"Come on, Mum. This is going to be a night to remember!"

CHAPTER EIGHTEEN

"I'M SO GLAD WE MADE the effort," Lexi said as she and Bob joined the vivacious crowd of guests that thronged the two glass-encased walkways spanning the bridge towers. "You know, I quite like you in that wig."

The jet black, shoulder-length pageboy cut framed Bob's warm brown eyes. His face was nowhere near as angular as a typical Ramone's. However, the T-shirt, clearly on display from inside his open, black leather biker jacket confirmed Bob's honorary affiliation with Johnny, Dee Dee, Joey and Tommy. Just in case anyone had any doubts.

Though primed to explain that she was supposed to be Joey's partner, Linda Ramone, Lexi remained content to be viewed as a generic 70s woman. That was what most people assumed until, inevitably, Bob put them right. She was already a little too warm in her white fake fur jacket, white patent leather boots and sunglasses. There was always the option to ditch a layer later if she got too hot, revealing the fine, long sleeved Indian print dress underneath.

"Gabba gabba hey!"

A remarkable Debbie Harry lookalike with a Liverpool accent clinked a glass of champagne against Bob and Lexi's. She wore a long black shirt over sheer black tights and black thigh boots. Her wig was perfect – an almost white peroxide blond with dark streaks underneath. However, the most striking thing about 'Debbie' was her makeup, which looked like authentic Harry. She was with a younger woman who wore a close-fitting silver leather catsuit, teamed with matching metallic platform boots, with her hair styled into something approaching a mullet.

"You sound like you're from my part of the world," Bob said, "And I don't mean Queens."

"You haven't got much of an accent," Karen observed suspiciously.

"I've been down here a long time. But really it's because I'm from the posh bit."

"Where? The Wirral?"

"Do you mind? No! I'm from Southport."

Lexi was fascinated to see how Bob slipped into a comfortable banter with this glamorous woman who somehow seemed familiar. It was probably just that she was pulling off her character so well. Still, coming from the other end of the country it must have been nice for her to find someone at the party with whom she had something in common.

"How do you know Ajay and Ayesha?" Lexi interrupted.

"I don't really." The woman smiled. "I'm Karen, by the way, and his is my daughter, P…"

"Portia," the girl said. "Nice to meet you. We're here because of me. I work with their grandson."

"Really?" Lexi was curious. It had not occurred to her, until then, that Sunil would be there. "I haven't met him, but Ayesha sings his praises all the time."

Portia glanced around the room. "He should be around. Mum and I only just got here."

There was a minor commotion as four friends dressed as members of the glam rock band Mud arrived in matching red stage outfits with flared trousers and even wider collars. A troupe of Bay City Rollers, in their trademark short jackets and cut-off trousers trimmed in tartan, came in next. They had to edge further away from the entrance to make space. Lexi was on the verge of saying something cutting about how 70s fashions looked rather ludicrous, but she held back when Karen marveled, "Hasn't everyone gone to a lot of trouble?"

Bob replied, "They've certainly kept the wig makers busy. And there I was thinking I would be the only one in a syrup."

"Sorry?" Karen queried. "Syrup?"

"It's cockney rhyming slang, Mum." Portia explained. "Syrup of figs, wig."

"Well, I never! You've learned the language and everything!" Karen marveled, with a twinkle in her eye.

They spotted Ayesha and Ajay a couple of groups away. Their hosts made a touching sight as John and Yoko, dressed all in white with Ajay sporting the small, round signature spectacles and his wife with her hair parted at the center and held flat with a headband made of two rows of pearls. Ajay was joking about how he had wanted to get a white grand piano up there, but they had not been able to squeeze it into the lift.

The incongruous cluster of people around them included the TV sleuths Kojak and Jason King, the character Margot from the 70s British sitcom The Good Life in an elegant evening dress and elaborate hair do; a short old man in a waistcoat who was unmistakably Vito Corleone from The Godfather, and a tall black woman with an enormous afro, hoop earrings and a beaded evening dress who Lexi assumed had come as Diana Ross.

Lexi chatted on. "Do you go back home to see your family very much, Portia?"

"Not really, I'm very busy with work."

"I can imagine. What do you do?"

"Advertising and marketing. I'm on a grad scheme."

"Well done! Those places are notoriously hard to come by. Are you at an agency?"

"Yes. We specialize in niche consumer services." She was quick to add, "You won't have heard of us, though."

"Is it fun?"

"A lot of the time, yes. It's my first job since uni, though, so I've nothing to compare it to."

"And you've got somewhere to live?"

"Yes, one of the new builds. It's tiny, but it's near work and means I have my own space."

"Best of all, it's big enough to fit me on the sofa," Karen chimed in, "And quite posh if you ask me. I have to say it's lovely to have somewhere to stay in the big smoke."

"I bet your mum's very proud." Portia glanced at Karen, already knowing from her stance that she was bursting with pride.

"Too right I am," Karen said. "It's hard for them, isn't it? Do you have kids?"

Lexi said, "No. I'm a teacher. I worry. We do what we can to keep them happy and prepare them for what lies ahead in the world outside, don't we?"

Karen smiled. "Tell me about it. I've said to our Paula, no job's perfect, but we all have to keep going, don't we?"

Portia was starting to feel self-conscious as her mother began to discuss the generic category of 'the youth of today' (i.e. her) with Lexi. Bob loitered awkwardly. He flagged down a waiter to replenish their glasses and gave Portia a friendly nod. Just as she was about to speak to him, he said, "Ladies, do you mind if I leave you to it? I've seen someone I need to catch up with."

He headed over towards two older white men dressed head to toe in blue denim. One of them, in jeans and a waistcoat, walked with a stick and had long thin white hair in a ponytail that straggled down to the top of his back. The other was a little taller, in better shape with a blond shoulder length wig and a denim shirt.

"It's the Quo!" Bob said, heartily, giving each of them a firm handshake. "How's it going, boys?"

He had not seen the Rockstar Ending survivors Bryn and George for a few months, and felt guilty for not having kept in touch after setting them up in their new flat. It had been a pleasure to help them with a few devices to make life easier for them when they had moved in together. He had installed a smoke alarm in recognition of Bryn's troublesome history of kitchen fires, and a few offnet entertainment devices.

"Hey, Bob, nice to see you mate. We should have guessed you'd be here." George said slapping him warmly on the back. Bryn looked in the direction Bob had just come from. "Is that Lexi over there? Our intrepid rescuer?"

"Indeed it is. But best not to say too much about all that business tonight, lads. Why don't we see if we can find some beers?"

Now Karen had found a friend her own age, Portia decided it would be OK to leave her mother for a minute and look for Sonny. It did not take her long to find him.

"Oh wow, look at you!" he leant in to give Portia an air kiss on both cheeks. It was not what she expected, but as there was no one there from the office to disapprove, she decided it was OK to enjoy the moment. He was wearing that gorgeous perfume again and his soft dark hair had brushed against her cheek. Sonny stood back a little and looked approvingly at her outfit. "Nan will be so pleased when she sees you." He was still gazing at her. If it had been anyone else, she would have started to feel uncomfortable. But it was nice. "Did your mum make that?"

She tried to sound nonchalant. "What, this old thing?"

"It's fabulous. The catsuit, I mean. Not so much the wig – although I wouldn't be surprised if the legendary Karen could turn her hand to that, too. She's an enormously talented lady. Do you remember? Stella went on about your Kylie dress all night at the boat party."

"I know." Portia glowed a little when she thought about it.

"My parents haven't a creative bone in their body. They've hired Sonny and Cher outfits. It was really expensive and they don't even fit that well." He rarely had anything nice to say about his mother and father, although he was begrudgingly grateful for their money and connections that had got him his job. She sensed he was permanently disappointed that they were so conventional.

"Tell me, then. If I'm Suzi Quatro, who are you supposed to be?" Someone topped up their glasses again, and proffered cubes of cheese and pineapple on cocktail sticks.

"I don't really know who I am. Probably a Ramone. Or possibly John Travolta in Saturday Night Fever. I'd settle for generic rock-stroke-punk-stroke-biker guy. Looking to the past isn't really my thing. I just borrowed a mate's leather jacket to be honest. And I already had the longish hair. But you know that. Anyway, I thought that would be good enough."

It was true. He did not look all that different to his usual office persona. Only the jacket was different, atop the usual rotation of interchangeable jeans and a T-shirt.

"Probably. It works, but I can only give you two out of ten for effort. Funnily enough, Mum and I were just talking to another Ramone over there somewhere." She glanced around but could not see Bob. "Maybe he went over to the other walkway."

"I think the disco is setting up over on that side. And I mean full on D-I-S-C-O. Mirror ball, psychedelic light show, tribute band, the lot. They have really pushed the boat out tonight."

They were surrounded by pleasant memories. Portia remembered the work summer party that they had both enjoyed on the biggest superyacht she had ever seen. The dock where it was moored was not visible from where they now stood, but it was not far away. Over on the south bank The Shard pierced the sky. Brytely had taken them both to dinner at the penthouse restaurant to thank them for their first successful burst of work on the End-ings. Thinking about how much shared history they had accrued in so short a time made her happy.

"Maybe we can have a dance later?" Portia was em-boldened by the fourth glass of champagne. "I seem to remember you can just about hold a few shapes together."

"Can I, indeed?"

Just then, Ayesha spotted Portia, rushed over to the two of them, and gave her a big hug. "At last! Why has this boy been keeping you away from me for so long? It is so lovely to see you again. Did you bring your mother? I told Sunil you must ask her to come. She is here, isn't she?"

"Yes, she's talking to another lady over there. Thank you so much for inviting us both. This is the most amaz-ing venue."

"You're only seventy once. Well, twice if you count both of us. What are we waiting for? Let's find your mum so I can say hello."

Portia took Ayesha's hand and led her over to the corner where Lexi and Karen were still happily chatting. Sonny followed, hanging back a step.

"This is my good friend Lexi who I know through my charity work," Ayesha said, "And you have to be this lovely young lady's mother."

"Where are your parents?" Portia said to Sonny as the three older women drifted away to admire the view of the city. "Oh, they're about somewhere." She got the impres-sion he was in no hurry to introduce her to them. How bad could they be?

"Over there is my total pain in the ass of a little sister, Amina," Sonny said.

Portia looked at a young woman, her features and slender build similar to Sonny, just a little taller and a more feminine shape. She was wearing a short, high necked navy party dress with cutaway shoulders and navy patent heels.

Amina caught the two of them looking at her and gave them a forced smile.

"She's having a good day, as usual," Sonny said under his breath. Portia was already annoyed he had shown no interested in introducing her to his parents. She was not going to let him stop her meeting his sister.

"Come on! You can't leave her there all on her own."

Before he could dissuade her, Portia had marched up to Amina and introduced herself.

"So, you're the one who was bigging it up at Yuthfest with my brother," she said looking her up and down. "If it hadn't been for you, I would have been the one having fun."

Portia was not going to take the bait. "I'm not sure I'd describe it as fun. We were working. You honestly didn't miss much."

"I dialed into the livestream, but it's never the same as being in the room. What a weird business trip for a data nerd like Sunil." Amina sounded bitter, but Portia had made her mind up to get her talking and carried on regardless, as if it were a more friendly conversation. Sonny had followed her across the room, but she could feel him lurking at her shoulder itching to get away. "Or do you call him Sonny?"

"He's Sonny at work. Anyway, even data nerds need to get out of the office now and again. It reminds them that, in our line of work, the data is only a proxy for actual human beings."

Amina looked behind Portia. She was fruitlessly scanning the room to see if she could find anyone other than her brother's work colleague to talk to. Portia was going to ask her if she had brought a guest but thought better of it.

"This is so dull, isn't it?" Amina went on, her face combining exasperation and boredom in an unattractive expression.

"In my opinion, this is much more fun than Yuthfest," Portia said. "And by the way I love your makeup. Did you do it yourself?"

"Yep." Dammit. She had asked a closed question.

"If you don't mind me asking, is there somewhere else you'd rather be?"

"Anywhere." Sonny had now moved round so that Portia could see him, standing to the side of the two girls. The body language between him and his sister suggested a complicated relationship.

"What is it that you like so much about the Yuthies, anyway?" Portia asked. The girl might be hard work, but maybe this could be an opportunity to do some research for the Phase Two campaign. She was in the presence of a genuine fan, after all.

"Duh. It's obvious, isn't it? Yuthentic actually gives a shit about young people." Now she had begun speaking in whole sentences, Amina had the annoying habit of ending each phrase with an upward intonation. "We've only been waiting our entire lives to be taken seriously."

"Quite." Portia was wondering what Amina had to be so angry about. Their family had everything. Sonny had been right. Talking to his miserable sister was hard work.

"Have you really had it so bad, though?" She could not help asking. Sonny always seemed so chipper. How could the two of them have turned out so different?

"Well, I think I'll make my own mind up about that." Amina said. "But one thing is for certain. The Yuthies are on our side. They have convinced me and all of my friends. They're delivering on their promise. Freedom. Choice. Independence. Who could argue with that?"

"I've seen that memo myself once or twice," Portia said flatly. She glanced at Sonny, conceding he had been right. "It's been nice to meet you, Amina. I need to go and check my mother's OK. See you later, maybe?"

CHAPTER NINETEEN

"I DIDN'T KNOW YOU WERE COMING tonight," Lexi said, "It's so nice to see you again."

Jess had styled her hair into an impressive mane of Farrah Fawcett waves. She steered silently along the polished walkway. You had to hand it to her, Jess had captured 70s casual cool flawlessly with a bright red shirt and flared jeans.

Her champagne flute was almost empty, but she raised it nevertheless. "I was hoping I'd bump into you, too."

Lexi looked towards the distant skyline. "It's an amazing view, isn't it?"

"The city is so complicated. Sometimes I think it's more beautiful at night. You can see how it's flowing. How are you doing, anyway?"

"Oh, up and down." Lexi said. She was relieved that she didn't have to pretend with Jess. For a second she thought she might cry, and then she was alright again. Maybe it would be a good idea to ask for a glass of water next time someone offered her a drink.

"I'm not giving up, Jess." Lexi said softly. "I promised Bob not to go on about it tonight, but it's impossible to blot it out. Anyway, I know I'm safe with you, you know?"

"I'll take that as a compliment." Jess said.

Lexi barely heard her. "I've been having a hard time. I've thought about it all so much. Whenever I try to do what Bob suggests – you know – 'move on', think nice thoughts about flowers and butterflies and unicorns, I actually feel worse."

"I'd been leaving you alone," Jess explained. "We thought you'd been through too much. Nicky is really worried about you. Are you sure you still want to be involved?"

"There is no alternative. Yes. Yes, of course I do. And now they're targeting the kids and disabled people. What they did to you at Yuthfest was unforgiveable!"

Jess huffed. "Surely, you're not surprised? They've been going on about fixing social care for decades. But it's obvious that they'd rather find a way to fix people like us, permanently, so they don't need to think about us. I'm grateful all I got was a few bruises. Especially when you know the Yuthies are looking for more permanent solutions to make their problems go away."

Lexi bit her lip, "I'm sorry. Do you think that everyone who voted for the Euthanasia Act understands what they have done? I supported it."

"So did I."

"But I regret it now. We sleepwalked into coercing tens of thousands of perfectly healthy old people into dying. I am with you, Jess. But I'm reaching the end of my tether with trying to change the world by asking nicely. Look out there. There are millions of people, millions of lives, trillions of pounds all flowing every hour of the day and night. If we are going to change things, we're going to have to do something to disrupt it that nobody will ever forget."

CHAPTER TWENTY

" I CAN'T STOP OUT HERE FOR too long," Bob said as he trotted outside onto the bridge with George and Bryn. "Lexi will be wondering where I've got to."

"We're not planning to be all night," Bryn said. Although he moved slowly compared to most people, Bob noticed that Bryn was faster and stronger than the last time they met, when Bob had popped into their flat. Whereas Bryn had previously depended on a walking frame with wheels for stability, he now seemed able to manage well enough with just a stick. A wisp of white hair that had escaped from his ponytail blew across his craggy face.

The three men trotted along the pavement towards the north bank of the river matching Bryn's steady pace. Behind them The Tower of London looked like a model. City skyscrapers lay behind with their jagged misfitting shapes. The torpedo-like gherkin was set back from the skewed 'walkie-talkie' building that dominated the view. Soon they came to a flight of steps that descended to a pedestrianized area that ran along the river. They took it easy on the way down so that Bryn would not lose his footing.

"I'm afraid this reprobate has got me into one or two naughty habits," George said, "Which is ironic. He is leading me astray. What kind of thanks is that? It was my training program that got him his core strength back. That and a proper diet. Do you think that makes us co-dependent?"

Bob shrugged. "As long as it works for you guys, I'd ignore the psychobabble."

"It's true." Bryn said proudly. "All it took was for a friend to take an interest in me. If you've got something to do with your life, someone to chat to, why would anyone want to just give up and sit there? Or worse? I don't know what got into me, signing up like that for you-know-what."

"That's all behind you now, mate." Bob said warmly.

"Do you think we'll be OK on one of those benches?" George asked, looking around a little furtively. A row of seats was arranged in prime position for viewing Tower Bridge and the city beyond.

"For goodness' sake, man. It's personal use." Bryn said, reaching into the pocket of the overcoat he had slung over his denim ensemble. "And, in any case, there's hardly anyone around."

They sat together, three men loosely resembling the lost Ramone and two renegade members of Status Quo, cheerily sharing a spliff on the chilly embankment, gazing up at the intricate towers of the bridge, and following with their eyes the occasional boat that motored by. It was as if three ghosts had escaped from some celestial rock 'n' roll hall of fame for a low-key boys' night out back on

Planet Earth.

"Talking of co-dependency, how's the missus?" George asked. "You've got a good one there."

Bob looked up at the bridge where he expected the love of his life was most likely starting to miss him. He should really have told her he was popping out. "I know. She means the world to me. But it's not as simple as living on your own. Or even with a cat." Bob said, lifting a hand to decline a second drag. "I'm not used to it, but don't mind me."

"Did we tell you we've got a cat?" George said. "Cilla. She's ginger, naturally."

"Nice. I might pop over and see her." Bob missed his cat, poor Wotsit, dreadfully. Maybe he would bring up the subject of getting another cat with Lexi. She might be happier if she had something to care for.

"Is she still campaigning?" Bryn asked.

The last time they had all been together was at their PACE freedom celebration. Bryn, George and three other survivors had just received their compensation settlement from The Corporation. Henry, their lawyer, had negotiated them such a good deal that they all had enough money to stay alive for as long as they wanted. But they knew they were in a tiny minority. And despite their efforts, poor Mabel hadn't lasted five minutes. At least her former roommate, Mavis, was still enjoying life from her studio flat in Blackheath, and Meg was back in her comfortable home when not visiting her far-flung children. She had followed a long stay with Adam and his family in Texas with another long-haul trip to visit Alice and her daughter Dolly in New Zealand. Lexi, like Bob, was happy that

Bryn and George had found companionship, but the thousands of others who were not so lucky still kept her awake at night.

Bob sighed deeply. "She's red hot. I wish she weren't so het up about it all. No disrespect to what the two of you have been through, but it's been tough on her." He was relieved to finally have someone to talk to about his worries. With Bryn and George he didn't have to pretend. Something occurred to him.

"Sorry to ask, but you have both got your phones on dark, haven't you?"

"Yes, we've still got the bags you gave us. Well, I already had one." Bryn said. As part of his tech support for the boys, Bob had thrown in a couple of Faraday bags.

George looked concerned. "She should get some help. I've gone back to therapy for my PTSD a couple of times. It's a tough path. But it's very hard to deal with trauma on your own."

"You can say that again." There was a playful tone in Bryn's voice. He had earned the right to make light of George's night terrors by sitting with him when they had happened. "We had to do something about all that screaming in the night. God only knows what the neighbors thought we were up to! I was worried they were going to call the police."

"That or a BDSM helpline. Whatever your motivation, you old fusspot, you did me a right favor," said George. "All any of us can do is take one day at a time."

As they contemplated his words of wisdom in silent acquiescence the bridge began to move.

"Don't panic, you're not hallucinating," Bob said. As they relaxed on the bench, the road in front of them that crossed the river had split in half and was starting to lift. "Well will you look at that. Do you think they arranged it just for us?"

All the cars backed up on the approach were perfectly still. The sides of the bridge steadily opened, eventually easing to a halt, pointing at an angle towards the fixed walkways where the party was in full swing.

"Just think. They'll be able to see all the way down to the water, now, George said, "Through the glass panels in the floor."

"Hmm. I would say the sight is more impressive from here." Bob mused.

A Thames sailing barge, its red sail at full height, and decorated with strings of delicate lights, slid through the opening. That was why the bridge had lifted. On the deck of the boat, around half a dozen guests wrapped in winter coats and lifejackets cheered indistinctly as they passed through. Pedestrians waiting to cross waved and shouted. Once the vessel was clear, the bridge began to ease down again.

"How's work going?" George asked.

Bob sounded positive. "It's OK, actually. I'm not cooped up at head office anymore."

"Why? Did you upset someone?"

"No, nothing like that. They just move us around. It's all good." They didn't need to know anything else. "Well, this has been very special, but I should really be getting back to Lexi."

George and Bryn did not look like they were planning to go anywhere.

"I'll see you in a bit, then." Bob said as he eased back up onto his feet.

CHAPTER TWENTY-ONE

"**F**OR THE LOVE OF GOD, you've got to save me!" Karen grabbed Portia's arm urgently, "Kojak over there won't leave me alone. I've tried to get away from him, but he keeps saying 'Who loves ya baby?' and offering me a lick of his lolly."

"Him?" Portia peered in the direction that Karen had come from and caught sight of a bald man in a tight, tailored suit. He was standing on his own at the other side of the room with a lollipop stick poking out of his mouth.

"Don't make eye contact! You don't want him near you. Trust me."

"You do look amazing, Mum," Portia said. "The poor man can't help himself."

"Well he's not helping himself to me!"

A waiter passed carrying a tray loaded with nine up-turned grapefruit halves, each one stuck with cocktail sausages on a stick. Another followed with a plate of halved hardboiled eggs, filled with piped egg mayonnaise and topped with an anchovy.

Portia was relieved the food was finally making its way out onto the floor. She had lost count of the number of champagne top-ups the diligent waiting staff had poured. While her mother might be able to neck a whole bottle of – pretty much anything – without a sign of wear and tear, she knew she couldn't keep it up for much longer and stay vertical.

The lift was quiet when Bob rode back up the Tower. He doubted Bryn and George would follow him. They were enjoying chilling out on their own. It was good to see the lads settled and happy after all the two of them had been through. Ironically, their near-death experience had been the jolt they needed to shock them both into a happier life.

It was then that he saw his doppelganger, a man with his back to him, standing on his own. Bob wondered, what was the etiquette when you go to a fancy-dress party, and someone younger and slimmer than you is there in the same outfit? He considered the options for a moment, and as Lexi was not around to talk to, he plumped for the obvious one.

"Gabba gabba hey!" Bob said he approached the guy, taking a leaf out of Karen's book.

"Sonny? What are you doing here?" he said, shocked, as the young man turned to face him.

"Sorry, do I know you?" He looked confused.

"Yes, you do!" He still did not get it. Bob waved his hand in front of Sonny's face. "Look into my eyes, not around my eyes! Sonny! It's me. Bob."

"Bob! Man, you're in disguise!" Sonny started laughing.

"I know. You probably didn't recognize me with my clothes on."

"It's more the wig actually. How come you're here? I had no idea you knew my grandparents."

"Well, strictly speaking it's more my girlfriend, Lexi. She knows them."

"How?"

Bob shifted his gaze, thankful for the cover of the long fringe while he carefully chose his words. "Oh… the gym. Nordic walking. Something like that. She's big on keep fit." He did not want Sonny to suspect their connection with PACE. Anyway, it was true. They were members of the same gym and Lexi had met some of the Nordic Walkers, at least once.

Sonny looked relieved to have found another friend. "What a small world! I didn't mean to be rude, mate, but I just didn't expect to see you here. So, did they get you a new posting?" Sonny was fond of Bob. Their time together on Project Houdini, earlier in the year, had been largely enjoyable, even if it had been a bit weird.

"You'll laugh when I tell you what I'm doing now."

"Go on."

"I'm at CRAP. Aviation, drones, robots and that."

Sonny's eyes were wide, and he was grinning madly. "After we crashed that drone? Oh, Bob, that's hysterical!"

"I know. You couldn't make it up, could you? But I have to say I'm enjoying it. I might even get my pilot's license. How's work with you?" Bob hoped things were going well for his former colleague back in agency life.

"Good, all in all. We did a bit of work on the Blackpool stuff for The Corporation as it happens. Have you heard about it? You could be involved for all I know."

"Actually, most of the work on that was done before I arrived. Funnily enough, I have seen it in the wild. It's pretty impressive. Especially the dancers, if you'd call them that."

Sonny looked envious. "I've only seen the performance on video. Rumor has it Mason had a thing about Madchester. I can't exactly imagine the old silver fox off his face, can you?"

"That's very funny." Bob thought Mason had always seemed soulless. It was odd to think of him having musical preferences at all, never mind dancing like Bez.

"So, A&A are your grandparents? That's very nice," Bob said.

"Yes. They are."

Bob looked slightly puzzled for a moment. "Hang on. I didn't see Portia over there did I? From Brytely. That's her, isn't it? In the silver catsuit!"

"Yes, it is."

"She's a cracker. My girlfriend Lexi seems to have made friends with her mother. I didn't make the connection."

He waited for Sonny to say something else, but he was quiet.

"Are you two…" Bob was looking for a word that would suggest the two of them being more than friends, but that would not get Sonny in trouble.

"No. Nothing like that. We're just mates. She mentioned Karen was coming down this weekend and I thought it would be nice to invite her here. Just for the view, you know. It is fantastic."

"Very good," Bob nodded. He was sure there more to Sonny's relationship with Portia.

"I'm surprised you didn't come as Bowie, though, Bob. I would have thought you'd leap at the chance." Bob had given Sonny some of his Bowie merchandise as a parting gift when their project had come to an end. Anyone who spent more than ten minutes with Bob usually found out he was a big fan.

"I thought about it. But you know what they say. Don't meet your idols. And don't dress up as them either. I could never carry it off. In the end I thought a Ramone would be vaguely achievable while still saying rock 'n' roll."

Sonny grinned. "Snap!"

When the music stopped everyone was herded into the West walkway, with its view towards the center of town. Two cakes in the shape of the number seventy were on a podium. Ajay and Ayesha, whose birthdays were only weeks apart, cut a slice together. They had their backs to the city beyond and posed for pictures with their friends, making only the shortest of speeches. Dancing kicked off with John Lennon's 'Instant Karma'. The long room filled with psychedelic light. Jess was one of the first onto the floor with a handsome Robert Plant lookalike.

"Look – that guy over there is in a satin dressing gown!" Bob said, reunited finally with Lexi, as they lent against the glass watching the long, thin dance floor. "Are you going to tell him off?"

Lexi had already won that argument. "I think that's Jim. Do you remember? You met him at the first PACE meeting you came to."

"The one with the badge?" Bob said.

"Yep. It said, 'Lewisham pensioners go on forever' if I recall correctly. That's him."

"Ah, yes. He looks smarter tonight, though. Even in nightwear." Bob mused.

"Well. I think his hair is shorter. And the beard is gone. But I'm sure it's him. And anyway, that dressing gown is much longer than yours would have been."

"And it has Muhammed Ali on the back. I wonder if they'll play 'Black Superman'?"

A bunch of Nordic Walkers, who during the course of the evening had become a rather ragged Abba, dragged Lexi and Bob up to dance to 'Waterloo'. When they played 'The Bump', a novelty record that was a risky choice at a party where so many people were prime candidates for fractured hips, Bob pretended he needed the bathroom and left Lexi strutting. He found a piece of birthday cake which, once you dug underneath the sliver glitter icing, consisted of exquisite dark chocolate sponge with Black Forest filling (juicy morello cherries soaked in kirsch, floating in sweet, whipped cream). It was the best he had ever tasted. He grasped his plate like a talisman to ward off anyone who might have the audacity to try to get him moving.

Bob was happy listening to the songs he loved, from a decade of extraordinary musical diversity. No wonder his parents had so much fun. The DJ tried to play something to match everyone who had taken the trouble to dress up as a music icon. She even found some Suzi Quatro. When 'If You Can't Give Me Love' came on, Bob hoped Sonny would take the bait and grab Portia, but he could only see her dancing with her mum.

He thought he had got away with it, but when Bryn and George surprised him by coming back to the party, it was impossible to escape their clutches. They dragged him up to join in an energetic bikers' line dance when Status Quo's 'Rockin' All Over the World' blasted through the bridge. When Lexi joined in, he was amazed how quickly she got the hang of it, even though they had almost cracked heads at the beginning.

The only person he saw Sonny dance with was Karen. There was no way she was going to let him off the hook when Abba started up with 'Does Your Mother Know?'

CHAPTER TWENTY-TWO

ORTIA HAD NO IDEA HOW Karen managed to pack away so much booze and still stay sober. Far from letting her down, which had been Portia's secret fear, her mother had been the very best plus one she could have taken to the party. Karen was engaging, lively and gorgeous in a forty-something kind of a way. She could dance, too. Most miraculously, she had remained coherent after countless glasses of champagne and been delightful company throughout the evening. Not one slur.

The guests had been tipped out into the cool, dry night in small batches, as the lifts down from the high-level walkways ferried consecutive groups back down to earth. Each of them had been given a small bag containing mementos – a piece of birthday cake in a grease-free wrapper, and a replica set of three 1970s button badges.

Portia and Karen compared their little collections. Both had a Rock Against Racism star. They were in everyone's set. In the pale light in the back of the cab they could just about make out an Old Grey Whistle Test logo, which Karen was able to explain because her dad had an old poster; a John Lennon 'Imagine' album cover, a David

Bowie 'Aladdin Sane' face complete with lightning bolt, and finally one which had 'Mud on Road' in a red triangle. They instructed the car to take a detour via London Bridge so they could hop out and take a few selfies with Tower Bridge resplendent in the background.

"What a fantastic night!" Karen eased off her long boots and flexed her ankles, relieved to be sitting back on Portia's small foam sofa. One of her big toes had popped through her tights. She tugged at the hole in the elasticated fabric to relieve the pressure it was creating around her strangled digit. Portia busied herself twisting the top off a glass bottle of fizzy mineral water she had taken out of the fridge. She poured them each a glass with ice and a slice of lime, having learned her lesson from the last time her mum had come to stay. There were going to have some proper rehydration before bedtime.

"They must be loaded," Karen said.

"Yes. They had a food business. Sold it for a fortune a few years ago. But they're ever so nice, aren't they?"

"Lovely. Absolutely lovely. That's proper class, that is."

"And Mum, I have to tell you this catsuit is really comfortable. Tons of people admired it. You did a brilliant job. It's such a pity I won't get the chance to wear it very often."

"You never know. They might come back in again. Things do."

Portia refilled their glasses and steeled herself. "What did you think of Sonny?"

"He's a nice enough lad." Karen hesitated.

"But?" She could see that her mother was choosing her words cautiously.

"I couldn't really tell. It was a bit noisy to have a proper conversation by the time he came over. He obviously likes you, though, or he wouldn't have invited you, would he?"

"Not necessarily. His Nan's my biggest fan. She could have put him under pressure…"

Karen was shaking her head a little. "He would not have told you about the party if he hadn't wanted you to go. Maybe it was me being there cramping his style. You know, I could have come another weekend. You didn't have to take me."

"Don't be ridiculous."

"Well, our kid, I have had one of the most amazing nights out. And you did a good job of keeping the location a surprise." Karen drained her glass and leaned forward for a refill.

"You seemed to be getting on very well with – what was her name? The one with the guy from Southport."

"Lexi, you mean?"

"Yes. That's the one."

"I'll let you into a secret. I've met them before. They came in the arcade when I was sent over to work on Southport Pier. Do you remember? When our one was closed."

"I bet they thought that was an unlikely coincidence!"

"Probably would have. If I had told them."

"Why didn't you?"

"Paula, we were at a party at the top of Tower Bridge with all your posh new friends. They don't need to know your mum works in a gambling arcade, do they?"

Portia was annoyed that Lexi had not recognized her mother, but angrier at herself for being grateful for Karen's discretion. She felt obliged to contradict her, as much as anything to purge her own sense of shame.

"No, Mum. That's not right. You've always told me that all work is honorable. I'm so proud of you. You're one of the hardest workers I know. You've taught me so much." She was starting to feel emotional. There worlds might be far apart, but their values were the same, weren't they?

Karen could see her wobbling. "Anyway, I do look very different this evening. Master – or should I say mistress – of disguise, in my glad rags." She still had barely a hair out of place, and her lipstick was immaculate.

"So, what did you tell them you do?"

"Well, I mainly went on about the kids. Said I picked up bits of work here and there to fit in round my childcare arrangements. They didn't push me. And she was a teacher. Very interesting actually."

"I'm glad you had some common ground."

"Yes. We got on OK. But she had a bee in her bonnet about – of all things – euthanasia! Not exactly party talk, is it? Sounds like she's involved in a charity or something. I couldn't quite follow it. But she was obviously getting upset. Her Bob changed the subject pretty quickly when he came back."

"Sounds like he's a sensible fella."

"He was alright. Even if he thinks he's posh compared to the likes of me. They always say that. Southport might have been a glamorous resort a hundred years ago. But they need to get over themselves. These days it's not special at all."

CHAPTER TWENTY-THREE

LEXI LET OUT A BLOOD-CURDLING scream.

Seconds later, Bob burst into the bedroom wearing only his Ramones top. He had been in the bathroom across the landing when he heard the commotion. "What's wrong?" he gasped, wiping the dregs of toothpaste with the back of his hand.

"There's something in here!"

She was standing on the mattress in an outsize T-shirt which said: 'The Cure – Let's Go To Bed'. She stopped yelling when she saw Bob, but her jaw dropped, and she was struggling to catch her breath. The low bedside lights cast eerie shadows around the room. Oh no, Bob thought, the breakdown has finally happened.

"I can't see anything, Lex. What are you talking about?"

Her eyes were wide, and her voice fast and panicky. "It's under the bed!"

She was in danger of falling. "Easy, Lex. Can you just sit down? Nice and slow. That's right. Now tell me, what have you seen?"

"I didn't see it. I felt it. It could be anything. You need to have a look. Be careful, Bob!" Her breathing started getting faster again, and she gave an odd whine.

He took a small torch out of a drawer, and gingerly knelt by the bed to peer underneath. By now, he was convinced that he was just going through the motions to put her mind at ease. It was dusty under there. As the beam of light moved around the space he realized what had happened.

"Be careful Bob!" Lexi said again. "It touched my foot. Could it be a rat?"

"There's nothing alive down here," he said crawling backwards.

"I didn't kick it that hard, did I? Please tell me I haven't killed an innocent animal."

"Nothing like that."

Bob reached forward and grabbed his wig from where it had landed between two battered shoe boxes filled with old CDs. For a moment he thought about slipping it on to surprise her, but there was a load of fluff stuck to it. "I need to find somewhere to keep this if I'm ever going to wear it again. Panic over," he said only just resisting the temptation to pretend it was attacking him. He slowly lifted the wig above the mattress to put her mind at rest. "Sorry about that, Lex."

"You left it on the floor! Oh, for goodness' sake!" she said. "Why can't you ever put things away!"

He started to pick the fuzzy bits out of the hairpiece and smooth it back into shape. "I thought it worked rather well."

She looked at him, trouserless, perched on the edge of the bed, thoughtfully stroking the soft black clump of hair, and could not find it in her heart to be annoyed with him.

"Put it down or put it on, sweetheart," she said. "It's time for you to follow the instructions on my pajamas."

CHAPTER TWENTY-FOUR

PORTIA HAD TAKEN SONNY FOR lunch. She said it was to thank him for inviting her and Karen to the party at the weekend, but the real reason was that she wanted some answers.

The Bagel Bunker was only a short walk from where they worked in Shoreditch. The district had been famous for bagels for around a hundred years, and they were usually very good.

"I'm so glad carbs are back in fashion," Portia said, as she paid for what they had chosen at the counter. Stacks of ready-made bagels were piled high behind the spotless glass cabinet in front of her. Sonny picked up the tray and found them a couple of seats in a booth towards the back. They were cocooned by the usual polished concrete floor and exposed brick walls. They only had half an hour before their colleagues might notice they were both missing, so she got straight to the point.

"You've got to tell me. What was Jess doing at the party?"

He looked uncomfortable. Portia wondered whether she should have given Sonny a gentler preamble, but she had grown bored with small talk. There were too many big questions to fit in to a short amount of time. Surely, he knew who she was talking about? There weren't exactly hundreds of women like Jess there, on Saturday night. He was fidgeting now and avoiding looking at her. Portia was going to have to spell it out.

"At the party. Jess. Nicky Hartt's researcher. Farrah Fawcett. Did you know she was going to be there?"

Sonny still looked blank. After a few moments, he took his phone out and slipped it into a 'Man Who Sold the World' Faraday bag that he pulled from a pocket inside his jacket. He had given her something similar as a gift at the work summer party. At least, she supposed, that showed he was taking her question seriously.

He cleared his throat quietly and looked her in the eyes. "Do you have yours with you?" he asked, raising his eyebrows. That was embarrassing. She did have it in her handbag, as it happened, but it was full of tampons, and she wasn't about to tip them all over the table.

"No, sorry."

"Well. You'll have to share mine."

She dropped her phone into his hand and he stuffed it into the pouch alongside his. The fabric was tight, but it sealed properly, just about.

"Sweet," she said. "Now that's done, are you going to tell me why Jess was there?"

It was like trying to crack open an oyster with a plastic knife. Sonny snapped the ring-pull on a can of energy drink and took a long gulp. "I suppose she must know my Nan."

They had been there ten minutes and already he was driving her mad. "Obviously. It was your Nan's party."

"She could have been a plus one," he hypothesized.

"True. At least you haven't tried to fob me off with that excuse."

"Damn! I only just thought of it." He smiled. "Look, I'm pretty sure Nan knows Jess through one of her charities."

"And you don't need to be AI-enhanced to work out which one. I mean, they were both at the Select Committee FFS. It's got to be PACE, right?"

"I haven't asked her directly. We don't really talk about it. Surely you can understand how difficult things could get if she knew what we're working on. It was bad enough after Amina told her I went to Yuthfest."

It was unpleasant to be reminded of Sonny's disdainful sister. "What was all that about, then?"

Sonny shrugged. "It just came up, you know? I mentioned I was going in the family Splutter group. Mum and Dad had suggested us all doing something together that night because Amina was due to go back to uni later in the week. She was even more pissed off than usual with me because I didn't take her. She went round to see Nani and Nana the next day to say goodbye and ended up having a bit of a moan about it. Nothing out of the ordinary, just family dynamics. And then, out of the blue, a few days later I got this massive lecture from Nani about the Yuthies – how I wasn't to listen to any silly ideas. If I was ever feeling depressed, I could always talk to her. Honestly, it was excruciating. I've never had a suicidal thought in my life. And I've no plans to start now."

"You never said any of this before," Portia said. "I had no idea."

He looked a little more relaxed. "It's not the kind of thing I'd bring up in the office."

It made sense. She started to feel a little more warmly towards him. "Jess wasn't the only one there with PACE connections though, was she?"

"I think quite a few of their friends are involved. She's a bit vague about it. It's not like I've been exactly honest, either. 'Oh, by the way Nan. All those healthy old people you know who are dying, yeah? Well I'm the one persuading them it would be a good idea if they left the planet. And that Portia who you're so keen on? She's at it too.' How do you think that would work out for us?"

Portia swallowed her mouthful of smoked salmon and cream cheese bagel and took a quick swig from a can of passion fruit flavored mineral water. Any other time he had described them as an 'us' she would have been touched.

"I can understand your position, Sonny," she said thoughtfully. "You know, one of the others even said something to my mum. She thought it was a bit off, to be honest. Funnily enough, she wasn't in the mood for death talk."

"What more do you want me to say?" Sonny looked tired. He tipped back his head and drained the can. "I think I need another one of these before we go back. Can I get you anything?"

She looked up at the daily specials board. "Will you share a dark chocolate chunk banana rye bread with me?"

"Sure."

Ordinarily she would have looked at her phone while he went to the counter, but he had confiscated her device. She felt vulnerable sitting there, mulling over what they were doing for a living. It was a moment of unexpected calm in a day that was normally so crammed with things competing for her attention that she could not get too deep on anything.

"What is it with your sister?" Portia asked when he came back, cutting the cake in half and breaking a piece off her side. "Why is she like that?"

"Abandonment issues. She also thinks I'm the favorite. It's not true, by the way. But Dad recently made the mistake of telling her that everyone would like her much more if she stopped being so barbed and eye-rollie all the time."

"It's a fair point," she had to agree. "How old is she?"

"Twenty."

"Well, there's still time for her to grow out of it. It's usually insecurity that makes people…er…like that."

"My parents have never had a huge amount of time for either of us. Mum always seemed to be at the hospital, Dad at the office. I know they love us, but they don't tell us very often. They work really long hours. It's just how it is. But she has always found it harder to accept than me." Sonny had only taken a couple of bites of his cheese salad bagel and lost interest in it.

"She's a good-looking girl." Portia wanted to find something kind to say about his sister.

"It runs in the family." He flashed her a smile. "And she's not always so brusque. But if she doesn't know you, it takes a long time for Amina to let her guard down. And not many have the patience for it. I feel sorry for her. She's actually pretty lonely." He had never let Portia see his sad side before.

"Well, the Yuthies have impressed her. Maybe she can make some friends there."

"They have a massive student section at her uni."

"Are you worried about her?"

"What do you mean?"

"Phase Two. Disability, mental illness, youth…"

"She's not mentally ill," he said defensively, "And anyway, I can't see it."

"Which brings us nicely to the day job," Portia said. She had finished her half of the cake but was still hungry. Sonny's pile of discarded leftovers seemed such a waste.

"Do you want mine?" He caught her eyeing his untouched slice.

"If you insist."

Portia was glad that she had invited him out, and even more pleased that he had opened up a little to her. "Do you think we're still on track for 1 April? Lars seems to be convinced, but then he always talks like they're going to take over the world."

"Yes," Sonny said. "I know there's been a ripple of resistance in Parliament, but it was just one question. I really can't see it getting derailed now, can you?"

Portia was not so sure.

"There's a chance the research might throw a spanner in the works. We'll get the full results next week to present to Stella. Most of the new incentives will be aimed at people who are already marginalized one way or another. Even if they wanted to fight back it would be an uphill struggle. Physically. Mentally. They are sitting ducks. Just like the old people were. Actually, it's the open access option for the under-18s that's looking most controversial."

"A demographic too far?" Sonny nodded thoughtfully. "Maybe."

"Try to remember they're human beings, Sonny, not a data category."

"That was uncalled-for." Sonny said. "I thought you might be on the verge of resigning not so long ago."

Portia shook her head and shrugged. "I'm still uncomfortable with the whole thing, but needs must and all that. You're stuck with me. I've had a chat about it with my mum."

"What do you mean? Did you actually tell her what we do? About The Endings?"

"No! Of course not. I'm not totally stupid. Just about being generally unhappy with some aspects of the work. No specifics. You've got her to thank."

"To thank for what?"

"For your lovely lunch," she looked ironically at the pile of half chewed bagel in front of him. "And perhaps more importantly, that I will continue to be part of the dream team for the foreseeable future."

"Well, I'm pleased to hear it," Sonny said draining his second can of energy drink and scrunching it flat between his hands. "Now we need to be getting back."

CHAPTER TWENTY-FIVE

"**W**HAT DO YOU MEAN, THE groups say no?" Stella squinted dismissively down at them from the screen on the meeting room wall. Portia felt her hackles rise. How could this woman be so senior and yet, at the same time, so stupid? She explained again.

"Some of the details for the proposed Phase Two. They're not playing out very well in terms of public opinion, I'm afraid." It was taking all Portia's strength to control an overwhelming impetus to sound smug. Finally, her instincts, which everyone else around the table had consistently ignored, were being proved right. Running with the Youth Assisted Suicide Service (YASS), unmodified, could blow a gaping hole in The Corporation's reputation.

Lars eyed her coldly across the meeting room and fiddled with one of his sigil ear spacers. Sonny stayed quiet. They were in Anthrax this morning. It was 8am in London and 4pm in Singapore where Stella had gone to give the keynote address at a Global Leaders in Ubiquitous Marketing conference. Portia envied Stella, staying somewhere with a tropical climate, even if she would be at meetings indoors for most of her stay. The British autumn had turned chilly and wet, the mornings increasingly dark.

"I appreciate that this may not be what you want to hear," Portia went on, becoming bolder with each sentence. "But we need to tell the client."

"We've already done so much work on it," Stella said. "It seems rather a shame."

"Only at The Corporation's behest," Lars said, reluctantly beginning to hedge his bets. Everyone in the meeting knew that they had persuaded The Corporation to start work on the Phase Two campaign early, based on Lars' insider information that it was a political 'done deal'. His intelligence had always been accurate before. This time, however, it had landed them in a tricky place.

"And you have Brytely's reputation to think of, Stella," Portia went on, "If we are associated with something that could turn out to be this damaging."

Stella still looked baffled. She tilted her head to one side as she struggled to process what was being said. Portia thought she looked like a budgerigar that had been given an expensive asymmetric haircut and draped in extravagant designer jewelry.

"What I'm struggling to understand," Stella said, "Was why Jasper talked about it at Yuthfest if he wasn't absolutely certain how it would play out. He doesn't strike me as the kind of person to take big risks. I'm sure they would have done the research."

Portia shrugged. "Flying a kite? He was very short on specifics, wasn't he?" Sonny was silent but looked like he agreed.

Lars appeared ready to explode but only managed to mutter, "I'm not sure that's completely right."

"Let me show you a few slides," Portia went on, "which I recommend we use over the next few weeks to help the client understand the looming risk."

Onto the screen popped a graph which mapped public attitudes to active euthanasia against the age of the person receiving the 'service'. In the run-up to the meeting, Sonny and Portia had had a lively discussion about how best to describe their customers on the slides. Portia was so excited when she saw that the research backed up what she wanted to hear that she suggested calling them 'victims'. Sonny had talked her out of it. He was right. It would have been provocative.

"This is what we asked:

Please rate your level of comfort that humane assisted dying should be offered at an affordable price to healthy people in the following age groups:

- 85+   70%
- 75-84   65%
- 65-74   60%
- 55-64   50%
- 46-54   50%
- 35- 45   30%
- 18-34   10%
- Under 18   3%"

"What this data tells us is that none of the entities in the assisted dying ecosystem will be damaged by associating ourselves with the Endings program with its current scope.

"At the moment we are promoting it exclusively to the over-70s. Offering seniors an Ending package is not going to provoke serious moral outrage any time soon. It meets with public approval. Even if we ratcheted up our offer to make it even more irresistible for that oldest cohort, we would be on safe ground in reputation terms.

"As part of the Phase Two research, we also asked a few questions about the Disabled and Ill Social Segment. There, the results were broadly in favor of rollout with some highly polarized views at the edges."

Lars huffed. "Tell me again, where are you getting all this from?" he said.

"By asking the opinion of a statistically significant cross-section of the general public rather than your mono-cultural echo chamber of Yuthies," Portia snapped back. "This is what we should have done from the very beginning. All our research was geared to selling to the customer, not gauging reputation risks with wider society."

"So what do I do now?" Stella asked, blinking into the camera like a rabbit in the headlights.

"You need to take this to Mason," Portia said. She wasn't going to suggest Sonny go out on a limb this time. It all had to go through the proper channels. "He's the client."

"Oh, come on," Lars sneered. "This is ridiculous. All the political risk is taken by the Yuthies. Surely we have to continue? The Corporation is merely fulfilling a public sector contract that they tendered for. If they don't deliver the service another firm will. And probably not as efficiently, either. We have put so much time into making this work."

"Honestly, Lars, I think Portia has a point," Sonny said.

"But what about the people like Willow?" Lars said, showing an uncharacteristic glimmer of compassion, "Who see suicide as their…" he fished around for the most appealing word "kindest option. For them and their loved ones. Don't they have rights, too?"

Portia had been expecting that question. "Let me be clear. Among the general public, youth is a powerful trigger for negative sentiment when it comes to assisted suicide.

"If the Yuthies want to stay in power, they have to drop it. It will make or break them in the next election. Now I would suggest that it's for Lars to break the news to Jasper and his crew. Illness and disability remain a relatively uncontroversial area for new business. Perhaps we could suggest some process improvements to take some of the friction out of that decision path. I am sure, Lars, you could apply your AI expertise there."

"So you aren't saying we should pull out of helping The Corporation with the Endings business altogether?" Stella asked.

Oh, do keep up, Portia thought. "That is correct, Stella."

"And you're not saying we should stop supporting their plans to expand the service?"

"No, but it is a delicate situation. Stella, this is a brilliant opportunity for you to give strategic counsel to both The Corporation and Yuthentic. Firstly, the research validates their existing business, the Endings program targeted at the elderly which is the foundation of the Yuthentic wealth redistribution agenda. Only a handful of activists have any argument with that. Secondly, they can, with safeguards, start offering it to certain people who are ill or disabled. There is some resistance there, but they aren't getting much traction with the media. Thirdly, they should abandon the offer to the under-35s. If they really want to do something for the youths who claim that they would like to die, perhaps we could propose a more reputation-enhancing alternative?"

"Like what?" Stella said.

"How about a youth suicide prevention campaign?"

Lars could not contain himself any longer. "But that's not empowerment!" His voice was strained. "That is being sentimental, patronizing and over-protective."

"Lars, I know that's how it might come across to some people. But I have to argue that in the long term it will be more profitable for Brytely to associate our brand with something life-affirming rather than life-ending." Portia went on, while Sonny nodded in agreement. "Rockstar Ending is truly innovative, and we can all be proud of it. It is delivering unprecedented social and economic benefits. But we can't stretch the concept indefinitely. Not without provoking the kind of public backlash we can all do without. In business terms. In political terms. And, I think I can say this among friends, in career terms."

"But won't that lead to more wasted public spending? Keeping all the sick and weak people alive? Not to mention the impact on the happiness index?" Lars was not going to give up.

"Well," Portia explained, "We can still support Phase Two for the 'sick and weak' as you call them. That will certainly save some money. But we have to take children and teenagers out of the equation."

"There is another way to approach this," Sonny said. "What if we dangle the possibility of access to the YASS as a bet we are prepared to lose."

Stella was really struggling now. "What do you mean?"

"Well, if we do what Jasper did. He's very clever. You could tell him that. I'm sure he wouldn't mind. Float the idea of the YASS knowing that it will act as a magnet for negative sentiment. While all the do-gooders are trying to save the youth of today, we can quietly ramp up some other expansion opportunities."

"Can you please stop using acronyms?" Stella said. "It's hard to follow."

"Sorry," Sonny said. "To put it simply, what's left of the media will only have space for one argument. Let's give them something to get their teeth into, a staged battle that they can win. We could produce some very provocative material together to fan the debate. I'm sure Lars will know some ways to get that out onto the internet without our fingerprints. Then, while the chattering classes are busy saving the children, we can quietly start targeting sick and disabled people. The kiddie pro-lifers can fight it out on Splutter with the hardline pro-death activists, such as our colleague Lars, here. I'm not judging you by the way, mate. It's just who you are."

Lars looked happy enough to have had his tribe correctly identified. Otherwise he seemed deflated but resigned. "It's such a missed opportunity, but I have to be a realist and the data speaks for itself. I don't pretend to understand how the dark arts of communications work, but Sonny's idea sounds like it could hit the spot."

CHAPTER TWENTY-SIX

"**N**OW I'VE SEEN EVERYTHING," ARDUA murmured as ten knee-high robotic quadrupeds trotted in perfect step, two by two, down the empty school corridor in the direction of the playground.

There was the softest sound of ticking, like an arsenal of tiny synchronized timebombs, as their delicate rubber-tipped feet tapped quickly along the shiny floor. You could always count on The Corporation to put on a good show. The demonstration was exactly what Ardua needed to boost the school's media profile and it would be good for the students' job prospects. They were fortunate to have a long-standing relationship with such powerful friends.

"Head," Bob said proudly, "It's a privilege to be back."

Ardua offered him a limp handshake. When Bob had worked at Charlton Green, she had found him to be a maverick presence. However, she could not forget that his ideas for the creative use of their experimental child surveillance technology had helped her school become known as one of the best in the country. He had his uses.

"And thanks for the floorplan. Having the exact lay-out in advance allowed us to pre-program the best route through for this lot."

"Can't they find their own way around?" Ardua looked disappointed. "I would have thought that Corporation robots could make their own decisions these days."

"Not this model. You wouldn't want one escaping, though, would you? I think you'll find them impressive enough once we start the show."

Bob had arrived an hour earlier to cordon off a large area in the middle of the schoolyard using lightweight collapsible barriers. At each end of the pitch, he had placed a small goal. A ball sat in a center circle which Bob had sprayed on with temporary paint. An area had been fenced off at the side where a cameraman from the local TV news, a freelance reporter, and one of The Corporation's press officers had set up their equipment.

Opposite, a large pop-up banner, provided by some-one at HQ, read: "CRAP careers with The Corporation'. Around the edges of the ground, a few hundred teenag-ers began to bark in anticipation as soon as they saw the mechanical visitors walk out onto the makeshift pitch. He scanned the faces for Lexi and found her in a small cluster of teachers. They had a good spot for observing the kids, as well as the demonstration.

The robots peeled off from their phalanx and fell into a new formation of two opposing teams. Everyone gasped when their surface changed, one set taking on a zebra stripe, and the other large circular dots.

"Can I have a volunteer to blow the whistle?" Bob stepped onto the pitch. Surrounded by the machines, he seemed an unlikely referee. His physique was not athletic. The Corporation had provided him with a branded, hexagonal-quilted puffer for the occasion.

"Sir, sir!" An array of hands shot into the air. Bob chose one of the smaller girls and glanced across to Lexi in the huddle of teachers. She gave him a thumbs-up sign. He had been looking forward to showing her his toys.

"What's your name?" he asked the child as he carefully broke a small steel whistle out of a sterile pouch. It was stamped with The Corporation logo.

"Perfect."

"OK, Perfect. You can keep this by the way. On the count of three. One. Two. Three. Blow!"

Before the shrill sound had stopped echoing around the playground, the machines snapped into action. They were straight into an extremely fast game of five-a-side football, kicking with any of their 'legs', passing the ball between the different team members, and conducting all manner of positively balletic rolls, tackles, swerves and tricks. Students cheered and laughed as the show played on. Bob was absorbed in giving an intermittent commentary over the loudspeaker.

When the gameplay came to a halt, the winning team did a lap of honor, periodically standing up on two legs to bow and to entertain with more daring acrobatics. The losers huddled in the center, their body language cleverly programmed to convey the emotion of disappointment. It was hard not to feel sorry for them. Eventually all ten robodogs came together again, and flawlessly stacked themselves into a pyramid where they froze, creating the perfect backdrop for Bob's talk about careers in robotics.

Now and again, he would command the droid at the top of the pyramid to help him with a demonstration. It stretched and somersaulted into various positions.

The students were captivated when Bob started playing with the cuttlefish camo setting on the units' membranes and got them to blend into the tarmac in the playground. There was a short Q&A which produced a howl of disappointment when Bob had to reply that, no, rides on the robots would not be permitted. "Good question, though," he added with a wink.

As the teachers began to herd the students back inside, Lexi was nowhere to be seen. It took him a while to march the robots calmly back to their automated transport vehicle, their camo now reverted to Corporation branding. The truck pulled away, and Bob went back inside. He had promised to do some individual career advice sessions. Most of all, though, he was looking forward to seeing Tyson. They had bonded over a shared love of music during Bob's time at Charlton Green.

By the time he reached the assembly hall the students were crammed in, and the room was filled with an excited buzz which faded to an awe-filled silence as soon as the music began.

The audience was enchanted by the sweet sounds and hypnotized by Tyson's huge physical presence. He towered over the keyboard swaying in time to the beat, playing entirely from memory. Nobody saw Bob's flicker of disgust when Ardua headed back to her office in the middle of Tyson's medley, or heard him mutter 'philistine' under his breath.

Several years earlier, Bob had been horrified to discover that Ardua had sacked the school's much-loved music teacher, Francis, and sold all the instruments. The students were devastated. Although there was nothing he could do about it, it had bothered Bob that his office and control center had been installed in place of what had previously been the music room.

He looked around while Tyson played, hoping to see Lexi. Surely, she would not want to miss this? As discreetly as he could, Bob typed a short message: *Where RU?*

By the end of the session everyone was feeling inspired. Bob, however, was on edge, and messaged Lexi again. Maybe she would find him in the careers room later?

There were about a dozen desks spaced out for careers speed dating, each with a sign giving the name and business of the visitor. Most of the seats were already filled. The pupils politely waited their turn on benches arranged in rows in the middle of the room. Bob had forgotten how much he enjoyed chatting to young people. He told them about his job, and all the things that happened at CRAP. Tyson was popular, too, and got a couple of bookings for private keyboard lessons. It was thirsty and bum-numbing work sitting on hard school chairs and talking non-stop, but Bob didn't mind.

As the last pupil left the room, Bob sidled up to Tyson who was packing away his neat electric piano. They chatted about how much Tyson was enjoying college, and their memories of the good times they had shared in years gone by.

"I've had an idea," Bob said suddenly. "Before you go, will you come with me to have a look at the Fakesy Bowie? For old time's sake?"

"Sure," Tyson grinned, "Why not?"

At first Bob thought they had taken a wrong turn. It was a few years since either of them had been in the school. When he realized he had definitely come to the right place, Bob was horrified. "My Ziggy's gone!" he gasped, looking like he might burst into tears. Tyson was upset to see Bob getting into such a state and wanted to get hold of Lexi, but Bob said there was no point.

In place of Fakesy's Bowie portrait, which Bob had played a crucial role in getting installed in the school, was something else. The new picture had been done by an artist with far less wit and even less skill. Its subject, however, was unmistakable. David Bowie had been replaced by a full length portrait of Jasper, Yuthentic's party leader. He looked at them smugly, from beneath his fluffy fringe, holding in one arm a skateboard which bore the Yuthie sigil, and raising the other fist in a pastiche revolutionary salute.

Bob and Tyson were both taken aback.

"Man, he's not even holding the board right," Tyson said. "You never hold them by the trucks. What idiot came up with that?"

CHAPTER TWENTY-SEVEN

BOB WAS STILL SEETHING WHEN Lexi came home late that evening. Ardua had buttonholed her as she was leaving school to rave about how brilliantly the careers day had gone and she could not get away.

The media coverage of the robodogs had made the national roundup. It was glowing. Ardua had feared that the reporters might say something irreverent about the machines taking the children's jobs rather than providing them with fresh opportunities. She need not have worried. Every single journalist had been dazzled.

"It's been a successful day," Ardua had said, as the two women finally left. "Do pass on my sincere thanks to Bob."

Shortly afterwards, Lexi found him pacing round the kitchen.

"Where were you earlier?" Bob said pointedly, before she could even get out a quick 'hello'. "I was looking for you at school."

Lexi tossed her phone into the Faraday box and folded her arms.

"When?" she asked.

"After the match. I couldn't see you anywhere. You didn't reply to my messages. Where were you?"

Her face began to crease into a troubled expression. "If you must know, Bob, I thought I was going to have a panic attack." She was avoiding his gaze.

"What?" He stood perfectly still and stared at her. "I had no idea! Sit down, eh?" Bob pulled out a chair but Lexi stayed on her feet. "Come on. Tell me about it?" he coaxed.

She started to explain. "It was when your match kicked off. It must be to do with what they did to Mabel, you know?"

Bob drew a glass of water from the tap and placed it gingerly on a surface near her. "Has it happened before, Lex?"

"I had a bad moment when I saw the robots in Blackpool, but I didn't want to say anything."

"What?" Bob was furious with himself for not having noticed.

"You were enjoying it all so much. Both of us wanted it to be a fun night. Once we had driven past them I was OK. It was stupid. I was convinced it was just a one-off. But the second the football began today it started happening again. I thought I was going to be sick. So I went back to my classroom. I didn't want to spoil your show. I had the phone on silent, doing one of those meditations that are supposed to calm you down. And then, when I tried to leave, the head dragged me in."

"I'm so sorry. Are you sure you're OK now?" Bob had frozen to the spot and was directly facing her. "Lexi?"

"Yes, I'm fine. Honestly. Just promise me you won't bring one of them home?" Lexi was only half joking.

Bob edged closer and gave her a hug. "I promise. No robots here. Only in the lock-up," he said. She did not need to know about Wotsit2U, the small, stealthy quadruped named after his dead cat, that he had been building in his little workshop in his spare time.

"Anyway," Lexi went on, "It's your fault I'm late. I had to stay behind after school to bask in your reflected glory. Ardua even asked me to pass on her thanks to you."

"That stupid bitch!" She was shocked by Bob's outburst.

"She was speaking very highly of you." They both had their issues with Ardua, but she had never heard Bob be abusive about her before. It was hard to remember the last time he was nasty about anyone. She found herself suppressing a nervous laugh which she just about managed to catch in her throat. His face had darkened.

"What's up, Bob?"

He had a look of profound disappointment. "The Fakesy. My Fakesy. My Bowie. It's gone! But I think you probably know that. Why didn't you tell me Ziggy Stardust had left the building?"

She did not know where to look. "Oh, Bob," Lexi said quietly, trying to calm him down. As she watched him, he just seemed to get more wound up.

"Well? What has happened to it?" he demanded.

"I knew you would be upset. That's the only reason I didn't tell you. It was stupid really. I should have said something, but I didn't think you would ever find out."

Bob grunted. "When did it happen? Where has it gone?"

"Ardua sold it. Only a month or so ago. I believe it went to a private collector."

"Oh for fuck's sake. That woman knows the price of everything and the value of nothing. And why the hell is that Yuthie idiot there in his place?"

"Surely you can't imagine I approve of that?" She went on to explain the details.

"It was the new governor's idea. That Holly, the Yuthie Member of Parliament. She ran a competition for the kids to design a tribute to the Party. They seem to be rolling them out in a lot of schools. I don't think it's appropriate. But there's no point arguing. There were loads of brilliant entries. Some of them were very funny, actually. Then the sponsor said none of them were good enough. You would not believe how upset the kids were. Anyway, the Yuthies' design agency came in with that big stick-on transfer in the end. It's not even an original painting. I knew you'd be angry. I was, too. Nobody is sorrier than me that this has happened. Honestly."

"How dare they! Didn't anyone try to stop them?" Bob was starting to become calmer, but he was still baffled. "You should have told me, Lex."

"You told me not to go on about the Yuthies all the time." She thought that was a bit of a low blow, but it was true. "And anyway, it's not your room anymore. It's ages since you left."

"I'm going to talk to Channelle about it. The Corporation commissioned that artwork. It will be worth an absolute fortune. She was involved when it was done. She's an important executive now, with direct access to Mason. She needs to know!"

Lexi was adamant. "No, Bob. Don't get involved. Ardua squared it off with them. The removal of the Fakesy might seem like an act of vandalism to you and me. But for the school and The Corporation it's simply collateral damage in the campaign to curry favor with the Yuthies."

"Really? I find that hard to believe." Bob knew that corporate life could be shallow, but he had hoped that schools would have higher principles.

"I've already told you, the Yuthies are all over the school. I can't afford to make any trouble at work. I will never find a teaching job like this anywhere else. I'm the last of a dying breed. You should have heard Holly in our assembly this morning, going on about how young people's career prospects were better than they had been for decades, thanks to the Yuthies. All that was missing was for one of the kids to stand up and launch into a chorus of 'Tomorrow Belongs To Me'. Only then I remembered the last time we performed *Cabaret* was before Ardua came. When we still had a music department. Ancient history."

Bob was muttering angrily. "It's bloody disgusting."

"Too right it is. Just be glad you didn't have to sit through it. Holly made everything they are doing sound so innocent and positive. In comparison to all their other insidious nonsense, I'm afraid the loss of your Bowie painting is the least of my worries."

CHAPTER TWENTY-EIGHT

E VEN MASON COULD NOT FIND fault with what his team had come up with.

The Corporation's support for the Biking Executive Road Killers was something of a personal indulgence. He could not host the Spring Sprint without taking the opportunity to show off a little. And anyway, competition led to innovation. Everyone knew that, even if nobody still dared to admit that greed was good.

A few of Mason's visitors had been suspicious when he said The Corporation was going to provide all the bicycles. Thirteen of them, to be precise. It saved the participants from having to get their own bikes shipped, and the risks that entailed, and they were all invited to bring their own saddles.

In any case, who would not be curious to see what an organization as innovative as The Corporation could come up with?

Ricky had been working on the design with Bob, one of Lola's guys down at CRAP. They had modified a top-end racing bike so it could steer itself, navigating to routes that were dynamically optimized to meet certain criteria.

The options could be anything from simply avoiding traffic, to choosing the routes with the least pollution or the most interesting scenery.

A small unit – not unlike a conventional bike computer – was mounted on the handlebar of each bicycle, allowing the rider some basic controls – for most of the time, at least – and giving them an idea of the route immediately ahead.

Mason had decided what the navigation strategy should be. All the riders had to do was pedal. He had not been able to resist mentioning the project to a couple of his friends in venture capital. Already they were sending him investment proposals. They were certain the bikes could prove popular in tourist destinations. And he hadn't even told them about the clothing yet.

Using the cuttlefish membrane had been a stroke of genius. They had made it adhere to the frames and helmets, and even the clothing they had provided. Each rider could choose their own livery from a range that had been pre-programmed not to clash. There were also a few surprises in store that would get everyone talking.

On the day of the event, Ricky had brought along a friend from her days on the cycling circuit to help with the final checks, ensuring the tech was all live, the saddles at the right height, and the cleats on the riders' cycling shoes properly adjusted. Each bike was pre-loaded with a water bottle and a small bag of snacks and gadgets under the saddle. Coffee and pastries were set out on a heavy white tablecloth.

It was a nice touch that the marketing team had arranged for the riders' names to be written on the frames.

Mason, Tom, Lola, Luis, Chet, Garcia, Gennaro, Klaus, Birgitta, Sophie, Iris, Ben and Brenda arrived in good time at the marquee in Regent's Park. Their bikes were arranged on stands, angled along a wall. Behind them was a red-carpet backdrop peppered with logos.

Today, Mason wanted their tour to take in some of London's most impressive sights on their city-wide Easter Egg hunt. They would be warming up with a few circuits of the Outer Circle around Regent's Park, heading up to Hampstead Heath for a little hill work, making a few laps of Hyde Park and The Serpentine, then down the Mall and along the river, ending at Tower Bridge where they had all been booked into a hotel for a networking dinner which he would have to leave early to fly out to Bangkok.

When security tried to make him cancel, he refused. He had already invited the guests. Then they had tried to persuade him to stay away from some of his favorite parts of central London because a demonstration was taking place. He had said no, demonstrations happened all the time. It was the capital city after all.

Eventually they reached a compromise. The whole point of the bikes was that they would automatically steer away from any emerging disruption. With the addition of the cuttle camo clothing, they should be exceptionally safe. The risks were being blown out of proportion. And it would be such a shame to miss Victory Square.

In the end, he sold in the idea so effectively to his international chums that they had to auction the tour places, giving the money they raised to tr-AID-lib, a useful catchall social enterprise which was on the up. They might be a global elite being paid – collectively – millions of dollars, but their bike ride was going to help bring an end to child labor, slavery, climate crisis and animal exploitation.

Courtesy of the charity, they even had a victim of trafficking join Mason on the podium to tell everyone how grateful he was to have been rescued. Blake had been picked up by a criminal gang in the fast food restaurant where he had been dumped on leaving care. They had sold him into a call center where he had been forced to trick people into buying non-existent financial products with their life savings.

Blake was one of the lucky ones. Things were better now he was working at one of The Corporation's flagship depots. Mason lowered his head modestly as the BERKs listened to Blake's moving testimony to The Corporation's modest munificence and burst into spontaneous applause.

CHAPTER TWENTY-NINE

B OB WAS HOPING THIS WOULD be the last weekend for a while that he would have to go into CRAP. Things had been stressful at home, and then Lola had given him Project BERK.

While it was flattering to be hand-picked to drive an esoteric pet rock job for Mason, the pressure that came with it was intense, and he had struggled to find the time he needed to work on his Wotsit2U idea, which always helped him relax.

Working with Ricky, however, had been a joy, and a welcome break from trying to help Lexi manage her increasingly fragile mental state. He found himself thinking about Ricky a bit more than he should have. But Lexi had nothing to fear. Not only was Ricky half Bob's weight, ten times as fit, and more than twice as good looking. She was also madly in love with a paramedic called Trudy.

Today was the day when all the plans were supposed to come together. The timing could not have been worse.

Lexi had invited Jennifer to stay that weekend so they could go on the PACE demonstration. If he had not been working, Bob would have put on a balaclava and gone with them. Instead, he had to find other ways to help, promising to take them both out for a curry when they all got home. It should all be over by teatime.

At home that morning he had been up first. The house was silent. Before heading off to work he took them both a cup of tea in bed and left a surprise gift for each of them in a zip-up pouch on the kitchen table. Something from his growing anti-surveillance range.

Now, however, he was stuck in the CRAP control room. A few colleagues were around, but it was not as busy as a weekday with no manufacturing staff in. The delivery drones and droids, however, kept going all day and night.

Ricky had said she would call him from the starting area. Bob had arrived at CRAP in good time and flicked through various dashboards.

One of his favorite pastimes, in less busy moments, was looking at the map of London with all their robots marked on the screen. He could zoom in if he wanted. Or get the droid's-eye view of what was happening on the city streets. Someone less responsible than Bob might have taken advantage of the privileged panoptic viewpoint. The possibilities were endless and included both up-skirting and blackmail, but Bob had only ever been tempted to misappropriate a customer's food delivery. He had no reason to put his job and security clearance in jeopardy. Why would he, when he had the best set of toys in town, and was even allowed to take home decommissioned spares to play with in his private workshop?

Ricky's friendly face appeared in a video call. It looked like she was round the back of the tent.

"They're all here," she said. "Only there's a bit of a problem."

Bob tried not to panic. "How can I help?"

"Tell me, how many Ns in Gennaro?"

Bob was sure he had triple checked all the names on the bikes. "Oh no! We didn't get it wrong, did we?"

There was silence, followed by a giggle. "Nah. Only kidding. Sorry Bob, I couldn't resist. It's all fine."

Lola checked in with Bob from the marquee, too. She had been training for the ride for months and would have her hands full helping to host Mason's VIP guests. Until recently, she had been more of a runner than a cyclist, but she had come to the conclusion that such a solitary sport was not helping her career enough. Especially when the CEO and his corporate best friend Tom were such enthusiastic riders.

Without telling anyone at the office, she had secretly bought herself two fine wheels and hired a personal trainer to help her build on the fitness level she had already achieved from spin classes. When Lola casually let slip to Mason, how much she was loving her new pastime, he immediately invited her to join the BERKs. They needed more 'people like her' to get involved, and she could easily get the eyewatering membership fee paid by The Corporation as a legitimate business expense. She accepted graciously. There was no need to embarrass Mason by pointing out that it was screamingly obvious from the team photos in his office that there were no other 'people like her' involved at all. Well, nobody who was both Black and female.

And today was the day. "It's all looking brilliant," she reassured Bob. "The big man's pleased. There's just one thing…"

"Yes?"

"Can you sort out the weather as well? The forecast is disappointing."

"Hmm. I wish you'd asked me earlier. I'm all out of silver iodide. But there's a novelty rain cape in the little bag under your saddle. Would that help?"

"I knew you would have thought of something," Lola laughed. "Seriously, though, well done."

"I'm expecting you to come back with the yellow jersey," Bob said.

"Oh no. As far as today is concerned, I'm merely a domestique. We've already discussed who we need to win, and it's not going to be one of the home team. I've got to go. Just wanted to say a quick thanks."

"I'll be here all day keeping an eye on things. Good luck boss."

As the peloton set out, Bob sat back to enjoy their tour of London's beautiful parks. He had once loved driving around the city, before it got clogged with electric vehicles, and parking became almost impossible – even assuming you could afford to pay the congestion charge. All the bikes were mounted with unobtrusive cameras. The riders probably did not even realize they were there. And he had worked with the drone team to arrange aerial coverage from a series of UAVs that would take it in turns to follow the cyclists.

Bob could see Lola was chatting and taking it easy. It was harder to keep up the conversation when they all had to put in extra effort for the steep climb up to Hampstead. As they reached Whitestone Pond, the highest point in London, the leader's jersey flushed with the red dots of the King of the Mountains livery, and the others did the same when they crossed the same point. Everyone whooped with joy. Ricky thought it was fun when the camo on her scooter joined in, too. A small tent had been erected where a robot waited to photograph them in their ersatz victors' shirts.

When they entered the massive park, speed controls cut in on the bikes so they stayed within the legal limit. What they lost on the workout they gained in the chance to network. Ricky had to leave them at the entrance to the Heath, as her scooter was not allowed in, so a couple of low drones joined the party to keep an eye on them until they got back to a main road. Bob followed the footage and was able to look out for miles across the city.

As soon as Ricky was back on the cyclists' tail, Bob thought he would have a quick look at Victory Square. It worried him that Lexi and Jennifer had decided to leave their phones at home. It wasn't like they were looking for trouble, so it seemed an excessive precaution. He could not see them. Still, it was early, yet.

The BERKs sped down to Hyde Park for a few more laps, and an extended stop for a light lunch in their own exclusive pop-up pavilion overlooking the Serpentine. Everyone was buzzing and Mason invited Ricky to give them the inside track on her years in racing.

By the time the pack turned down Constitution Hill, along the side of Buckingham Palace, Mason was in his element. He was delighted to see that the bikes were taking them towards Victory Square after all.

As they skirted the Victoria Memorial and turned down the Mall, the bikes snapped into formation and their clothing rippled into union jacks bringing cheers from the passers-by. None of them could remember when they last had so much fun. They slowed down again so that they could take in their surroundings, and to give The Corporation drones time to capture the magical moment on camera, with the Palace in the background. The sky had turned deep, menacing grey, a low rumble of thunder sounded, and a fork of lightning flashed from the direction of the river.

As far as Bob could tell, the official demo would consist of a few speeches and a bit of placard-waving. PACE had wanted to do a balloon release – one for every thousand deaths delivered by the Endings Program since it began – but it had been ruled out in case the balloons interfered with aerial traffic. In areas of the city where footfall was most dense, the deliveries increasingly went through the skies rather than across the pavements. The doggie droids only really got more numerous to the west of Parliament Square, in the residential areas that stretched down into Pimlico. He could see them trundling along delivering shopping and takeaways. Just like a normal Saturday.

An alert appeared: a severe weather warning. Looked like it was going to rain on Mason's parade, after all.

Bob dropped a quick message to Ricky and Lola. They knew that Mason would be annoyed, but he wouldn't let any of his guests see what was going on behind that enhanced poker face. Ricky had some folding, lightweight umbrellas on the scooter. They had even matched them with the cuttle camo. Never miss an opportunity to show off.

On the bank of screens that surrounded him, Bob could see the Central London UAVs starting to head for harbor. The storm warning had triggered their self-protection mechanism. They would be hiding away in the depots until it was safe to go out. Urgent deliveries would have to switch to the roadside droids. It was just as well. A gust of wind or a lightning strike could easily bring down a drone on someone. So far, no one had successfully sued The Corporation for drone injury, but it was bound to happen one day.

Bob had been hoping to use the drones to keep an eye on Lexi and her friends. When they began to retreat it made him uneasy. He started to listen to 'Riders on the Storm' by The Doors with one ear to help him keep calm before slipping out his personal device and glancing down at an app. He might not be able to watch Lexi on the surveillance cameras, but the backup pet tracker would show him exactly where she was.

It was only when they drew close to Admiralty Arch, at the opposite end of The Mall to Buckingham Palace, that Mason began to feel uneasy. The drones had disappeared. There seemed to be some kind of commotion after all, up ahead in Victory Square. Traffic was starting to back up, and he could hear shouting.

As the bikes speeded on, he was starting to worry that he could be leading his esteemed associates into a dangerous situation. He tried to remember if there was a manual over-ride on the computer, but the peloton was in such a tight formation he did not dare take his eyes off the road. A pile-up would ruin their day. Especially if there were anarchists on the loose.

He breathed a sigh of relief when, just before they reached the entrance to Victory Square, all the bikes peeled off to the right into Horse Guards Road. The tranquil ornamental gardens of St James's Park lay on their right, and the bleached expanse of the Horse Guards Parade stretched away on their left, surrounded by grand buildings hewn from pale grey stone.

Mason's instincts were still telling him that something was wrong back in Victory Square. Fat drops of rain fell on his arms. The thunder was rumbling closer. Suddenly, they were in the middle of a torrential downpour. It didn't seem to affect the cuttlefish camo colors, but the rain was cool, and he could feel it wicking into his socks.

The bikes were taking them away from Parliament Square through some backstreets by the park. Rainwater was swilling around inside his cycling shoes now. He heard one of the guests joking about British weather.

Then, the cuttle camo thought it detected nightfall and switched to the brightest imaginable palette of Day-Glo colors. It was like an explosion in a neon paint factory. No one on the road would miss them. Mason was losing count of the number of times the riders had gasped with joy. He heard Gennaro say, "Bravo, Mason!"

But he was still uneasy and pulled alongside Lola. He knew she would have a channel to the control center on her embedded headset. "Do you know what's happening?" he said. "This is hardly a tourist route. Government buildings and mansion flats? This isn't the London I wanted my guests to see. Can we divert back?"

"The demo's getting out of hand and our bikes are optimized for the safest route. Don't be distracted. Follow the bikes. My guess would be we're heading for Lambeth Bridge."

Before he could argue, they swung left onto Horseferry Road, and the bikes began to lead them towards the river. The route was briefly more scenic, but soon they were crossing Lambeth Bridge in the lashing rain and the bikes steered them away from the river as they started to head east, behind Saint Teddy's Hospital.

Tom drew up alongside him. "Some of the guests would like a group photo with the Houses of Parliament in the background. The rain doesn't seem to bother them. Do you think we can do it?"

"Of course we can."

Mason accelerated to the front of the peloton, water cascading from his helmet down his back. When they reached the approach to Westminster Bridge Road, he gave a hand signal in good time to tell the other riders to slow down and stop safely on the slippery tarmac. They were still a way from the river, at a low point on the corner by the massive hospital which obscured their view.

"I've had enough of being told what to do by the AI," he muttered to Ricky. "If the bikes won't let us ride onto the bridge, we'll walk."

"The safety routing function is there for a reason, boss," Ricky said quietly.

"But look," Mason said. "The bridge is practically empty. We can't come to any harm if we just stop to take a photo. But we need to get closer."

"If you get too far from the consoles you'll lose the colors. The camo is controlled by units on the bikes." Ricky was clutching at straws, but she had a nasty feeling she would get the blame if it all went wrong.

"We can push them." Mason snapped, before shouting to his friends, "Wheel them up here! Ricky can take some photos. Come on!"

The Day-Glo warriors began to follow Mason onto the bridge, pushing their bikes. Ricky cut the power to her scooter and heaved her considerably heavier contraption up the sloping approach road towards the Houses of Parliament.

CHAPTER THIRTY

"FUNNY HOW THEY RE-NAMED IT Victory Square, isn't it?" Jennifer said as she and Lexi walked along The Strand from The Aldwych where the bus had dropped them off. "I wonder where that came from? It used to be Trafalgar Square, didn't it?"

Lexi started to explain but was distracted when she spotted Ayesha and Ajay waiting for them, as arranged, on the corner opposite a busy Charing Cross station. Ayesha was holding a placard which read, 'CHOOSE LIFE'. As soon as they saw Lexi, they waved and smiled, but Lexi knew them well enough to tell that something was not quite right.

"That's them," she said waving back, "I can't wait to introduce you."

Ajay radiated a warm and jovial presence. He and his wife of some decades both wore light hexagonal-quilted navy jackets, jeans and trainers. They had followed the PACE advice to dress incognito. Ayesha carried a large, lightweight matching bag across her body, and Ajay a backpack. Lexi knew that Ajay did not like demonstrations, but he had insisted on coming in case he needed to protect Ayesha. From what? He had no idea.

"I left some of the leaflets on the train," Ayesha said, indicating that there were still quite a few of them weighing her down, "You never know who might need them. Shall we go up to the square and see what's going on?"

It was a busy spring weekend with tourists, locals and protesters wandering slowly around the heart of the city, gazing at the sights, oblivious to the intentions of whoever may be standing next to them. In a corner of the vast pedestrianized square stood a tiny permanent stage with a pathetic, monochrome screen in front of it which said, in writing almost too small to read, 'Victory Square welcomes PACE'. The platform was swamped by the grandeur of the surrounding buildings and historic ornamental fountains.

"Couldn't we do better than that?" Jennifer said. "It looks so uninspiring!"

"Too many rules," Ayesha explained. "You can only book the square if you agree to certain conditions. No inflammatory language. Some of it is quite sensible to be fair. I mean, none of us wants hate speech, do we? Keep the visuals on the podium to a minimum. Limit the numbers of attendees. Submit their names in advance. It goes on and on."

"We were lucky to get a slot at all." Lexi wanted to back Ayesha up but picked up on Jennifer's disappointment. Jennifer had travelled a long way to be there and must be starting to wonder whether she should have bothered. But what did she expect? Dancing bloody robots? It wasn't Blackpool! "They've tightened up a lot of the rules around protest," Lexi went on. "Since the Yuthies decided they didn't need to protest about anything anymore."

"Well, they aren't stopping me putting my flag up." Jennifer reached into her backpack and pulled out a thin, telescopic carbon fiber tube to which she clipped a lightweight yellow flag, and then extended it to its full height. The banner had been cleverly vented so it just caught the wind enough to display its message without becoming hard to hold.

"If they think little old ladies aren't serious about stopping this nonsense, then they need to think again," she grinned as a skull and crossbones rippled above her head, encircled with a red starburst, and the words 'EUTHANASIA? NO THANKS!'

"I feel like I might have seen that before somewhere?" Ajay squinted up as the flag waved in the breeze.

"That's probably because I based my design on the iconic international anti-nuclear-power badge 'ATOMKRAFT? NEIN DANKE'."

"Of course. 'Nuclear Power? No thanks'. I see it now." Ajay nodded approvingly.

"And my banner," Ayesha said, giving it a little jiggle, "Is based on Wham's Katharine Hamnett T-shirt from around the same period. 'CHOOSE LIFE'. Do you think we might be showing our age?"

"That's kind of the point, isn't it?" Ajay said, shifting from foot to foot. "How long have we got until the speeches start?"

More people were gathering around the unremarkable podium.

"Twenty minutes I think," Jennifer said.

"Anyone want a sweet?" Ajay pulled a tube of cherry drops out of a coat pocket and offered them round. Other people nearby had small hampers from upmarket food stores. A couple behind them shared a smoked salmon and rocket baguette and swigged from a miniature bottle of prosecco.

"How was your journey down?" Ayesha asked Jennifer, "You've come a long way!"

"Not too bad. It was nice to see Lexi again." She smiled like she meant it.

"Remind me, how do you know each other?"

"Bob went to school with my son, and we met when they were visiting. And then we found a common interest in all this." She indicated the protest. "Just last year."

"Where is Bob today?" Ajay asked, "Not that I mind being surrounded by women, but it would have been nice to see him. Such a decent fellow."

"Oh, he's had to work." Lexi said.

"He's not still having to go in weekends, is he?" Ayesha asked.

"This is the last one. Or so he says," Lexi did not look convinced.

"And Jennifer, are you married?"

"Yes. But my husband would not be safe in a crowd like this. He can't stand up for very long."

"One thing's for certain, nothing stops *that* woman," Lexi pointed to the stage where Jess was moving towards the microphone. "Nice to see her taking a lead for a change, instead of doing all the backroom work."

She and Ayesha had got to know Jess when her boss, Nicky Hartt MP, had started helping PACE. Since then, they had become aware of Jess's own influential position in the disability rights community. While she was an expert in getting things done by quietly lobbying people in power, Jess was also fearless when it came to using direct action.

"She's the one who got roughed up at the Yuthie conference, isn't she?" Jennifer said.

Lexi nodded. "Yep. She tried to press charges, but they said she was on private property and there was no CCTV. The Yuthies have got the police in their pocket as well as everyone else, if you ask me."

"Hello there, Lexi!" said a man with ginger hair who appeared younger than most of the other protesters. He wore a steward's waistcoat over his jacket, which was open at the neck revealing a clerical collar.

"Father Aloysius! Fancy seeing you here!" Lexi had heard through the grapevine that the priest's bid to join the speakers on the platform had been flatly turned down. PACE had decided that he wasn't secular enough for a mixed crowd. At a previous event, he had broken into prayers for the dead, despite having been instructed by the bishop himself to tone it down. People had walked out. Someone had even thrown a vegan matcha shake at him. Increasingly, he was being viewed as a loose cannon by the movement.

"All those terrible things are still going on. I cannot be a bystander. Every life is sacred," the priest said. "And please, call me Al." He nodded hello to Lexi's entourage.

Lexi made eye contact with Jennifer to stop her saying anything. She couldn't face an argument. Not today. "Of course, Al. But it's Easter weekend. Isn't that your busiest time? Shouldn't you be turning water into wine, or something?"

"We don't do that on Easter Saturday. Not until sundown. There is a lot to do in the parish, for sure, but this protest is just as important. The Son of God might have been able to come back from the dead in three days. But that's not an option for any of us, is it? Certainly, my superpowers don't stretch that far. Unless we do something about it, tens of thousands more are going to have to start on a premature wait for the resurrection of the body. So many of them non-believers, too. And Judgement Day is a long way off."

"Hmm. I see what you mean." Lexi was often confused when Father Al peppered his conversation with what she assumed must be tenets of Roman Catholicism. "It's hardly ideal."

"Well said, Father!" Jennifer joined in. "One of my sons lost his mother-in-law thanks to that lot. There was nothing wrong with her."

"Would you like me to…" he pulled a string of pale jade rosary beads out of his pocket and was about to offer to get down to it, when his walkie-talkie went off. Before he disappeared to deal with some overcrowding by a plinth, he promised that he would remember Jennifer and her family in his prayers.

"That was a narrow escape," Lexi muttered the second he was out of earshot.

Ayesha was more sympathetic. "I know he can go on a bit, but he's on the side of the angels," she said. "Remember when he put everyone up in the Presbytery? It can't have been easy."

The reminder of the Endings escapees' time in their safe house gave Lexi the chills. She still could not stop thinking about what had eventually happened to Mabel, and how she had not been able to save her a second time.

"Well, I have to say I'm quite glad I came," Jennifer said, casting her eye over the growing crowd. "I've been feeling isolated recently. It's nice to know you're part of something. We're offline a lot of the time, you know, to avoid the pressure. But I can't help thinking we miss out on a lot because of it."

Ayesha nodded in recognition. "I'm glad it's not just me. Since we turned 70 last year, we've really noticed them turning up the heat, haven't we Ajay?" she said. "I'm sure you're doing the right thing. But I don't know how people manage to get right off the grid. I want to live in this century, not the last one!"

"It's tough," Jennifer's tone was blunt. "They've been nagging away at me and my Andy for almost two years now. Since all this nonsense first began. Because of his condition, they think it's acceptable to use even more underhand tactics. I could only leave him because my son's keeping an eye out. He'd have the set on in no time if he was on his own. And as for targeting you two! How dare they! You're a pair of spring chickens. It's all wrong."

She could be open with Lexi's new friend, Ayesha thought. "At least Phase Two was dropped, I can't begin to tell you what a relief that was for us. I mean – the under-35s? What the hell were they thinking? We have been very worried about our granddaughter. She's been spending way too much time with that Yuthie lot. We were terrified they would suck her in. You just hope they have a good head on them, don't you? It doesn't bear thinking about."

"There aren't many young people here today." Lexi said, glumly. "Though I suppose I shouldn't be surprised. It would just be nice to have a bit of solidarity for once. The way they go on about it, you'd think boomers were worse than serial killers."

The crowd was indeed a sea of showerproof outdoor wear, grey hair and flat unbranded shoes. Even in subtle, dark colors that would not mark them out from the crowd, the four of them punched above their weight in the style stakes. She suspected there would be an over-representation of elderly, plain clothed nuns in among the throng, too.

A couple more speakers had joined Jess on the plat-form. Lexi explained to Jennifer that they were Henry, the human rights lawyer who had helped them persuade The Corporation to widen their escape clause, and Liz, the first Endings escapee, who seemed to have carved out a niche for herself as a motivational speaker since her appearance at the Health, Euthanasia and Legacy Planning (HELP) Select Committee.

"This is all prematurely triumphalist if you ask me," Jennifer huffed, after Henry gave an account of what PACE had achieved to date. "It's all very well going on about stopping Phase Two, and how brilliant it is that people can cancel their booking right up to the point of departure. But it's not exactly a mini break we're talk-ing about here, is it? It's an appointment with death, for goodness' sake! They shouldn't be allowed to sell it in the first place! Not to anyone!"

"I have to agree with you," Lexi said, "There's always this underlying sense that old people don't count, isn't there?"

"Every single day we see this stuff it's like we're being slowly poisoned." Jennifer grimaced.

From the stage, Jess reminded them that people with disabilities were still included in the Endings target list, as long as they were 18 or older. Her words were moving and feisty, packed with examples she could cite, from years as an activist, of how people with disabilities had been let down. "We were already living shorter lives, on average, than people without disabilities. And now they want to shorten them even more. How can that be right? Join with us and fight!"

"Finally, someone who is prepared to tell it like it is." Jennifer declared. There was a ripple of applause. Jess carried on.

"As you know, our commemorative balloon release was banned today."

"Pathetic!" someone shouted. It sounded like Father Al.

Jess continued, her face determined, looking confidently at the crowd.

"So, we are going to have to do something else to commemorate those who have already sadly died, aren't we? They cannot be forgotten. And we refuse to stand by and watch while our friends and family are coerced into believing that their life is no longer worth living. Come with me! Let us all march from here to Parliament Square, right now, and leave a wreath outside the Department of HELP. Together, we must show the Government that we will not forget those we have lost, or be thwarted in our determination to end this diabolical killing spree. Follow me!"

"I'm coming with you!" Jennifer yelled at the top of her voice. "This is for Iris!"

With that. Jess moved gracefully to the front of the stage. She turned her back to the audience for a moment. A beautiful wreath of inter-woven black blossoms was strategically placed on the back of her chair. As the crowd cheered, she swiveled to face them, and a moving platform lowered her gently to pavement level.

Back on stage, Henry was looking nervous. They did not have permission to march on Westminster. Jess had not told him what she was going to do. As PACE's lawyer, he could never have agreed to it. However, he still wanted to cover her back. The police in this part of town, so close to Parliament, had permission to shoot to kill. It only took him a few seconds to make the call.

"I'm so sorry," he explained to the duty police officer in the public order team. "I had no idea she was going to do this, but can I ask that you let her through? You surely can't think this demographic will cause too much trouble?"

As he looked down into the crowd, they gently parted to let Jess through. At the South side of the square other people with disabilities were waiting to take the lead, with Jess, down Whitehall. The sea of casual wear and grey hair formed itself into a procession behind them.

"There's only a few hundred of them," Henry went on. "No, I haven't counted, but surely you can see? I can get our marshals to follow and make sure they don't get out of hand."

The marchers were already on their way down White-hall, slowly edging forward, chanting: "Who's next?" "Granny's next!" "Who's next?" "We're next!" "Who's next?" "You're next!"

Jennifer stooped down low among the crowd. When she stood up again she was wearing a hooded grey cape, and she had her face covered. "What are you doing?" Lexi said.

"I'm doing what Jess did. I'm taking matters into my own hands. Here, will you look after my banner?"

Lexi eyed Jennifer's backpack. Panicking now, she exclaimed. "Please tell me you haven't got a bomb in there!"

With Jennifer's face covered she could not gauge her reaction, but she thought she heard a muffled sigh of disappointment.

"Of course not! Nobody is going to get hurt. I'll see you back at home if we don't manage to meet up again today. Wish me luck!" She slipped away into the crowd.

Lexi was livid. How could Jennifer plan a solo operation without involving her? And she had dumped her stupid sign on her. She felt used. Like she was running a free B&B for people with more courage than herself. Wishing she could call Bob, she regretted having left her phone at home. Probably just as well, though, if Jennifer was going to do something crazy.

While Lexi walked slowly forward with Ajay and Ayesha, Jennifer slipped back, against the direction of the march, back towards Victory Square. A police escort had assembled and was following the back of the crowd, trying to close in around the edges so that they could control it if necessary. It looked like every available officer had suddenly been assigned to the demo. Back in the square there did not seem to be any of them left. The PACE sign had gone from the podium, and some technicians were setting up for the next booking.

Jennifer knew exactly what she wanted to do, but she didn't know where she would be able to do it. Although she had a range of possible scenarios in her head, the scale of the monuments and buildings was daunting. She turned around and set off back towards Parliament Square.

She reached the Department of HELP just as Jess crept forward to lay the wreath. That place had rubber-stamped the Endings program that had killed so many. It was suddenly obvious what Jennifer had to do. Not yet, though. It was too public. She would have to wait. But at least now she had a plan.

CHAPTER THIRTY-ONE

A MINA HAD TOLD THE FAMILY that she was going to visit an old school friend for lunch. It was the kind of normal thing that a normal young woman would do if she was home from university for Easter weekend.

She had been looking forward to meeting Lars again. He had come to the campus during the autumn term to run an empowerment workshop for student members of Yuthentic. The chair of the Yuthentic Society had been thrilled that they had been sent a speaker who was so closely involved in shaping the party's agenda. Amina had arrived early. After missing out on Yuthfest, she was determined to swing her own ticket next time, instead of being let down by her selfish brother.

The students had spent a day in a shabby meeting room in the Union building. Perched on battered chairs arranged around scratched Formica tables, they divided into several groups where they ran through a set of challenging questions. The process, Lars explained, had been designed with Jasper's personal input to help them decide what freedom, choice and independence really meant to each of them. It was only by being deeply committed at a personal level that they would truly benefit from the Yuthentic values.

At first, she was frustrated. Half her group had made it to Yuthfest back in September and found it hard to keep on the meeting agenda. It was as if they were compelled to keep reliving a shamanic experience. She could not stop them going on about what a transformational evening it had been. Luckily, she had quietly caught Lars' eye and he stepped in to get the discussion back on track.

Once each of them had written down their personal definitions, he mixed up the groups and told them to start to work on a personal action plan that would equip them to live their lives based around the three principles. "All Yuthentic can do," Lars had said, "Is shape what the government delivers. But ubiquitous, sustained change can only come from embedding the principles in your everyday life. It's down to you. You are the future. And – for the first time in history – with Yuthentic you can truly believe that the future is in your hands."

By the end of the day, they were all standing up and committing. Lars had encouraged them to be radical in their thinking and apply the three principles to every aspect of their life, whatever the cost. However, something about his demeanor suggested he was disappointed that, in most cases, the young people's commitments had ended up being more mundane than revolutionary.

What did he expect? Amina thought, sensing from the downbeat way he reacted to their hard-forged promises, that he felt somehow let down. It would take more than a day's workshop to fire up this lot's imagination. Simply to get to university, they would all have had to knuckle down and conform. They weren't going to suddenly sprout courage and imagination from nowhere. If they had ever had it at all, it was probably beaten out of them by relentless studying and being assessed every five minutes. To expect them to set the world on fire would have been as futile as hoping people would become anti-racist after a two-hour unconscious bias workshop.

Nevertheless, Lars brought himself to round up the day by concluding that they had all made a good start and invited them to join him in the Thunberg bar for a quick drink. That was when she had asked him if they could stay in touch in a private Splutter Splinter room. She would get that Yuthfest ticket if it killed her.

For a few months they had traded occasional messages. If she mentioned that she was feeling down, he sent her funny cat videos. She was surprised. It seemed out of character for someone who had come across as so serious, but she was touched that he was taking an interest in her. When he invited her to attend an event, and meet him at his flat in Vauxhall beforehand, she had been quick to accept.

Her parents would not approve of her plans. Lars was exactly the kind of guy they would hate, with his straggly goth hair and piercings. She had never got to know anyone who was passionate about a political cause before. Until recently, though, she had to agree with almost everything he said. Freedom, choice, independence? Well, it was a no-brainer, wasn't it?

They had chatted in the run-up to Christmas. She had told him about day-to-day life at uni and had a moan about her family. She had even invited him to her grandparents' 70th birthday party. The night would have been so much more bearable if she had been able to rustle up a plus one. But he would not give her a straight answer. Then, at the last minute, he said he could not make it, leaving her in a foul mood for the entire evening. She had never asked him whether he had a partner. Maybe that was it. He did not volunteer much information about his life outside the party.

In the New Year something changed. Lars was still a member of Yuthentic, but he had become disaffected. At first, he didn't want to talk about what had made him more critical, but Amina subtly persevered. He began to open up. It seemed that he had been trying to persuade Jasper to adopt more radical policies.

"But the Yuthies have already done so much," Amina said, trying to make him feel better. "You've really changed things for people like you and me. Finally, we're getting a share of the nation's wealth. You have so much to be proud of already. We, I mean."

Lars told her that she had no idea what she was talking about. He had been convinced they were about to do something 'extraordinarily humane' and 'a game-changer'. At the last minute, however, he said, "That pretty twat bottled it." Everything had come to a head with Jasper after he saw some research that suggested the new initiative was likely to halt the growth in the support the Yuthies were starting to attract from the wider public. The plan to democratize death had been diluted. It had all made such beautiful sense to Lars, but now his proposal had fallen at the last hurdle. Freedom? Choice? Independence? They were only words. The Yuthies were, 'only playing at it', he said.

Like Amina, however, he stayed a member of Yuthentic, but he was starting to organize his own internal faction. His day job in data analysis and artificial intelligence programming equipped him to drive a few followers to his Splutter Splinter, and to experiment with recruitment techniques. Given their radical remit – to remove the age of consent for everything, including euthanasia sign-up – even Lars knew that it was only a matter of time before the Yuthies would ask him to leave, he confided in Amina. Before that happened, he was planning to pull out all the stops to get attention.

That afternoon, he was going to march into the city with his followers. It was the weekend before the changes he had yearned for would have come into force if it hadn't been for the stupid focus groups. When that interfering MP and her mates kicked up a fuss Yuthentic had backed down.

There was some consolation for Lars that the Endings program was still running like a dream, routinely culling any old people who applied. Yuthentic had, at least, managed to expand the offering to one or two other categories of people the general public had never much cared about. Well, not until it happened to them, or one of their so-called 'loved ones'. Lars had tried doing things their way. Today, he was going to give them something to remember.

Amina had never been on a demonstration. Her grandmother, Ayesha, had told her stories about some of the ones she had been on in the past, and she had seen news reports of people in street theatre outfits or being carried away by the police. When Lars asked her if she would come with him on Easter Saturday, she thought, why not? She had no other plans. And anyway, she was intrigued by him and had enjoyed chatting with him about his political obsessions over the past few months.

She arrived at the flat an hour before the demo. He buzzed her in through the front entrance and she took a small elevator up to a narrow corridor with rows of identical doors leading off it. One of them had been left slightly ajar. The number on the open door matched the one Lars had given her. She pushed it open just enough to squeeze in, after the bottom of it caught on a small, heavy rucksack that had been left on the floor.

"Hello!" she said cautiously, stepping gingerly towards another doorway directly in front of her. It swung open and Lars was suddenly there, taking up most of the space. He was so close she could smell coffee on his breath and some kind of synthetic herbal cosmetic scent. It wasn't wholly unpleasant.

"Hi!" he said, "Welcome to my humble abode."

He sprang back to allow her to pass into a small living room. She had been in the Yuthie new-builds before. This was much the same as everyone else's. Well, everyone under 35. It was the kind of box Amina knew her brother Sonny was hoping to get if things continued to go well with his job. Except Sonny would not have decorated it the way Lars had. Black net curtains diluted the light, and the walls were black. It was sparsely furnished in somber tones: a small dark grey sofa, a screen, and a few shelves where Lars had symmetrically arranged photos of what looked like an island in a lake, covered with pine trees.

The two of them were still quite close to each other, but it was more a function of the confined space than a deliberate attempt at intimacy. Lars looked more tired than when she had last seen him.

"Would you like a drink?" he said. "Coffee – or maybe one of the special things I brought back from Sweden at Christmas? There's herbal tea or Arrack Punsch. Not much in between."

"Erm… what are you having?"

"Black coffee with a shot."

"OK. Why not?" It was five past midday, so strictly speaking it was the afternoon. She followed him and loitered in the doorway that separated the tiny kitchen from the capsule living area. He turned on the heat under a black enamel coffee pot already sitting on the ceramic hob. From a high cupboard, he took a couple of small glass science beakers and half filled them with alcohol that came out of the freezer. It was no surprise when he gave her a mug, identical to his, with 'Slayer Nation' written on the side. Just like his T-shirt.

"It's quite near here, isn't it?" she said.

"Yes, unfortunately." She had forgotten that his voice had a slight Scandinavian intonation.

"Why…?"

"We made an application for the protest stage in Victory Square, but they said it had already gone. Booked by another group. I suppose it was a bit late. We're just learning the ropes, really, now Yuthentic won't help us with the logistics."

"Shame. Still, I'm sure it will be a success." She found his bitterness unsettling. The first time they met he had seemed more positive.

"It's not over yet. Maybe we'll head up to Westminster afterwards," he went on. "It's not like they can stop us. This is supposed to be a free country, after all." He snorted dismissively.

Amina had been expecting Lars to cheer up after the rally, but he became more antagonistic.

Fewer than 50 people had turned up. It was not a good sign of the movement's potential. Willow, their guest speaker, was furious about something. Amina assumed she was annoyed because the audience was so small. After her gig addressing 20,000 people at the O2, a few dozen misfits huddled in a corner of Vauxhall Pleasure Gardens must have been something of an anti-climax.

Once she had finished speaking, Willow pulled Lars aside to berate him for not having done enough publicity. She made him take down the banner he had pinned to the railings. "I'm not being seen anywhere near that. What sort of slogan is 'suffer little children'? Just wait until I tell Jasper about this."

"It must have been the algorithm," he complained to Amina after everyone else had gone. "Sabotaged! The Yuthies have so many connections. I bet the bastards poisoned my data set."

"But you organized it all through a secure group, didn't you?" Amina said. "How can that be?"

"You have no idea how these things work," he said bluntly. Realizing how rude he must have sounded he quickly added, "I'm sorry. I just thought we were going to make history with the Yuthies, but it's all over."

"I can see why you think that Lars," Amina ventured, "But in all honesty I'm so grateful to them. Haven't they given you your flat?"

"Not given, exactly."

"No, but they got it built, right? And my uni fees. The under-30s are in a much better place…"

"But it's not enough! Can't you see? They are just playing at it. Little more than a bunch of well-meaning amateurs."

She wasn't sure she wanted to be around Lars much longer. He was becoming angrier by the minute. Had it not occurred to him that maybe people just didn't like his ideas? It was one thing quietly persuading old people to end their lives early. But mass suicide was never going to be a vote winner. And saying it was a good idea for children would be the kiss of death for any political movement.

As she watched him violently stuff the useless banner into a bin, Amina began to question what she had ever seen in Lars. She was glad they hadn't got any closer. There had been a fleeting moment in his flat when she thought he might be interested in physical intimacy. They had half an hour to kill before setting out, and there was nothing on the TV. She thought it might just clinch her Yuthfest tickets for next time. But Lars had missed her signals. He just put on a Slayer playlist and carried on talking about politics. Thank goodness nothing happened, she thought. Otherwise, she would be up to her neck in revulsion by now.

He was still wanting to head into town. They were walking along the Albert Embankment towards Westminster. The wind gusted from the river and almost took her breath away. He carried on muttering, but she was not really listening anymore. Once they reached Parliament Square she could get onto the Tube and leave him behind. She had a feeling it was going to rain.

It was then that Amina remembered her grandparents would be in town. Nani had said something about it. Maybe she could shake off Lars and try to meet up with them, instead? If nothing else, today had reminded her that it can be reassuring to be around someone normal. While her parents got on her nerves, she could never say that about Ayesha and Ajay. It would be too late for them to book afternoon tea somewhere fancy, but she was sure they could find a place for cake and a chat. She zoned out Lars' ranting and pulled out her device to send Ayesha a message. If they didn't reply she could make her getaway at Westminster.

After sending the message she glanced back at Lars. He was still incandescent.

"Why are you so angry?" Amina said, giving it one last shot. "You're using up a lot of energy, and it's getting you nowhere."

"Life is one long series of disappointments. Human beings cannot be relied on. In the end they all let you down."

"Who? Who has let you down?"

"Today? That idiot Willow, obviously." Lars was overflowing with contempt.

"Who else?" Did he mean her? He hoped not. She did not think she had led him on.

"Holly."

Surely, he could not mean the Yuthentic Member of Parliament? The one who had died unexpectedly just before Christmas? Poor thing, she was only 27.

"What happened with Holly? Was she your girlfriend?"

"Some would call it that. We were close. For a while we were able to help each other to find satisfaction in a number of ways."

She wondered whether he knew anything about the circumstances of Holly's death. It had been all over the news. The inquest was still going on.

"And then what?"

"Our political differences came to a head. Looking back on it, she was always too mainstream for me. It took me too long to find out."

"I'm sorry for your loss." Amina could not think of anything more appropriate to say in the circumstances. Lars' response was brutal.

"Don't be. I'm sorry I wasted my time. And then Willow said she'd help me. I gave her the chance to be immortalized today. I thought she was ready. But when she saw we had such a pathetic audience all bets were off."

Immortalized? Had she heard him correctly? That seemed a bit aspirational, even for someone as deluded as Lars. She decided to stop asking him questions. It felt like the answers could lead her to a nasty place.

Was there any chance Lars might turn his fury on her next? She looked around to see if there was anyone about who she could ask for help if she needed it. There was a group of twelve people, but they were firmly belted into a speedboat which flew past them on the river. They were laughing and screaming at the same time. She waved at them half-heartedly and they waved back. No. From this distance there was no chance they would pick up on a nuanced hand signal. Even if they did, there was no easy way for them to scale the embankment to help. She wasn't about to risk provoking Lars by showing him he was starting to scare her.

"Do you think if I jumped off a bridge it would make the news?" Lars said suddenly.

"What? No! You're joking, right?" He had her undivided attention now.

He ignored her question. "I asked Willow to do it. She's always saying she wants to die. Acts like she has a lot of public sympathy. Poor Willow. Willow's in pain. Willow's dying. Just not quickly enough. It's her specialist subject. But when it comes down to it, she lacks the necessary courage. I gave her the opportunity to tick two boxes at once, to end her life in the public eye and actually help others get the right to do it humanely. What happened? The attention-seeking bitch pulled out. She's a fake. A total fake!" There was icy vitriol in his voice.

"I'm sorry you're feeling so let down," Amina said. "You shouldn't be so hard on her, though. Willow is still relatively healthy…" she was struggling to find the right words, "… it's a lot to ask."

"You give people choice, and they are too scared to use it. Pathetic." Lars' face was a picture of disgust.

"Maybe she was scared of dying?" It seemed increasingly futile to try to get Lars to empathize.

He acted as if he had not heard her. "Why did you even come today?"

Amina was surprised how easily she was able to answer his question. "I was curious, I suppose. We've had some good conversations. I wanted to catch up with you. I'd never been on a demonstration before. But it didn't turn out like I expected."

"Same here!" Lars gave a sharp, snigger.

It felt like the right moment for Amina to leave. "Look, I'm going to meet my grandparents. They're in town somewhere. I just got a message from them. Will you be all right?" She had already decided that she wasn't going to invite him to meet them this time.

"Of course."

By now they were on the south side of Westminster Bridge facing the Houses of Parliament. Big Ben struck 3pm. There was a rumble of thunder in the distance. The sky was changing from dark green to dark grey.

"I'm going to make a run for the Tube before the rain starts," Amina said, "Are you coming? You were only joking about jumping, weren't you?"

"I'll probably just walk back to the flat." Lars looked across the bridge. "Will you be able to get out? It looks like they've closed it off on the other side."

"Oh, I'll be fine. I'm sure they'll be letting pedestrians through." Now he had reassured her that he was heading home, she did not want to wait another second to get away.

"See you, then."

With a smile that was half apologetic and half pitying, Amina turned and began pacing quickly over the bridge. It had been a narrow escape. Meeting Ayesha and Ajay for tea was just the tonic she needed after such a peculiar morning. There was no way she would look back over her shoulder. All she needed to do was persuade the police to let her through the cordon. The tearoom was only ten minutes away.

CHAPTER THIRTY-TWO

A s soon as he was sure that Amina was not coming back, Lars began to follow her across the bridge. A flash of lightning from behind him reflected on the clock tower that housed Big Ben, and the thunder rolled again. The storm was getting closer. Heavy droplets of rain began to speckle the pavement. Around him, tourists scrambled in their bags for umbrellas and rain capes. He was going to get wet.

There was no traffic. Something was definitely wrong up ahead. Not even a bus or a bicycle was being let through. Could he hear people shouting? He hoped they were still letting pedestrians out at the other side.

Amina had disappeared. Lars hoped she had made it through to wherever she was going. He stopped halfway across.

Over on Lambeth Bridge to the west, a group of cyclists in the brightest colors he had ever seen moved south in close formation. It reminded him of a box of luminous marbles he had been given as a present when he was a child. Be seen, be safe. What a joke!

'If you want something done you have to do it yourself. Or do the programming yourself. Time for Plan B,' Lars thought. He began to pull a tripod out of his backpack. It was easy to find things in there after he ditched the stupid 'suffer little children' banner. If Amina had not been there he would have set it on fire. Maybe Willow had a point. Well, it was too late now. He was a data guy, not a words guy.

Lightning illuminated the Gothic façade of the Palace of Westminster once again. The rain was falling harder now. Some of the tourists were trying to run for cover.

He quickly extended the legs of the tripod and placed his handset in the grip at the top, moving it into a position that would allow him to appear in front of Parliament while he spoke. Annoyingly, the lens kept focusing on the distance, so he asked a tourist wearing a long yellow hooded waterproof coat if they would mind standing in front of the camera for a second so he could get it set up.

By the time he got in position to speak, the rain was torrential. He could not recall ever seeing a sky this dark during the day, other than during his years in Scandinavia. Try as he might to make himself heard, the sound of the storm was drowning him out.

CHAPTER THIRTY-THREE

A MINA WAS THE LAST PERSON they let through the cordon before they closed the line. The face scanner the police officer was wearing advised that she did not represent a threat. Even without the AI he would have assumed that she was too young to have any sympathy with the protesters.

As she slowly made her way against the flow of the crowd towards Parliament Square, she spotted her grandparents. She had to look twice, having believed until then that Ayesha's protesting days were long gone. But even though they had the hoods of their matching coats up, she was certain it was them. Ayesha was carrying a placard in one hand and had her other arm linked with Ajay's. It was the first time in her life that she had seen them look afraid. She managed to slip through to the place where they had come to a halt.

"What are you doing here?" she asked. "You said you were going shopping."

"It's a long story," Ayesha said. "But I might as well tell you now you're here. We're trying to stop them killing people like us."

"No one's going to kill you, Nani!"

"Don't be too sure, Amina. Some terrible things are happening."

"Oh, come on! I'm sure that's not true. Anyway, why didn't you say anything before now?"

"I didn't want you to worry. And you seem so taken with Yuthentic. They're behind it all. But I don't want to fall out with you, my darling. Family first." Ayesha gave her granddaughter a hug.

"This is nothing like Black Lives Matter!" Ajay said. "That's the last demo Nani brought me on. It was so civilized. All spaced out. Respectful. The police are reading this situation all wrong."

The crowd was getting denser. They were finding it hard to keep their balance as more people poured in from Whitehall. The wet pavements were slippery underfoot. "They need to let us onto the bridge, or somebody is going to get hurt." Ajay said. "We all need to stick together."

"Why are they hemming us in like this?" Amina said, "We just want to get out, now, don't we?"

Ajay agreed. "That would be safest, yes."

Suddenly there was a loud bang near the Houses of Parliament. They could not see what had happened, but the crowd surged forward instinctively to get away from the terrifying sound.

"Well, if it's a suicide bomber, one thing's for certain. It won't be one of us," Ayesha said, grabbing Amina's arm. "Does anyone know where Lexi has gone? I can't see her anywhere."

"Hang onto me, Nani! You don't want to go over."

They were being jostled from all sides now.

The police, shaken and distracted by the noise, and fearful there would be more trouble if they continued to hem in the crowd with a shooter on the loose, gave in and released the cordon, letting the protesters flow forward onto the bridge.

Those at the front were propelled forward by the mob behind them. A couple of protesters were thrown onto the ground when their wheelchairs were tipped over. Other demonstrators formed a cordon to stop them being trampled. The police retreated to a position halfway down the bridge to make more room for the crowd.

The group at the front including Jess, Lexi and Father Al were pushed further forward onto the bridge by the weight of the mob behind them.

"We need to get back into town," Amina was having to shout now to make herself heard. She had decided that she did not want to see Lars ever again.

"Not through the Square, though. It's better to run away from an explosion rather than towards it," Ajay said. "Our safest option is to go onto the bridge."

CHAPTER THIRTY-FOUR

BOB WAS WORRIED.

He was watching a news bulletin about a group of disabled and elderly activists who were trapped in Parliament Square. It was all kicking off. A reporter stood on Westminster Bridge struggling to stop her umbrella turning inside out while she talked to the camera. Behind her, a row of police officers had linked arms and were preventing the crowd from moving any further forward.

Having slipped the pet trackers into Lexi and Jennifer's emergency kits alongside their nut bars and anti-surveillance camera accessories, Bob could see they had been separated, which did not make him feel any better.

Lexi was stuck in Parliament Square. She had been there for fifteen minutes now, right by the bridge. She would hate being squashed in so tightly. Jennifer seemed to be moving around on Whitehall away from the crush. How could she have left Lexi on her own after they invited her to stay, especially when she knew that Lexi was in a fragile state? He could only hope that Ajay and Ayesha were still with her.

"The police have been taken by surprise this afternoon," the reporter said. "Sources at Scotland Yard are blaming the algorithm. Apparently, the AI failed to predict that old and disabled people would be capable of this level of civil disobedience. Police are now panicking as the computer is telling them to go in with maximum force. I don't think I have ever seen the police looking more confused. There will be a lot of questions in the coming weeks about why they have made the decision to contain a group of elderly and vulnerable people so forcefully."

Anyone with an ounce of common sense could see that all they needed to do was let the protesters onto the bridge. As if Bob did not already have enough to worry about, Mason and the BERKs were over on the other side, well away from the action. Bob tapped into the feeds coming in from the cameras on the bikes. He overheard some of the execs talking about the demonstration. Eventually one of them turned their bicycle to an angle that gave him a good view of the bridge. It was practically empty.

Bob had already activated his support plan. A small cohort of delivery robots was arriving in Parliament Square. The police were too stretched, dealing with the human troublemakers, to worry about a surfeit of fast food. No one would suspect anything until it was too late. It was going to be hard to make this look like a coincidence, but Bob had always managed to get away with it before.

Apart from the small area where the protesters were trapped, it was unusually quiet. Thank goodness the rain had put off most of the pedestrians. He didn't want anyone to get hurt. Maximum disruption, minimum injury.

That was the idea at least.

In Smith Square, five minutes away from the demonstration, a driverless vehicle, parked there since dawn, opened a side door. Bob was sad that this would be his last chance to play with Wotsit2U, the homemade robotic quadruped who was his pride and joy.

He was pleased to see its steady view of the pavement as it tiptoed along, carrying its heavy cargo, without being dragged down by the weight. Bob's pulse quickened when a woman shot out of a doorway right in front of Wotsit2U and then slowed again as the robodog skipped to one side and trotted right past her. The cuttle camo was working like a dream. The woman had not seen it. People were used to seeing delivery cubes, but robodogs were hardly commonplace. Looking back through the rear camera, Bob could tell that the passer-by had heard the robodog, but she could not work out where the sound had come from.

Everything was coming together nicely in Parliament Square. The cubes were now clustering together on the pavement in front of the St Stephen's entrance. There were ten of them in total, arranged in a tight semicircle against the solid metal anti-terrorism barrier that separated the pavement from the road.

Wotsit2U was speeding along Millbank, avoiding the occasional pedestrian with grace. Bob found himself whistling 'Singin' In The Rain'. It deftly crossed the road and drew close to the cluster of delivery droids, which were starting to spread out into a wider semi-circle, and leapt into the center of the space, just as a policeman on duty at the St Stephen's entrance noticed that something was wrong and began to walk towards the railing.

Bob was proud he had managed to build such an effective machine. For all he knew about the perils of anthropomorphizing robots, his heart sank a little as his finger hovered over his pocket detonator button. Wotsit2U had served him well. He told himself it was not a living thing. Not like poor Wotsit number one. The regret he felt in the pit of his stomach was about his invention only being used for one mission. He had already disconnected the cameras from the delivery boxes and wiped the footage of their journeys there. The electrical storm might provide cover for a data wipe-out. He checked one final time that Lexi was a safe distance away and activated the detonator.

Wotsit2U's feed immediately went black.

Before he could do anything else, Ricky phoned him.

"Bob, can you see anything from there? I'm with the guys – well I'm sure you know where I am – and there's been an explosion. Some of them want to try to help."

"How could they do that?"

"Splutter's gone mad. It's suggesting an explosion in Parliament Square. Any footage?"

"Sorry. All the drones were grounded half an hour ago by the weather, and the wheelie droids are being interfered with by the electrical storm. All I've got is the same web news you can access. I really would advise them to head off in the opposite direction."

"I'm losing that one, I think. But thanks anyway. The bikes have been a huge hit, and the camo was an inspired addition. Sorry, I have to go."

CHAPTER THIRTY-FIVE

"NO HEROICS," WAS A SUGGESTION the BERKs were not prepared to countenance. They ignored the message from Mason's head of security, relayed by Ricky, who already knew how they would treat the advice. Nobody was going to tell them what to do. They shouted garbled instructions for Ricky to mind their bikes while they headed onto Westminster Bridge, determined to 'help'.

As they moved away from their bikes, their neon clothing faded to a pale grey.

Ricky tried to keep her camera phone trained on them. If it all went bad, at least she would have some evidence. Lola was the only one left beside her. "Even I'm getting close to the limit of how far I'm prepared to go for this job," she said.

When they heard an explosion, they were both glad that they had stayed back.

'Finally, something good happened,' Lars thought as he watched a plume of smoke rise above The Houses of Parliament. He could not see any damage to the building.

Shame. More smoke billowed up. The vista already provided an excellent backdrop. If the whole building blew while he was speaking, it would be even better.

The worst of the storm had passed over, and was now flashing away to the north, behind the Gothic palace. More great visual material. But he had to get in front of the camera now. He faced the lens and was about to speak when something else caught his eye.

At first he thought the group of athletic-looking people running towards him might be a triathlon club on a training run, in their matching skin-tight grey sportswear. Surely they would at least have changed their shoes, even if they had not abandoned their helmets? Their cleats kept clacking and sliding on the wet ground, but somehow they managed to maintain momentum. But why on earth were they running towards the explosion?

What had been an engaging backdrop for Lars' political broadcast was fast turning into a battleground. At the side of the bridge closest to the Houses of Parliament, police were now edging backwards away from the crowd, any attempt to contain them becoming more half-hearted by the minute. A few protesters had fallen and were being trampled by others forced forward by those behind them fleeing the blast. The police did not help. They clustered together behind their riot shields and radioed for instructions, leaving civilians to help the injured.

Lars switched his camera to livestream. Realtime footage was bound to get him more eyeballs. He assumed PACE had set off the explosions and, for the first time, had to admit that he admired them a little. At least they had the courage to take their struggle seriously. But it had all backfired. The idiots had given him the perfect honeypot. He could use the unfolding lawlessness to win followers. Everyone knew this kind of video was clickbait gold dust. He spoke straight to camera:

"They say they are pro-life – but look what they have done! Blowing up innocent people! These so-called humanitarian campaigners are intent on causing chaos and disruption. They are all fake. Fake! Where is the humanity in trampling the disabled and elderly underfoot? This is exactly the kind of bad ending you don't want for your loved ones. It should be planned, not random. We need to take out these anarchists. They have already tried to steal our future."

Bob found Lars' live Splutter broadcast and began to play the Led Zeppelin song, 'Trampled Underfoot', into one of his earpieces. It seemed like the perfect soundtrack to the confusing scenes unfolding behind his crazed former colleague. He sent the Splutter link to Ricky. The perspective from halfway across the bridge might be better than nothing if she had to keep an eye on the executive tearaways.

By now, the BERK superheroes had reached the first wave of protesters. They started to lift those who had fallen back onto their feet. Beneath their helmets and eye protection, nobody would be able to recognize any of the individuals.

Mason noticed the goth talking to the camera and tried to stay out of shot. The board would be furious when they found out he had brought some of their most important business contacts into such a potentially dangerous situation. He was not overly concerned for their safety, and they all seemed to be enjoying themselves so much. Talk about immersive! Normally cosseted in a VIP lifestyle, policed into never having an opinion unless it had been triple-checked by lawyers, his guests were having more fun today than most of them had experienced in years. It was only when Mason started to read the placards that he realized he might have some explaining to do.

The goth guy started climbing up onto the plinth that supported one of the ornate wrought-iron streetlamps. Mason's euphoria shrunk down a notch. A suicide would take the edge off the afternoon. At first, Mason started to walk towards him. If he moved quickly enough, he was sure he would be able to stop him. Then he realized the guy's camera was still running. No. It wasn't worth the risk. If he saved him, it might work out, but there were no guarantees. What if there was a struggle? It could end badly. The second he realized a tragedy might be imminent Mason's highly tuned self-preservation instinct kicked in. It was one thing ministering aid, but now he had to focus on keeping his rescue party away from the unfolding horror. Anyway, they'd had enough excitement for one day. He found Tom and told him to help round up the others so they could get them back south of the river.

Glancing sideways to see if the jumper was still there, he caught sight of a woman in a balaclava putting down a banner that read 'EUTHANASIA? NO THANKS!' She was walking slowly towards the potential suicide. It was reassuring that she would be able to help him.

"Hey! What are you doing up there?" Lexi shouted.

Lars looked down at her disdainfully. "Taking in the view. What do you think?"

"It doesn't look very safe to me."

"That's the whole idea."

"Come down, won't you? You're drenched."

"No. Leave me alone. This is my choice."

Lexi stepped a little closer. "Oh no! You're not one of those, are you?"

"Those what?"

"You're a Yuthie, aren't you? All that choice nonsense. It's a con. Please come down."

"Maybe I was once. I said keep back."

"OK." Lexi looked up at him intently. "I've seen you somewhere before. That T-shirt looks familiar."

"They're very popular. There are thousands of us Slaytanists."

"Oh, come on! Nobody listens to them anymore."

Lexi tried to edge closer. She was sure she could keep him talking.

"Hey, boomer! Stay back!"

"Do you mind? I'm not that old!"

"Yeah? Well, you can't expect me to tell under that balaclava. Why else would you be marching with those useless old fools? Don't they know what's good for them?"

"Hang on a minute. That's hardly fair. I'm as pro-choice as the next person, as it happens. But the odds have been stacked. You know, I'm sure I'm not the only person in the world who would prefer it if you chose to live. What's your name?"

"Stop trying to talk me down. I know what you're doing."

"Come down. You're not going to achieve anything if you give up now. There has to be another way."

He stood still. Come on, lad, Lexi thought.

The spell was broken by Amina running towards them, and shouting, "Lars! What are you doing?"

Lars inched closer to the edge. It was embarrassing that Amina had found him here. Wasn't she supposed to be having tea at The Ritz?

Lexi turned to Amina. "Do you know him?"

"A bit. Not very well. Lars, get down! You're frightening me!"

Lars edged even further away. He had one hand on the lamp post and was leaning out over the water.

"Please, please get down!" Amina was shouting now.

Lars shook his head. "No. it's too late. I've tried to tell them. Freedom, choice, independence? No one really knows what that means. I'm going to show them."

Still with an arm around the wrought iron post, he turned to the camera and shouted.

"If you're watching, Jasper, I want you to know – this is all your fault. You've deprived your followers of the chance to die on our own terms. It's time for you to learn what horror looks like. Why should the old folks get all the good endings? You have left me, and thousands like me, with no alternative."

"No!" Lexi shouted, moving to grab his leg, but suddenly Jennifer was there pinning her arms to her side.

"Get off me for goodness' sake. He's going to jump! We have to stop him!"

"No. You can't take a risk like that," Jennifer said. "He could take you with him. I promised Bob I'd bring you home safely."

Ajay had caught up with Amina. "Please don't jump, boy," he shouted. "I am sure there are people who care about you and who will miss you very much."

"It's not about who cares about me. It's about my independence, my rights. My right to choose. My right to claim the ultimate freedom."

And with that, Lars threw himself off the bridge into the swirling river.

CHAPTER THIRTY-SIX

"I T WAS ALL GOING SO well until that idiot emo jumped," Ricky sighed as she walked into the control room where Bob was hanging on for the final debrief. "I have to say it soured the day a bit."

"More thrash metal than emo, judging by his T-shirt," Bob said.

"If you say so. Not my thing. Any of it."

"It's ironic though. When you think it was one of The Corporation's own anti-suicide boats that may have saved his life. Something else for Mason to boast about to the BERKs?"

"That could be premature. Last thing I heard the guy was still out of it. Is there any update on him?" Ricky asked.

Bob had been on the case. "I saw on the system monitors that the ASBO crew cleared his lungs and put him on a ventilator. The good news – well, depending on how you look at it, is that he's young enough to get sustained treatment. And he jumped into the Thames on the doorstep of St Teddy's Hospital. They got him into intensive therapy right away. He's under 35 – in the ResusPlus category.

There won't be any pressure on them to turn him off for a while yet."

Bob had not been able to get the Pink Floyd song, 'Brain Damage' out of his head. Knowing Lars of old, however, he thought the situation merited Eminem's rather more distressing track with an identical title.

Ricky scanned the control center screens but she didn't know what she was looking for. She was determined not to end their day of glory on a low. "The bikes did great. He got a bit frustrated with the safety features, but by the time their adventures were over, I think he finally got it."

"Hard way to learn," Bob said. "I've had to file a report on the explosion. Some Corporation property was damaged. No injuries there, though."

"That's good news. I'd say the star of the day was the cuttle camo. It was terrific."

"It's neat, isn't it? I've got the AI to edit together a little video showreel. If it feels right, we can share it with the BERKs. I've sent the link to Lola. That's more her pay grade than mine."

"The bikes are back downstairs. I'll come in one day next week to check them all over, if that's OK." Ricky said. "I'd really like to get off now."

"Any plans?"

"Just meeting up with some friends. Not sure I feel like it, to be honest. But I'm sure I'll be OK when we get there. How about you?"

"We were supposed to be going for a curry. Might get a delivery instead. We only lost ten droids so Saturday night eating in will not be cancelled."

"I bet you're glad all that weekend work is over."

"Kind of. It's an anti-climax, though, isn't it, when a big project like this comes to an end?"

Behind the casual façade, Bob's mind was racing. He knew it was Lexi who had tried to talk Lars down from the plinth, even though nobody else would have been able to recognize her behind the balaclava he had slipped into her emergency kit. As soon as it looked like things might kick off she had put it on, just like he said. She had trusted him to protect her. She always did. He could not let her down now.

CHAPTER THIRTY-SEVEN

B OB STAYED GLUED TO HIS pet tracker as his bus edged along the Old Kent Road, watching Lexi and Jennifer's dots moving together in the same direction, only ten minutes behind him. He was apprehensive about their homecoming. How would Lexi's state of mind be?

He put the kettle on and looked for some music to play. He let the soothing electric heartbeat of Pink Floyd's 'Dark Side of the Moon' wash over him as he continued to monitor the women's progress on the app. Once they were close, he turned the sound down to background levels and waited at the half-open front door.

"Well done, girls," he said quietly, giving Lexi a little hug and only tearing himself away because they had a guest. He put his arm around Jennifer's shoulder for a couple of seconds as they went into the house. "You ladies had me worried earlier. Don't know what I would have said to Trev if you had not come back."

He guided them into seats in the living room while he made some tea. "Unless you'd prefer something stronger?"

"You know what, I could murder a beer," Jennifer said.

Bob was in the kitchen opening the fridge before she finished. "I've always got some Another Place. How about you Lex?"

She said nothing. "Lex?"

"Maybe a nice cup of tea?" Jennifer replied on her behalf, as Lexi sank onto the sofa and closed her eyes. "I'm guessing you two might not feel like going for that curry," Bob went on.

When he brought Jennifer's beer, they were checking the news channels on the big screen. "Do you really think you should be watching that, Lex?" Bob said, nervously. "Haven't you had enough distress for one day?"

"I'm not a child," she snapped. "Anyway, we want to know how accurately they've reported what happened. You know how biased the mainstream media can be."

Lexi and Jennifer looked so fragile, perched on the sofa together. Genuine armchair radicals, Bob thought, only these ones have the courage of their convictions. While Jennifer's exhaustion was overlaid with exhilaration, Lexi just seemed flat.

A reporter stood close to the spot where Lars had made his last, desperate broadcast.

"Scenes today, here on Westminster Bridge have been quite extraordinary. The police will be facing intense scrutiny over the coming weeks after what started out as a peaceful – albeit unauthorized – demonstration, ended in tragedy with at least one person in critical condition and many more injured. Chaos ensued after an impromptu march, instigated by the pro-life group People Against Coercive Euthanasia, was trapped by the authorities. As a result, a number of protesters, many of whom were elderly and disabled, were hurt.

"An explosion in Parliament Square is also under investigation. Nobody was injured by the blasts. While the loud bangs caused some initial panic, they provoked the police into releasing the hemmed in protesters onto the bridge. According to those who had been kettled, the opening of the cordon avoided greater injury. I'm joined by one of the organizers of the PACE rally, which began in Victory Square earlier today, and which the police are suggesting may have been the cause of today's tragic events."

"It's Jess." Lexi said, "Look!"

Her fellow activist had a graze down the side of her face, but in spite of it she managed to look sharp, if a little shaken.

"The researcher for Nicky Hartt, MP and has been named as one of the individuals who was responsible for initiating the illegal protest. Is that true, Jess? Can you tell me what happened?"

Jess launched into an articulate and impassioned attack on the circumstances leading up to the riot. She talked about the continued coercion of older people into ending their lives and the unacceptable pressure on those with disabilities to do the same.

"Too bloody right," Jennifer said, draining her beer. "Any chance of another one of those, Bob?"

On the screen, Jess was spelling it out. "If they had not penned us all into such a tight spot, everything would have been fine. One of our stewards, a Catholic priest, was seriously injured while attempting to protect those more vulnerable than himself. It's a disgrace. The blame for today's terrible events lies squarely at the hands of the police."

"Not Al! I hope he's OK!" Bob exclaimed.

"And do you have any idea who would have placed an explosive device in the square?" the interviewer continued.

"None whatsoever. We are a peaceful protest group. Any risk to human life is the complete opposite of everything we stand for."

The broadcaster cut to a montage of the damage. A pile of smoking debris by the St Stephen's entrance to The Houses of Parliament. Graffiti on the wall of the Department of HELP reading 'Abandon hope all ye who enter here'.

"Beautiful work, Jennifer!" Bob marveled. "It works so much better in English."

Back in the TV studio, a newsreader filled in more details.

"As if today's incidents in Westminster were not already shocking enough, it has now been confirmed that a man in his early 30s jumped into the Thames while live streaming on Splutter and arranging for the film to be replayed. It is estimated that several million people watched his video before it was taken down.

"So far, we are not clear how – if at all – the man who attempted suicide might have been involved with the other disturbances. He directly addressed Jasper, the leader of Yuthentic, who has made himself available to help police with their enquiries. The unconscious man was rescued from the Thames by one of The Corporation's anti-suicide boats that are permanently moored under the bridge. He is now receiving treatment at St Teddy's Hospital. The police are keen to interview him although nobody knows when, if ever, he will regain consciousness.

"If you have been affected by anything in this story, The Corporation have made their counselling service available free of charge for the next 48 hours in view of public concern. You can contact them, in complete confidence, at …"

"It truly is a miracle that no one was killed." Jennifer said.

"The fat lady's not sung yet," Lexi said. "That poor lad. His name was Lars. And we don't know about that daft priest yet, either."

Bob swapped Jennifer's empty beer bottle for a full one and walked back into the kitchen to sling the empty. There was a clink as it came to rest among the other glass.

"If we're going to have a takeaway we need to order soon," he carried on. "You know how busy Two Sisters gets on a Saturday night."

"Is that all you ever think about?" Lexi snapped. "That poor young man. You know, I'm convinced he's the same one I saw on the Yuthie stand at the Summer Fayre. It would make sense, wouldn't it, from what they are saying? Always in a Slayer T-shirt. He couldn't be that Lars you used to work with, could he? Wasn't he creepy?"

"It's a very common name." Bob perched on the arm of the sofa next to Lexi, his eyes fixed ahead on the screen.

The reporter was back with more breaking news.

"There is now growing speculation that the person who jumped from the bridge may have had something to do with the explosion. He was seen earlier in the day at a rally for a splinter group denounced by Yuthentic for their extremist tendencies, although they seem to have been recruited from within the mainstream party.

"Jasper, the Yuthie leader has now issued a statement. It reads as follows:

'Yuthentic and myself would like to distance ourselves from the actions of this unfortunate individual. While we fully support humane suicidal assistance for elderly and other suboptimal people, Yuthentic is fundamentally opposed to the Endings service being made freely available.'

"This is quite extraordinary. Some would say a complete U-Turn from Yuthentic's position only a couple of months ago where it was rumored they were poised to launch assisted suicide on demand. Strong words indeed from Jasper who must realize the future of their party could be in jeopardy."

"I hate them," Lexi said. "I fucking hate them."

Jennifer grunted. "Join the club. Suboptimal people? How dare they! That's my Andy! And most of those idiot kids' grandparents! You're lucky your mum and dad are in Thailand, Bob, away from all this nonsense, you really are."

It was not the first time Jennifer had made that point. "I appreciate what you're saying," he said. "But I'm still concerned about everything that's going on, you know. You, Andy, Jess and all the rest of them."

He shifted his position. The arm of the sofa was uncomfortable and one of his legs was going to sleep. But he wanted to be close to Lexi, and Jennifer was on her other side. He would have liked to have put his arm round Lexi, but he was worried she would push him away. "I know it seems trivial, Lex, but we do really need to sort out something to eat. You are both exhausted, and Jen's our guest.

If you don't want to think about it, I can order for all of us."

"Sounds good to me," Jennifer said. "We haven't had anything for hours, apart from Ajay's emergency supplies."

"He's sound, that bloke." They had not spent a lot of time together, but Bob had warmed to Ajay at the 70s party. "Generous to a fault."

"He was more scared than the rest of us when it all kicked off. He's not hardcore like us. I don't think he expected things could get so badly out of hand. We were pretty surprised too, weren't we Lexi? You should have seen Ajay trying to help that Lars, Bob. It was heartbreaking."

"None of us managed to stop him, did we?" Lexi finally piped up. "You'll never believe this, Bob. Their granddaughter knew Lars. Goodness knows where she met him. At uni I think. It was surreal."

"Well, I'm sure Ajay and Ayesha will give her all the support she needs now."

Bob was overruled by the others when it came to deciding what film they would watch that night after their meal delivery. He was all for Terminator Five, but Jennifer wanted Thelma and Louise. It was her favorite film, but she could not watch it at home in case the ending gave Andy any silly ideas.

It was not late when they turned in for the night. Jennifer had let Trev and Andy know that she was safe and they seemed to have had a good day together. She asked if it would be OK for her to have a bath as her back was aching. "Of course you can," Bob said. Fond though he was of Jennifer, he had been looking forward all evening to having Lexi to himself.

While Jennifer busied herself across the landing, Bob and Lexi lay on their bed talking in hushed voices.

Lexi's mind was racing despite her exhaustion. She had been keen to phone the hospital to see how Lars was doing, but Bob said he was sure any change in his condition would be reported. In any case, what help could she offer? Even worse, what if they started asking her questions? She was in too fragile a state to cope with that. It would be different if putting her head above the parapet could make any difference to Lars' prognosis, but it was all up to the hospital now. They could not risk their previous actions being uncovered when nothing she could say or do would affect Lars' survival.

"I'm as angry as you are about this whole thing, love," Bob said. "And the police behaved despicably today. If they had just let you all make your point it would have dispersed naturally. Especially in all that rain."

"Did you see us?"

"Parts of it, yes. The Corporation drones were all grounded because of the storm, but I watched the news coverage and caught the tail end of Lars' message to the nation. He came across as quite insane."

"Do you think that will influence how much they help him?"

"He could well pull through."

"I wanted to stop him, Bob. I really tried. If I had moved faster, if Amina hadn't panicked and shouted, it could all have turned out differently."

"Yeah? And if me aunt had bollocks she'd be me uncle. All these 'ifs' are no good. They are tying you in pointless knots. You did your very best, Lexi. Like you always do.

I'm proud of you, keeping up the fight. I really am."

"Hmm. I can sense there's a 'but' coming."

The bathwater had stopped running and the house was now silent. Bob lowered his voice to a whisper.

"I love you, Lexi."

"I love you, too, Bob. But you can't distract me so easily. What's the 'but'?"

"But…I can't stand by and let you self-destruct. Don't take this the wrong way, but have you ever asked yourself why you have this compulsion to save everyone?"

Lexi was lying on her back. Silent tears began to spill from the sides of her eyes and pooled in her ears. Her limbs felt leaden, and she could not bring herself to move as the final dregs of her adrenalin ran out. She began to sob quietly.

"Oh, Lex. I didn't want to upset you. It's dreadful seeing you like this."

"It's OK. You were right to ask. I'll never break the pattern unless I talk about it. I've known since that very first night in the Mews, when we rescued Meg and the others. I do it because …"

She could not get the words out. Lexi's breathing became shorter and more erratic. She wept silently and turned to rest her head on Bob's chest. He knew it was safe to put his arms round her now and waited in silence for her to find a moment of calm to speak again.

"I know why. It's because I lost my parents."

"Go on."

"All these years since the accident. I've just been putting on a brave face. When I promised Alice that I'd try to stop her mother killing herself I had no idea what emotions it would unlock. I mean, I never even liked Meg all that much. She never seemed to be around for Alice and Adam. It's hardly surprising they've both built their lives thousands of miles away. Their dad did most of the parenting. Paul was a lovely man. None of Meg's edges. We did the right thing by Alice, saving Meg. But then when Mabel was suffocated, I suddenly felt so powerless. The anger was overwhelming. Like all the good we had done in rescuing the five of them had been wiped out."

"That's not true though, Lex. Look how happy Bryn and George are. They've never had a better time in their lives. Meg has settled back into being a glamorous yoga bunny. And she's never off a plane."

Lexi shifted a little. "Yeah. We don't need to worry about her anymore. I think her kids are glad she's back in London, though. I was talking to Alice about it last week. We know from those few days when she was staying here, don't we? Do you remember?."

"Yeah, she was too stuck-up to bunk up in Lazarus House with the other survivors." Bob was grateful for high maintenance Meg as he detected a hint of amusement breaking through Lexi's distress.

"No wonder Alice has never had the easiest relationship with her mum. Therapy has helped. She's still working a few things through, even now. She's invited us to go over, you know? I think New Zealand might be nice."

Lexi had stopped crying now, so Bob seized the moment. "It's you I'm interested in. You need to be a bit kinder to yourself. There are countless others PACE has helped. Some you won't even know about. But you just can't win them all."

"I do know that in my head. But in my heart? It's hard to shake off this dreadful feeling of failure. I can't ever win, can I? Death and taxes are the only certain things in life. All we can ever do is postpone the inevitable. But that still does not make it right for them to be killing all those people. And they are still doing it."

"I know." Bob's T-shirt was damp from Lexi's tears, but he didn't want her to move away. All he wanted was for her to feel safe.

The silence was broken by a gurgling sound. "Was that your stomach?" Lexi said, lifting up her head. "Maybe you shouldn't have had that second Peshwari nan."

"Do you mind? No! It was Jennifer letting the water out of the bath." They giggled for a second, and then heard the click of the door opening.

"Goodnight, you two." Jennifer disappeared into the spare room and the house was quiet again.

"I've been worried you're going to leave me, Bob."

"Honestly? Oh God, don't start crying again! You've nothing to worry about. Come here! Don't be silly!"

Lexi was serious. "Things haven't been right, though, have they?"

"I've been thinking about us a lot, too. Especially when you keep having a go at me about working for the bad guys. And I was very upset about the Fakesy, but I know why you hid it from me. And I still want to be with you. I used to be a harmless nerd having an imaginary relationship with David Bowie, as you have observed in your less charitable moments. Why wouldn't I want to be here with my lovely girlfriend? I could get another cat, but it wouldn't be the same. Would you rather go back to being on your own?"

"No. This is good. Most of the time this is very good actually." She rubbed her nose on his shirt, "You can even double as a handkerchief!"

"I'm a man of many talents," he kissed the top of her head, relieved that she seemed to be recovering. "Several of which I have been deploying to help your cause today."

"You could tell me, but you'd have to shoot me?" Lexi whispered softly and fell into a deep sleep.

CHAPTER THIRTY-EIGHT

P ORTIA KEPT TELLING HERSELF IT had to be a different Lars, but the man's name was released to the media on the day after he jumped. The story kept rolling, with Jess and Jasper slugging out the moral issues in the columns of the Easter Sunday papers, although Jasper had declined any live interviews.

The Brytely office was closed for Easter until Tuesday and by the middle of Sunday afternoon Portia could not wait any longer to talk to Sonny about whatever Lars appeared to have done. She sent him a short message: 'Are you free? Work thing.'

Within half an hour he was on his way to her flat. They had both zipped their phones into their matching Faraday bags, just in case anyone might be tracking them.

Even though Portia had lived in her apartment for two years, the only other person who had visited her there was her mother. They had just finished building the units when she moved in, tiny modern flats earmarked for young people starting out on promising careers, just like her. Brytely had a connection with the property developers and was able to fast-track her to the top of the list. It never ceased to amaze her how Stella was able to pull in favors.

The main advantage of living in a bijou pop-up box was that it was easy to clean. Thinking about it, that was probably the only upside. Still, with Sonny's arrival imminent that was something to be grateful for. While she ran a cordless vacuum cleaner over the floor, she put on Madonna's Greatest Hits which always cheered her up. Her mum used to play it when she was little, and she remembered Karen, on good days, dancing with her in the kitchen to 'Express Yourself'.

It was not long until an image of Sonny's face appeared on her TV screen, captured by the cameras on the front door. She buzzed him up, leaving the music playing softly in the background. It was odd having another person in the space that had been exclusively hers for so long. She was allowed visitors but hadn't felt she knew anyone well enough to invite them back. How well did she really know Sonny? They had been getting on better since Phase Two had been dropped, the various threat scenarios having become more distant – for Portia's immediate family, at least – but since their post-party lunch she had felt less drawn to find opportunities to socialize with him. And here he was, in her minuscule living room.

"It's pretty hot in here." He was looking at the sealed windows.

"Yeah. Design fault." Portia shrugged, resisting the urge to apologize for the size of her home. Sonny unzipped his jacket and looked for somewhere to put it that wouldn't swamp the sofa.

"There's not much room, I'm afraid. Just give it to me." Portia popped it into the bedroom. She caught a waft of the subtle pleasing scent she had noticed before.

Sonny was staring out at the Spring afternoon when she came back, fat clouds moving fast across the patchy sky, the light constantly changing. She could not remember ever seeing him so preoccupied. Had it really taken Lars jumping off a bridge to make him want to spend time alone with her? He didn't exactly look pleased to be there. Sonny squatted nimbly to rummage in his bag, still on the floor where he had dropped it, and pulled out the sealed Faraday pouch dropping it on the table without a word.

"It's him, isn't it?" Portia declared.

"Hundred percent."

"I never suspected he could do anything like this." She shook her head. "He just seemed like a permanent fixture."

"It was him alright. The idiot."

"Don't you think that's a bit harsh? I mean, we have no idea what he must have been going through. Maybe if we had been nicer to him, included him more, not just written him off as the office weirdo, this might never have happened."

"What planet are you on, Portia? You honestly think he did this because he was lonely? We're all bloody lonely. It doesn't give you the right to traumatize everyone else."

Portia watched him begin to pace the room. It only took a few steps from one side to the other, and that was avoiding the furniture. She leant against the wall with her arms crossed. "I'm sorry you're so upset," she said, "I had no idea you cared about him this much."

Sonny's face half twisted into a half-hearted sneer. "That's not why I'm so wound up! You won't believe it when I tell you. My stupid little sister knew him. She was there. On the bridge. Grandad tried to talk him down. She's in a terrible state. Grandad's not much better."

"No way! What were they doing there?"

Sonny explained how three members of his family had ended up in the wrong place at the wrong time. His grandparents had been at the PACE demo, and his sister had gone to 'some dumbass rally with that vile piece of shit'. Everything had converged horribly on the bridge.

"Amina thinks he jumped because he was in love with Holly. I can't see it myself. I mean, could someone like Lars actually care about another person that much? Did we miss the signs? Looking back on it, he had a massive bee in his bonnet about democratizing death, didn't he?"

"Slow down. Are you saying he was in a sexual relationship with Holly? I thought they were just fellow Yuthies."

Sonny's raised eyebrows confirmed that was precisely what he meant. "It's hard to imagine. But from what he's said to Amina I think they probably were close in that way, yes."

"Yikes." She had never credited Lars with having feelings like other people. In the office there was a tacit assumption that he had a borderline sociopathic personality disorder which had made him good at his job. An AI would have highlighted it as a strength in the recruitment process.

She shifted awkwardly. "Erm, I hope you don't mind me asking, but … well, Lars … not with your sister as well?"

"No! Not even Mina would be that stupid." Something in Sonny's tone suggested that he might not be completely convinced.

She wasn't going to embarrass him further. "What a mess."

They were quiet for a moment before Portia said. "I'm sorry I haven't even offered you anything. Do you want tea or coffee?"

"Whatever's easiest. That would be great." He followed her while she made the drinks in Brytely branded crockery, sniffing the milk before she added it.

"So, you don't need to be anywhere in particular this afternoon?" Portia said, handing him a mug which bore the strapline 'Portia – you rock!' on one side, and the company logo on the other. "Thanks for coming over, especially when you must have a lot going on with the family."

Sonny relaxed slightly and explained, "I'm not used to my parents being home. They work such long hours that it can be unsettling when they show up. Team formation dynamics. It's worse than usual today. Amina is in a right state, and they're worried about the grandparents, so it's totally manic. It was great to have an excuse to get out. An emergency work meeting is the trump card. They'll never argue with that."

He was starting to smile, looking directly at Portia, and picked up her flicker of disappointment.

"Sorry, Porsh. I've been totally self-absorbed. Thank you for inviting me over. It's nice to be here. It really is."

"Sounds like a nightmare back at the ranch," she said. "You know, you're welcome to hang out here for a bit. I've no plans." She wondered whether she had sounded too casual, aware suddenly that they were two people, alone in a room, who had once had a near miss with a potential romantic encounter. Sonny shifted around the confined space with its forced intimacy and fixed his eyes on the screen.

"You've got – like a subscription, yeah? Maybe we could watch something? Take our minds off it for a bit. I mean, there's nothing we can do, is there?"

"Sure." She had really wanted to talk, but now he was here she realized he was not in the mood for listening. "I could order in some food later. The fridge isn't exactly fully stocked." Not like his grandparents' house, overflowing with all manner of treats.

To be precise, all Portia had to hand was the container of milk that was beginning to smell slightly cheesy (she hoped he had not noticed), a handful of dinners for one in the iced-up freezer, three large cans of Sauvignon Blanc and a bottle of champagne left over from a work teambuilding event. She could really do with a snack. Absorbed in the news coverage, she had not gone out to pick up breakfast. as she usually did at the weekends.

"I'm not really hungry," Sonny said. Without asking, he picked up the controller and flicked the screen onto the entertainment menu. He was clearly surprised at some of the suggestions that popped up, based on Portia's recent viewing history.

"Jeez, girl!" he said, as he quickly flicked back to 'new releases'.

Portia bristled. He had been there five minutes and was already taking over the remote and passing judgment on her viewing habits. They both watched as he scrolled through the suggestions of what they might like to see.

"That one!" she said.

"A rom com? Seriously? No way! How about this?"

"No. No zombies."

"How about a Marvel?"

"Maybe. Not Wolverine though. They're too sad. All the kind people die."

"True. Black Panther Four?"

She had watched the first one when she was at school, but lost track of the sequels. The enforced negotiation with Sonny was winding her up a little but, in the end, she felt it wasn't too tragic a compromise. "OK. Yes. I can go with that."

The sofa was intended for solo box-dwellers and felt unstable with two people on it. They perched on it gingerly, shifting to find a balance. Sonny was immediately engrossed in the film. Portia was finding it hard to read the situation. They were both so tense. It was more than just concerns about Lars. She cast her mind back to that New Year's Eve in his grandparents' attic, re-examining every tiny detail. That pleasant scent. His shoulder length dark brown hair almost brushing against her face. His kindness in staying with her when she had to keep her twisted ankle elevated all night. Could this even be the same person?

Portia had imagined this scenario more than once. Except it wasn't like this, him dropping into her flat for a matinee because their colleague was in intensive care and his sister was on the verge of a nervous breakdown.

Without giving him the opportunity to turn it down, she fetched two cans of wine.

"Oh, cheers," Sonny said snapping off the ring pull and taking a swig. "That's quite nice."

She let her leg fall against his and the sofa overreacted by detecting her fractional movement and tipping her body weight closer to him. She tensed her core to compensate, keen to stay upright. Slumping over and bowling him right off the sofa was the last thing she wanted to do.

Sonny continued to stare at the screen. He did not pull away. She wondered whether he had even noticed that she was touching him. She took three big gulps of wine. There was only one way to get through this.

"Letitia Wright's amazing, isn't she?" he said.

"Stunning. She's stayed in brilliant shape."

The film came to an end and her entertainment system switched back to playing Madonna. As 'Justify My Love' began to play, Portia fetched the final can of wine and drank several large gulps herself before passing the rest to Sonny.

"You don't mind sharing?" She wondered if she could ever tease back out the kind, attentive person he had been when she had spent the night with him at his grandparents' house. He had slept chastely on the same bed, made her breakfast and made sure she got home safely the next day. Maybe just being close to Ayesha and Ajay had made him nicer.

"Oh, thanks. I zone out when I'm watching a film. Always have. It's nothing personal."

"Well, you've got a lot on your mind. Are you feeling better?" She hoped she could find a way to get him to open up. They had drained the can of the wine and she wanted to get her bottle of champagne. She had gone past eating now.

"Yes. Thanks. Sorry I've not been the best company."

"The night is young." Portia was getting bolder. "Let's have another drink. I've got one thing left."

She washed out the mugs and brought them back with the bottle of fizz. "I know it's not appropriate, but it's all I've got," she said ripping off the foil and starting to release the tension on the cork, holding over it a commemorative tea towel from the 'Pete Burns: Freak or Fashion Icon?' exhibition.

"So. Absent friends." They clinked mugs but it was not sustained enough to drown out Madonna's heavy breathing. Now, they were very close together.

"I want to ask you something, Sonny. What did you mean earlier, when you said we are all lonely?"

"It's just the human condition."

"So, are you lonely?"

"Sometimes. Everyone is."

She waited for him to return the question, but he didn't. She supposed that was because he had already guessed the answer.

"There's a guy who lives not far from Mum in Liverpool. He's got a pickup truck and a caravan. In the summer he's always on the road. He's got a sticker on the rear window. it says, 'ONE LIFE – LIVE IT!'." They moved closer. The substandard memory foam beneath them shifted.

"I don't know about you," Sonny said, "But I think we're in grave danger of injuring ourselves. Can you think of anywhere we might be more comfortable?"

"There is such a place nearby. It's only a short walk. If you'd care to join me?"

CHAPTER THIRTY-NINE

Portia had never been so grateful for a holiday Monday. To distract her from the weekend's developments, she took herself off to the shops, and spent an hour on the phone to her mother in the evening.

"I hope you weren't anywhere near those troublemakers." Karen had heard about the events on the bridge. Her tone was more concerned than critical. Once she was reassured that Portia had been on the other side of town when it all kicked off, and was now safely home, she was happy.

Portia had been toying with the idea of telling her mum about her evening with Sonny, sparing her the more intimate details, but perhaps hinting at what had gone on. He had left at around midnight, at which point she had finally got to defrost a lasagna. There was no arrangement to meet again. They had a pact to ignore the work rules on intimate contact with a colleague. Once would not count, would it? Neither of them thought that reporting what had happened on the PUSSI app, designed to Prevent Unwanted Situations of Sexual Intimacy, would help their careers. It had been fun, but not so much fun they were in a hurry to risk flouting the rules again.

Before she had time to say anything about Sonny, however, her mother had some bad news.

"I'm not going to be working for a while." Karen tried not to sound downhearted but Portia knew every penny counted back home. It would be almost impossible for the family to survive on only one income.

"No! Are you OK?"

"It's my own fault." Portia heard a long sigh.

"I can't believe that. What happened?"

"Oh, it is. I should have realized Bernie next door was struggling. She's helped me out so much with the kids over the years. Makes you grateful for your health, when cancer creeps up on someone you love. It only came out after our Sean said he'd seen her crying."

"And you didn't think to tell me sooner, Mum?"

"You've got enough on your plate. Anyway, I was hoping to find another way to manage the kids when I'm working, but I've run out of time. Bernie's treatment is about to start, and my hours are too varied to find someone to job share at short notice. I'm so annoyed with myself. I should have known something was wrong, but I'm always in such a rush."

"Why didn't Bernie tell you she was going to have to stop? If you don't mind me saying it was a bit selfish, wasn't it? Leaving you stuck like this. I mean, I know she's ill, but…"

"No. I won't have a word said against her, Paula." Karen was uncharacteristically sharp. "In fact, you'll never guess what she was thinking! Honest to God, I can't believe it myself!"

"Go on."

"They'd only gone and offered her money to take one of those Ending things! Can you believe it? She was thinking of accepting the offer and signing over the cash for us and the kids, because she wouldn't be around to help. It was only a few grand as well. What kind of a world are we living in where someone who might get another ten years is contemplating suicide because they think it will help out a neighbor? And she's a Catholic! Dead before her time, and as if that wasn't bad enough, she'd be facing a miserable afterlife. Talk about hitting someone while they're down. Cash for corpses, that's what it is!"

Portia felt sick. The ghastly business of what she did for a living was uncomfortably close. After Phase Two was abandoned, she had thought her community was out of danger. She had breathed a sigh of relief when it was announced that The Corporation would not be targeting younger people with depression, having seen the medication that both her mother and her partner had been prescribed. But Bernie was effectively part of the family circle and Karen's only practical support.

Portia remembered shamefacedly how she had stolen aspects of that kind woman's life for the Endings campaign. The Catholic ephemera that filled Bernie's small house had inspired a range of Ending memorial merchandize ranging from snow globes to jewelry.

"If our Seanie hadn't told me... well it doesn't bear thinking about, does it?" Karen was appalled. "Luckily, I could tell her to ignore them. I'll be keeping a close eye on her from now on. And I thought that Lexi at Ayesha's party was a conspiracy theorist! I take it all back."

"Terrible," was all Portia could say. "Is Bernie OK now? Please tell me she's not going to sign up."

"Not if I've got anything to do with it. And nor am I for that matter, so don't you worry about that either."

"What? Mum, you're not even in the target group!"

"Well, it didn't stop them sending me a letter as well, did it?"

"You're joking!"

"It's true. I phoned them up and told them where to go. How they keep so calm I don't know. What do you mean, the target group? How come you know so much about it?"

"Oh, I think it must have been on a documentary or a podcast or something."

"Right. The letter came not long after I handed in my resignation. Reminds me, I need to sort out my antidepressants now my private health cover has gone. That's the only aspect of the job I'll miss, to be honest."

"I don't understand how The Corporation thought it was OK to target you."

"Apparently anyone who loses their job on Merseyside gets the same letter. It's a new thing, since they built the new Kindness Centers. What a cheek! We might be working class but we're not stupid. And I for one certainly don't want to die. Anyway, I reckon if I'm around at home for a bit I can manage the kids and keep an eye on Bernie. She's done enough for me over the years."

"Jeez. How can I help, Mum?" Portia ventured tentatively.

"Well, one thing's for certain. You're not to come back up here. It's all happening for you down there. We don't even have a bedroom for you anymore. Don't get me wrong, it's always lovely to see you, but you can't turn your back on your future. Anyway, I was thinking maybe I could do a bit of dressmaking on the side, like you said, to bring in a few extra quid. If you know anyone who needs anything made, like."

"Deffo." She knew, however, that would not be enough. Not at first. "Mum, at least let me send you some money, eh?"

Karen hesitated. "I didn't want to ask." There was shame in her voice which made her daughter well up. Both women took a deep breath, then Portia cleared her throat.

"It's no problem. Like you said, helping out with the bills makes more sense than me packing in my job, Mum." She was certain she heard a faint sigh of relief.

"Aw. Thanks love. I'm not in a position to turn you down."

"And maybe I could get you private healthcare?"

"Don't be daft. It costs a fortune. No, anything you can send will go straight into paying the rent and feeding the kiddies. They have to come first."

By the time she made it into the office after the four-day weekend, Portia felt far from rested. The dull head-ache she had put down to dehydration after her evening with Sonny had stayed with her for more than twenty-four hours. The atmosphere at Brytely was uneasy. Colleagues who normally sat all day staring at screens, using their headsets to repel contact with other humans, were clustered in small groups and talking in hushed tones. She had not even taken a seat before Sonny dragged her into

Anthrax. There was no flirting this time. He wanted to talk about Lars.

An overwhelming wave of melancholy hit Portia as she looked up at the mural of the thrash metal band that differentiated Anthrax from the other meeting rooms. Everyone knew Lars had rigged the employee competition to decide the naming convention. Now he might never set foot in one of his creations again.

Before they could say anything, the door opened. It was Drew, one of the senior Brytely employees who rarely acknowledged them, but who was on edge today.

"I hope I'm not interrupting anything important," they said, loitering in the doorway and nervously pushing their sharply-cut silver bob behind their ears, "But a police officer has turned up in reception. She's asked to speak to Stella."

"What's that got to do with us?" Portia asked. "They'll have to call her in Bangkok, won't they?"

"I suggested that, but she had an entry warrant. It's to do with Lars. We thought, maybe, as you guys knew him better than anyone else, you might be able to have a word with her?"

"You're joking, right?" Sonny said as Portia looked on, equally incredulous.

"I'm sorry but I didn't know what else to do. She's on her way up."

The police suicide liaison officer, Juliet, had arrived at Brytely without any warning.

Unable to prevent her entering their offices, the staff had been so unhelpful at first that Juliet assumed she was being deliberately given the runaround. She had chosen her charcoal grey tailored trouser suit because she wanted an air of authority, but it also made her seem a bit like an undertaker with her angular, sallow face.

When Drew eventually led her into Anthrax, Juliet could tell from the pair's faces that they had already been talking about Lars.

There was a particular kind of sadness she had come to recognize in the people she interviewed who were on the periphery of a suicide. These two had been identified by their colleague as those who had worked most closely with the victim. While neither of them would admit to knowing him well, they were keen to find out how he was doing in hospital, which suggested a tie.

"He's still unconscious," Juliet explained. "I can't say any more than that at this stage."

"I'm surprised you didn't just ask us to fill in an online form," Sonny ventured.

"We used to do that, but it got a lot of complaints."

"You probably didn't invest enough in the emotional components," Sonny said. Lars was a specialist in designing such interfaces. It did not look like he was going to be able to help them with it now.

Juliet shrugged. "Not my department, all that."

"I hope you don't mind me asking," Portia said, "Why are you here? I mean, if he wanted to jump, right, it was his decision, wasn't it? Not like he was pushed."

Juliet had explained her presence in such circumstances many times before. "You might think that. And I can see why. But when someone attempts a messy DIY job like your friend has, we have to investigate it. Especially when they are this young."

"Do you investigate all the, what did you call them, 'DIY' attempts?"

"No," Juliet grunted. "That would be impossible with our limited resources. There are agreed protocols. When the subjects are older, and in some other circumstances, there are fewer grey areas. The hospital will simply make them comfortable and finish the job they started themselves. Humanely, obvs. My unit would never get involved if someone were over seventy, for example. Not even if they were a member of the royal family!" She laughed a little, having used that example more than once before. "Your associate Lars is a trickier case."

"Lars was, sorry, *is* more of a colleague than a friend," Portia said. "We don't really know him very well."

"As you wish." Juliet was still skeptical. "He has attracted some attention. If he really wanted to die, he would have been better to arrange it more discreetly, not throw himself into the arms of a rescue bot."

"How difficult can it be? See, I told you he was an idiot," Sonny muttered.

"Either that, or very clever," Juliet said. "He was revived quickly. The media are still sniffing round after his broadcast. Nobody is in a hurry to let him die. Invoking Jasper was arguably a stroke of genius if he wanted to stay in the public eye. Your Lars is also relatively young, so that's another factor weighing in his favor, depending on how you look at it. Did you know he's on a list for having exceptional data skills? It's all over his immigration record. There have been unprecedented levels of interest from more than one government department."

Not like someone expendable, who works in an amusement arcade, Portia thought. "So, what do you need from us?" She knew there was no way she and Sonny could escape involvement now.

Juliet placed a recording device on the table in front of them. "Is there any reason you can think of why Lars would have wanted to jump from the bridge?"

"He was never exactly a laugh a minute," Sonny quipped, "Even on his good days."

Given the seriousness of the situation, Portia thought Sonny was being too flippant but still nodded her head in reluctant agreement.

"Did he tell either of you anything about his personal life?"

To stop Sonny from making more inappropriate comments, Portia jumped in. "He went back to Scandinavia occasionally. Lived in a Yuthie unit. One of the lucky ones, you know, with his own place. Well, up to a point…"

"Did he talk about any friends?"

"Only Holly."

"And she is…?"

"Was. His friend Holly was the Yuthentic MP."

"The one who died last year? Were they close?"

Sonny butted in, "I would assume so. But he wasn't … sorry isn't … the kind of guy who talks about his feelings. Not even when he's conscious." Portia wished Sonny stop making wisecracks. She knew he was nervous and addicted to energy drinks, but they were with the police. Surely, now of all times, he should have the good sense to button it.

"I think what Sonny is trying to say is that Lars never struck either of us as someone who was going to die of a broken heart. He is quite a cold person."

"I see." Juliet was periodically glancing at her device, clearly running through a checklist. "You might be able to help a bit more with this one. Was there anything at work that might have led him to consider taking his own life? Bullying? That kind of thing?"

"Not bullying, no. Not that I can think of. But you should check with HR. I'm sure they would have records. They like to think they know everything about us." Portia said, feeling her neck flush a little.

"Ah, yes. His job. What was it, exactly?"

"Sonny, Lars and I were working together on the Endings program. We have been for a few years, now. The client is The Corporation."

Juliet wrote something down and drew breath for a moment. "Mason's outfit? Hmm. Let me get this right. Are you telling me that the subject – sorry, Lars – was promoting assisted suicide as his day job?"

"Yes. All three of us worked on it. It's aimed at old people mainly, though. Lars was looking at some other categories. He was big into the freedom, choice and independence mantra. That's how he saw it. If anything, the guy was the Endings program's biggest fan."

Sonny was coming across as disrespectful. "Remember it's called humane assisted suicide," Portia clarified for Juliet's benefit. "Nothing has ever been released that would be appropriate for an able-bodied person in Lars' demographic."

"And I thought my job was macabre." Juliet let out another snigger. She regained her composure and turned back to her prompts. "That's very helpful. Now, tell me, Portia, do you know whether your associate Lars was involved with any extremist groups?"

"He was a Yuthie. Everyone knew that. It was how he met Holly. But that's mainstream, isn't it?"

Portia paused to give Sonny the chance to talk about his sister, but he said nothing, so she carried on. "More than once Lars said that he believed in democratizing death. You can ask anybody. Now I come to think of it, he was very excited about Phase Two and in a bad mood for weeks when it got scaled back."

"Phase Two?"

"The plans to widen access to assisted dying. Most of the proposals were abandoned just before Christmas. Too controversial."

"Ah, yes. And had Lars been heavily exposed to this – what did you call it – Phase Two campaign?"

"We all lived and breathed it for a good few months." Portia's mind began to race as she wondered whether the material they had worked on together had damaged Lars more than any of them had realized.

"It was his favorite subject," Sonny added. "Everyone knew he was angry when it got dropped. But we thought – well – that he wanted to democratize death for everyone else. I would never have thought he wanted to be a candidate himself. He may not have seemed conventionally cheery, but suicidal?"

"It seems to me you may have been wrong, there." Juliet observed coldly, typing a couple more characters, and then starting to pack up while she summoned her final words.

"I've heard enough to decide that we will need to take this investigation further. You have been very helpful. I will be instructing the AIs to trawl for more evidence as soon as I get authorization from my commanding officer. We will need access to all your internal systems to check compliance with the laws on anti-bullying, Control of Systems Hazardous to Health; Prevention of Unwanted Situations of Sexual Intimacy; and protection for those who are exposed to toxic content and datasets. I will be speaking to your CEO within 24 hours. Is that clear?"

CHAPTER FORTY

"WHAT THE HELL DID YOU tell them?" Stella was seething when she appeared on the screen to give the 'dream team' a piece of her mind. She was wearing a red silk dress with a silver pattern woven through it, and a large chunky necklace that screamed expensive in the most vulgar way.

Portia was unsympathetic. She had tried to tip Stella off discreetly over the weekend, but her calls had been ignored and it was not the kind of thing you could put in writing. Especially when the bots were about to start crawling through all the company data. Stella would never have had the sense to be careful. Much though Portia loathed the woman she did not want to set her up. In any case, Stella would think nothing of pinning the blame on her underlings, if it came to it.

"Maybe you could send her a text saying it's a matter of life and death?" Sonny had joked. Perhaps she should have done. The compromise 'PLEASE CALL ME URGENTLY' had yielded nothing.

This video call had been scheduled for weeks. It was supposed to be a quick update on the Endings campaign, as Stella was due to meet Mason for drinks that night. Phase Two had been modified, but there was still a mountain of business going through the books targeting over-70s.

"That suicide liaison officer actually got the hotel to wake me up in the middle of the night! How dare she! Someone actually came up to my room."

If Stella had taken Portia's calls, which would have reached her in Bangkok at a more civilized hour, she could have got a step ahead and enjoyed uninterrupted sleep. But Portia knew better than to point that out.

"I'm travelling on very important business!" Stella ranted on. "You can't expect petty officials like her to understand how international commerce works."

"We really didn't say all that much, Stella. But she insisted on going to the very top." Flattery and reminding Stella of her stratospheric status usually helped to calm her down. The CEO took a big sip from a spectacular red striped cocktail, overflowing with dry ice and cherry blossom, before carrying on.

"I've told her Lars was eccentric. You two know that better than anyone, right? Not client ready. I mean, you give these unconventional geniuses a job and they throw it all back in your face! The idiot! If he comes back from all this, we can't even sack him, now. Not even if he has brain damage!" She was working herself up again.

"This is going to be extremely tiresome. That Juliet seems to have got it into her head that it was exposure to pro-suicide material in the course of his job that may have given Lars the idea. With his IQ, how can that even be possible?"

Portia wanted to diffuse the tension. "Well, we've both been all right, haven't we Sonny?"

"Well, here we are," he piped up, "All in one piece!"

Stella barely heard him. "I'm going to have to check all his training records, whether he's up to date on his mental health program. All that blah blah blah. Please tell me you've both done it?"

"Yes. We're both fully compliant as of this morning." Portia had been keeping up her mandatory training as she went along, whereas Sonny had spent twelve hours in the previous twenty-four banging out online quizzes like they were going out of fashion. Still, what she said was true. They had completed everything, with the deliberate exception of an entry on the PUSSI app.

"Apparently when they closed down the youth aspects of Phase Two, they also tightened up the regulations prohibiting the promotion of suicidal ideation to under-35s." Stella sounded like this was news to her. If she had done her own training, read the briefings she demanded, or even watched the news occasionally it would not have come as such a surprise. "It's not as if it ever got rolled out, is it? I can't be expected to keep up with all these things."

She drained her glass. The straw sucking up the last drops of alcohol made a noise like a miniature drain. Only someone as practiced as Stella could drink something so crammed full of decorations without stabbing herself in the eye.

The three were silently (and unusually) united by fear that Lars' actions could result in disaster for their careers. They could not let the blame for his existential crisis fall on Brytely. Sonny threw out a lifeline. "Some think he might have been depressed because of Holly…"

"Oh, that stupid girl," Stella said, "She should have gone to Doc for her procedures. I could have put them in touch. He's the best in the business and they were on a parliamentary committee together. I'm sure he would have given a good deal to such an influential client. Such a waste."

If anyone knew the best place to get cosmetic surgery, it was Stella. She went on: "It's not been in the press, but everyone in the know knows. She went to one of those industrial estate body shops. It's one thing being allowed to do Botox and veneers after a three-hour course. But liposuction and gastric band under general anesthetic? What's wrong with these people? Does nobody understand that you only ever get what you pay for!"

"Indeed." Portia shuddered, thinking about what had happened to some of the girls she knew back home in Liverpool. Paying a Rodney Street consultant would never be an option for them unless they won the lottery. Like Holly, they had gone to budget operators and more than one of them was now permanently disfigured. They were all still alive, though, as far as she knew.

"I'm going for drinks with Mason shortly. What do I need to say?"

Sonny had already provided Stella with the dashboards which Lars had been responsible for maintaining and a steer on how to present them to Mason. "You just need to stick to the usual format. The numbers are up to date as of Friday. We're in good shape. The enhanced financial incentives are proving popular. There we are a couple of files I wasn't so familiar with on Lars' drive. It looks like there are some new services being trialed in the North-West. They're tied in with the levelling-up agenda. It's all on the dashboard."

"Hang on a minute? What's that?" Portia looked confused. "What new services?"

"I just found out about them this morning," Sonny said, "I'll tell you about it later, Portia. It's a bit complicated to go into it now."

Stella was scrolling through the dashboards on a handheld screen. "There's lots of lovely green here," she drawled. "Super. The figures are good, and we all know how much Mason loves his numbers, don't we? And what about this incident? What do I say?"

This time Portia was ready with the answer. "Say nothing, Stella. It hasn't come out publicly that Lars even worked here. Not yet, in any case. Mason has never met him. He does not even know his name."

Stella nodded. "Of course. Not client ready. Thank God I got that right." She pulled a twisted wooden twig out of her glass and bit into a red Maraschino cherry speared on the end of it before announcing, "Right, I'm off." She heaved herself onto her towering red patent ankle boots and slipped out of the stuffy little VC suite, leaving behind three empty cocktail glasses and an untouched bowl of wasabi-coated nuts as the final image fading from the screen.

Mason was waiting for her in the most exclusive cocktail venue in town. It had become the place to be seen since it had been used as a location for a Jason Bourne film. Stella sidled up to him and proffered her usual two air kisses. Bathed in violet light, their reflection danced in fragments between the rows of bottles that adorned the mirrored wall behind a troupe of flawlessly attractive bar staff.

"Mason, darling!" she drawled, almost overwhelming him with Polarizing – a pungent modern scent with hints of cilantro – developed by one of her other clients. He held his breath and tried to pull away a little. It was no use; it would be too obvious.

"Your speech was incredible. As always, you are quite the star!" There was something a little salacious about the way she eyed the rippling biceps beneath his crisp shirt. He flashed her a smile optimized for suggesting modesty – his eyebrows raised a little, the corners of his eyes just crinkly enough. His teeth picked up the violet light in a way that was quite unsettling. "Classic gin and tonic?" he suggested. "Oh yah. Perfect choice. Double."

"I have had the most ghastly call from home," she confided after the first sip, so disarmed by Mason's compelling charm that she disregarded Portia's advice not to bring up Lars. "Something to do with an unfortunate incident on Westminster Bridge. Have you heard about it?"

He nodded, expressionless, and waited for her to continue.

"The silly man has a connection of sorts to Brytely. It seems that your friend Jasper has intervened to stop them turning the fellow's life support off. No one would want to upset the head Yuthie, would they? The idiot addressed his final words to him, so now he won't let him die."

Mason looked at her directly. She thought she might have blushed.

"Jasper always gets what he wants," Mason said.

Stella decided, then, that it would be best not to say any more about Lars. It was obvious. The more distance she could put between the idea of him and Brytely, for the time being at least, the better. Mason did not need to know that Lars had been working on The Corporation account, did he?

"That's enough about me," Stella emptied her glass and signaled the barman to bring another. Mason's was still full. He put his hand over the top of it. "I'm training in the morning," he said, "With a local chapter of the BERKs. We like to get out before the sun comes up. Too hot here otherwise. You should come with us."

"Not my thing." Stella never exercised in public. She liked people to think her trim, sculpted physique was effortless. Mason understood the truth better than most, but then they both knew a few of each other's secrets. Casting around to get the conversation away from Lars, she thought she should attempt to say something intelligent about the news. The cover of an international business magazine she had seen in an airport business lounge popped into her head.

"China is ever so worrying, isn't it?" she ventured.

Mason nodded sagely, "Indeed. Where will it all end?" he said. She decided that could not possibly be a literal question and switched the conversation to a lighter subject she knew was dear to Mason's heart.

"How is your art collection coming along?"

"Very well." His grey eyes sparkled.

"I had wondered," she leant towards him furtively, placing an icy manicured claw on his warm arm, "Whether you might be the mystery collector who bought that recovered Fakesy. But then again, Fakesy collectors are just as elusive as the artist, aren't they?"

CHAPTER FORTY-ONE

"**W**E HAD HOPED UMA WOULD be a doctor,"
Ayesha confided in Lexi as their car sped
across South London to St Teddy's Hospital. As soon
as she got the call, Lexi had gone to collect her friend,
finding her waiting at the gate in a subtly stylish grey
tr-AID-lib leisure suit and bronze trainers, her black hair
tied into a neat French plait. "But all the tutoring in the
world could not get her good enough grades."

"She's a tremendous credit to you," Lexi countered,
unzipping her hoodie a little. She was starting to find the
car stuffy. "No one makes it to chief pharmacist at a top
London teaching hospital without being one of the best.
If she were one of the kids from my school, I would be
shouting it from the rooftops."

Ayesha nodded, "You're right, of course. I shouldn't be
so critical. It's not as if Ajay and I followed conventional
professional careers. Our parents were terribly disappointed when we decided to get into franchising. Fried
chicken takeaways were hardly the dream they had for us
when they sent us off to university. But when we were able
to sell the business for millions and never have to work

again, we were fully vindicated. I didn't want Uma to end up in catering, though. It's repetitive work. And now with all the food laws, well, all I can say is we sold at just the right time."

"Her working at St Teddy's has worked out pretty well for us today," Lexi said. "Are you sure she will be able to get us in?" She needed to keep talking if only to take her mind off the feeling of dread that she could not shake off. As far as she was concerned, it would be the best result if they failed to gain admission. It was hard to turn Ayesha down, as it was the Easter holidays, and school was closed. Bob was at work and thought Lexi was at a Pilates class. Her friend had been there for her when she needed support. Now it was her turn to repay the favor.

"Uma used to manage the drugs for the patients in intensive care. She knows everyone in that part of the hospital and was able to make a few enquiries. Apparently, Father Al has already been transferred out to a private Catholic medical facility, specializing in treating paraplegics. His injuries were so bad that he would have gone straight to palliative care in this place. The bishop intervened. As for Lars, it seems they are at a loss to find his family or indeed anyone who was close to him. When I explained that I had met him…"

"You said that?"

"Well, it's true! Admittedly, not for very long. Anyway, I told them that Amina had been to his flat and had given me some ideas for helping to bring him round. That was what clinched it. They were pleased to make arrangements. Uma is not exactly overjoyed that her daughter has been involved with this fellow. But she can't say no to her mother."

At the entrance to Chris Whitty Ward, they went through the usual hospital decontamination procedures. While being held in an airlock, they were bathed in ultra-violet light and sprayed with a disinfectant gas that left a faint metallic taste in the mouth.

"I'm not sure I can do this," Lexi said suddenly as the inner doors slid open. Her legs felt like they were going to buckle, and cramp was starting to grip her gut.

"Of course you can," Ayesha grabbed her hand. "All we are doing is paying him a little visit. Look, here's Uma."

There was no mistaking Ayesha's daughter. She had the same warm smile and casual elegance as her mother, although her hair was cut shorter and her figure a little more curved. "This all seems a bit crazy," she said after introducing herself to Lexi and dropping her professional façade for a moment. "I'm glad it's you two here and not Amina. She pretends to be tough, but you don't have to be her mother to work out how upsetting all of this has been."

Lexi smiled sympathetically. "Don't beat yourself up about it. The Yuthies are all over the place. We've even had them showing up in school. It's impossible to keep their poison away from the kids. But I'm sure Amina will be able to put all this behind her. She has the support of a wonderful family."

"It's kind of you to say so." Uma's voice betrayed her self-doubt. "Anyway, you'll never guess what else has happened today. Jasper actually came in. The whole hospital has been talking about it."

Lexi shuddered, wondering what further punishment the Yuthie leader might want to inflict on Lars, after he had the temerity to criticize him in his monstrous tirade.

Ayesha leaned close to her daughter. "Are you serious?"

"Oh, yes. He had a meeting with the chief exec," Uma confided in hushed tones.

"Lars is still alive, isn't he?" Lexi asked, "Only it wouldn't surprise me if ..."

Raising a hand to reassure her, Uma said, "He's fine. Well as fine as anyone can be if a machine is doing their breathing for them. The only way he'll die in the near future is if there is a decision to turn him off. That's highly unlikely now. Jasper came here to make sure Lars lives. That poor man resigned his own right to freedom, choice and independence the second he hit the water. Jasper was adamant. No one is to activate the Do Not Resuscitate policy. It's an exceptional situation. They normally turn off attempted suicides within 48 hours. Right now, he has a chance of recovery, but if he's not come round in the next few days, they'll put him into deeper sedation which is harder to come back from. If he were over seventy, he'd be in the mortuary by now."

"So, if he were my age his number would be up! Charming!" Ayesha exclaimed.

Her daughter put her right. "Not if I had anything to do with it, Mum. In this case they had to promise Jasper that Lars would be kept alive indefinitely. Otherwise, he was going to kick up an almighty stink. After what happened to Holly, the Yuthies are keen to avoid losing any more high-profile party members. One casualty can be written off as an accident, but two starts to look careless.

It's a big turn-off for the voters. I'll take you to him. You should have about an hour before anyone comes to check on him. He's being remotely monitored. We don't have a lot of human staff in this department. In any department, really."

The last time Lexi had seen someone on a ventilator she had ended up being plagued by terrifying nightmares for months. Now, just as her sleepless nights had been starting to abate, the riot had triggered a relapse. Nevertheless, she kept putting one foot in front of the other, still gripping Ayesha's hand tightly. By the time Uma left them at the entrance to room number 101, Lexi's throat was aching from tension and the rest of her body felt numb.

"Come on," Ayesha said, sensing her friend's fragility. "We've got this. You and I are the only ones who can help him, now. Take a big, deep breath."

Lars lay limp on the bed, the top half of his scrawny body slightly elevated. From the top of his chest down, he was covered in a pale, disposable hospital sheet that did nothing for his grey complexion. Wisps of his thin, black hair splayed out on the pillow. Seeing someone so young hooked up to so many tubes felt all wrong.

"I've only ever seen him wearing a Slayer T-shirt," Lexi said. She wondered what they had done with Lars' clothes and the jewelry from his piercings. His chest rose and fell with the regularity of a metronome as the machine filled and emptied his lungs. She was reassured by the temporality of the pipes and mask that were held in place with a few elastic ribbons and pieces of tape. If it came to it, he would have a better chance of survival than poor old Mabel who had been suffocated by an iron unit which no human being could prize away.

Ayesha pulled out a small speaker along with a bulging Yoko Ono Faraday bag.

"That's the one Bob sent you after the party, isn't it?" The thought of that night on Tower Bridge lifted Lexi's spirits. If this room had a window, they might have been able to see the river. But they were shut in a box with no natural light. Why would St Teddy's waste the view on someone who might never wake up?

"And what a lovely thank-you present it was, too. I'm going to have to get my phone out to play him some music, so we will need to be careful what we say," Ayesha explained. She set up the speaker close to Lars' head and started looking on her device for the music which Amina had told her he liked. "Goodness me. This all looks horrible!" she said, "Have you seen these titles?"

Lexi looked down at the screen "I wish Bob was here. He would know which ones are ... erm ... best," Lexi said as she scanned down the list. "Why not put it on shuffle?"

"Good idea. I'll kick off with 'Angel of Death', though. Amina mentioned that one. She remembered him playing it when she went round. What a Romeo! Quite a catchy title, don't you think?"

"But not such a catchy tune!" Lexi gasped as the sound of thrashing guitars and drums filled the room. Both women pulled pained faces before bursting into a fit of nervous giggles.

"I'm going to give him my headphones." Ayesha said, digging them out of her coat pocket and resting them alongside her phone, right next to his ears. The room became more peaceful again, dominated by the soft rhythm of the ventilator. Only if you listened very carefully could you detect the faint leak of fast paced guitar and intense vocals from the vicinity of Lars' head. It was hard to know which sound was more sinister.

"Hello Lars," Ayesha began, giving a quick aside to Lexi, "We are supposed to talk to him to help bring him round. They say he might be able to hear us. That's why I didn't put them right into his ears.

"My name is Ayesha. I'm Amina's grandmother, the one she was going to meet for afternoon tea after she came to your flat. Well, it didn't work out like that in the end, did it? We all got sidetracked." As her friend chattered on, Lexi was soothed by the gentle monologue and began to zone out, absorbed in her own thoughts.

Poor Lars. He had seemed so happy, if a little weird, when he was canoodling with Holly on the Yuthie stand at the Summer Fayre. For two years running, Yuthentic had set up their booth opposite PACE. The first time she saw him he was out at the front, chatting and sniggering with the other kids. Then, last summer, he had spent most of his time at the back of the stand in cahoots with the MP. It was a world away from the deranged behavior he had exhibited on the bridge. In well under a year, something had turned him from a lovestruck misfit into a maniac with a death wish.

"Lexi?" She had slipped into a world of her own. "Lexi?" Ayesha was tapping her arm. "Did you see that?"

"Sorry, I drifted off." Lexi yawned. "It's been a long few days."

"It's just I thought I saw him move."

They both looked hard at his face. It was motionless.

"You can't have done. He looks away with the fairies to me."

"Maybe I imagined it. Did I imagine it, Lars? Can you hear us?" Ayesha touched his shoulder very gently, but he did not register any response.

"We can't go on like this indefinitely," Lexi said. "I mean, if they're not going to turn him off, why are we even here?"

"They might have put him on oxygen, but with no stimulation he has little chance of recovery. This is the only thing we can do," Ayesha said. "Look at him. He probably has parents out there. I'm sure he will feel differently when he knows that someone cares about him."

Lexi was getting restless. Try as she might she could not bring herself to have any sympathy for Lars. He was a Yuthie. As far as she was concerned, that meant only one thing. The enemy. He wanted all the old people to die. Surely this was his karma? To be neither living nor dead. If only the world and his wife hadn't intervened, Lars's wish would be granted by now. And good riddance. Not that she could say any of that out loud. Not to Ayesha. And not with her phone on listening mode. All Lexi wanted was an excuse to be somewhere else.

"Shall I go and get us some coffee, Ayesha? We could both do with it, I think."

"Ah. Thank you for reminding me! I've brought a flask of espresso and a bun. You look like you could use a blood sugar kick."

As Ayesha rummaged in her bag, she carried on talking to Lars, telling him what she was doing, nattering about the reassuring mundanities of life, listing what she had with her – coffee, a plastic box containing a couple of Waitrose hot cross buns and some packets of chocolate mini eggs.

"I have nothing to say to him," Lexi said blankly.

"Look, why don't you sort out the snacks and leave the talking to me?" Ayesha passed across the makeshift picnic and Lexi unenthusiastically arranged the items on the bedside trolly. She was won over when she twisted the top of the flask, and the enticing aroma filled the room. There were a couple of stacking rose gold espresso cups, too.

"That's such a great smell," Lexi said as she handed across Ayesha's little crucible of sweet black liquid.

"Ajay roasts his own. Gets the beans direct from tr-AID-lib. You know what incorrigible foodies we are." She grinned a little. "Do you want one, Lars?"

The ventilator gave another non-committal response on Lars' behalf, filling and emptying his lungs right on cue.

"It's the little things in life that make it worth living, isn't it?" Ayesha declared to Lexi and Lars simultaneously as she savored each tiny sip.

"For us, maybe. A lot of kids don't have enough space in their life to appreciate things like this." Lexi was thinking about the young people she saw every day. Half of them were overwhelmed with anxiety caused by the burden of their parents' expectations, while others seemed permanently lost, finding comfort only in the digital realm despite her unrelenting efforts to convince them of more real-world joys. It was a far cry from her beginnings as a mathematics teacher. "What if he really doesn't want to wake up?"

"You know, young people can be manipulated, too." Ayesha had a stern note alongside her compassion.

"I suppose so. But don't you think it's cruel to keep him alive like this? He's trapped, and all on Jasper's whim."

A loud buzz startled them. For a second Lexi thought it might be a medical alarm, but it was only Ayesha's phone.

"Ajay's with Amina today," she explained. "She has not gone back to university yet. Uma didn't want her to be left on her own after everything that has happened, and her brother Sunil isn't being much help. I need to give Ajay a quick call back. Can you at least try to have a chat with Lars?"

As Ayesha disappeared into the corridor, Lexi tried to force herself to move closer to the bed but instead began pacing the room. Small talk was not her strong point.

"Hello Lars," she began hesitantly. "It's me, Lexi. What do you mean, you didn't recognize me without the balaclava? You can't even see me! Yes, that's it. I'm the annoying woman that tried to stop you jumping. Sorry about that. Still, you can't get away from me, now. And with friends in high places like yours – assuming you'd call Jasper a friend – you could be stuck here for some time."

What else could she say? The sound of the softly whirring machines made her nauseous. It really was just like the sound of the ventilator that suffocated Mabel. She just made it to the chair by the side of Lars' bed as her legs turned to jelly. Breathless and angry, Lexi gripped the side of the bed.

"Do you think I wanted to come here today? Of course not. I've been through a lot recently and I don't like hospitals. Dad looked just like you after the accident. He never regained consciousness. He never knew that Mum was already dead. She had lost so much blood there was no point in even trying. It wasn't fair. They had so many people who loved them. I may have been technically an adult, but I was still their child.

"Dad didn't have influential friends like yours. It was only a couple of weeks before the authorities started saying they were going to disconnect his life support. I wanted to stop them, but the doctors had already made the decision. Nobody else got a look-in.

"For years I have asked myself whether I tried hard enough. If he had been the Prime Minister or somebody famous, they wouldn't have let him die after two weeks, would they? If we'd had lots of money, I could have flown him to a private clinic. But I was just an ordinary teacher. A kid barely out of university trying to hold it together. How I managed not to cry in front of the children I was teaching I'll never know. I went into school every day because I needed to be somewhere normal. Somewhere that wasn't all about the people I loved most in the world being all mangled up. I needed to forget about them, for a while at least, if I was to have any hope of carrying on living myself."

Her breathing was getting faster.

"If you don't mind me saying so, I'm angry with you, Lars, for all this attention-seeking nonsense. Not to mention all the other people you put at risk on the bridge. Goodness only knows what a girl like Amina saw in you.

I think you've blown it there, by the way. But that's no reason for you to give up, is it? Third time lucky?

"I saw you once, with Holly. Quite a conspicuous couple. You with all your half-assed goth get-up, and her with that mane of red hair. You seemed excited to be together. Don't get me wrong, I found her ideas loathsome, but I'm still sorry she died. Body dysmorphia is an illness. They've needed to clamp down on rogue firms offering cosmetic procedures for years. But rich people never die on an operating table in an industrial estate, do they? No one ever goes to prison for it. From the way you looked at her, I can't imagine you ever made her feel bad about herself. You were fond of Holly, weren't you? I'm sure it wasn't your fault she ended up butchered. Don't blame yourself."

Lexi's face was now just a few inches away from his bony shoulder. She wondered whether she was crediting him with feelings he did not have. She held the edge of his pillow. If she wanted to suffocate him, that was all it would take. He was utterly helpless. It would be over in no time. He could get the peace he so obviously craved.

"So, what are you going to do, young man? You need to decide. The hospital will only keep you ticking over until Jasper loses interest. You could be lying in limbo until after the election next year. Whoever wins, you won't matter to anyone in power by then. The tick boxes that are holding off your DNR order will default to clear. An AI will power down your ventilator and you'll be off on a trolly to the hospital furnace. But before that happens, you'll have a year of hallucinations and nightmares, just to keep that sociopath Jasper out of the headlines. Surely that can't be what you want?"

With a decisive jerk, Lexi tugged out the pillow and hugged it tightly into the pit of her stomach, rocking a little on her chair. Lars' head bounced on the mattress. His tubes were swinging around with the sudden change in height, but they remained attached. There was plenty of slack in the pipes and cannulas to compensate for his change in position.

She stroked the mask that was keeping him breathing.

"Why is it you get one of these when Mabel didn't?" she whispered in his ear as she ran a finger round the seal.

The ventilator continued its rhythmic pumping.

"What makes you so special, Lars? Do you have any idea what they did to her? I saw it with my own eyes. All of it. No one cares, of course. You don't care, do you? As far as you're concerned Mabel was just another worthless boomer, and all the old people who have bought into the Endings are simply ticks on a spreadsheet."

Still rocking on the chair, Lexi put her head in her hands and began to wail. It was as if she was back on the floor of the Disposal Center, looking at the bodies queued for the furnace. Why hadn't she been able to get them all out? Why had Mabel not wanted to carry on? The tears flowed fast, and her nose was streaming. It was hard to catch her breath between the sobs.

She lifted the pillow out of her lap, smothered her face in it, and slumped forward, trembling, onto the edge of Lars' bed, where she passed out.

CHAPTER FORTY-TWO

"We've had some weird days in this office," Portia said, huddling with Sonny at the back of the crowded open plan space, "But this knocks the rest of them out of the ballpark."

Every member of staff had been told to come in to Brytely for a compulsory briefing. This had never happened before, and the space was too small to comfortably hold everyone at once.

Instead of being able to breeze through the turnstile, which normally snapped open as soon as it detected the employees' credentials, they were greeted by three stern security guards. Each arrival was patted down and any devices capable of recording sound or images confiscated before they could set foot inside. A short email and non-disclosure agreement had been distributed the night before. Anybody who had not already returned it was marched to the reception desk to sign on the dotted line.

There was an anxious buzz in the room as several dozen young executives were forced to rub shoulders. Worried that Brytely might be about to lay them off, they took some comfort in being part of the crowd. They talked in hushed tones, taking care not to spill their beverages on their fashionable outfits, or to get too close to the sharp edges of the glossy furniture.

Stella tottered on her pale mauve suede ankle boots to a clear lectern at the front, preparing to read from an autocue. She wore a somber black dress, high at the neck with cutaway shoulders and three quarter-length sleeves, unseasonal for the bright June morning. Her wrists were layered with nests of bracelets which jangled when she moved, and those boots would never survive the lightest shower of rain.

Everyone knew that Stella would have preferred to brief them all offsite. She liked any excuse to throw a party in a string of luxurious London locations. And she wasn't normally one for speeches. Today was going to be different. The subject matter had been judged too sensitive to be discussed anywhere but on their own premises, never mind the space constraints.

"I don't think I've ever seen her look scared before." Portia was sure that Stella's hands were shaking. "Am I reading this right?"

"It's got to be about Lars," Sonny said. "I can't think what else would make them go to all this trouble, can you? Certainly not our Endings stuff. Now they've made a big noise about protecting the children it's all back on track. There is even growing support for opening up the Kindness Centers to new categories of consenting adults, provided of course they keep up the rigorous safeguards."

"How much confidence do you have in that, then? The safeguards, I mean?" Before Sonny could answer, Stella called the room to attention.

"The board of Brytely has asked me to give you the following news," she said, her eyes glued to the script to avoid meeting the apprehensive gaze of people who worked for her.

"In response to an incident involving one of our team members, the agency recently commissioned an independent audit of safeguards for the small number of Brytely staff who may be exposed, during the course of their work, to systems or datasets that may be hazardous to health.

"Today, I am pleased to report the auditors' findings. They have concluded that the agency is actively discharging its duty of care and could have done nothing to prevent the unfortunate situation that occurred on Easter Weekend involving one of our employees. Brytely has always maintained that it goes beyond the letter of the law to safeguard its staff. This expert endorsement substantiates that claim.

"While the agency cannot be held responsible for the actions of its team members in every circumstance, we are of course deeply saddened that one person's mental health reached a crisis point. Our employees are our greatest asset. The wellbeing of every single one of you is critical to Brytely's future." She cleared her throat and looked up, trying hard to look like she believed what she had just said.

"The audit recognized that some of our most admired work involves pushing the boundaries of behavioral science. We have always believed that, while developing and implementing such powerful technology, we have a duty to behave ethically. This is especially relevant where we design highly persuasive advertising services to assist our clients' customers in making important life choices."

"Doesn't she mean death choices?" Portia whispered to Sonny, who hissed back, "Shush!"

"All our staff undertake compulsory training and certification in ethical compliance. I am proud to report that every one of you has demonstrated the required understanding in this area. Keep up the good work!

"We have appraised our client, The Corporation, and Yuthentic, who boldly pioneered the humane assisted dying laws, of the results of the audit. They are satisfied that we have acted responsibly at all times, and I am pleased to tell you that, our work on the Endings programs continues." Stella could not hide her relief.

"Finally, I know many of you will be concerned about our dear colleague Lars and the prognosis for his recovery. He is much missed, every day, both for his superb data skills and for being a noteworthy character around the office. Our welfare team is in regular touch with St Teddy's, and we continue to monitor his situation. Lars is in our thoughts and prayers, and we hope very much, one day, to be able to welcome him back to the Brytely family so that he can continue his ground-breaking work.

"Finally, on behalf of the board, I would like to thank you all for your loyalty, your creativity and for making Brytely a privilege to lead and a great place to work.

"Thank you."

Stella lifted her line of sight, forced a smile over the heads of her minions, and headed for the door.

CHAPTER FORTY-THREE

"I NEVER USED TO BE FRIGHTENED of flying," Lexi said. She had just thrown up in the public washrooms in the Departures area of Terminal Two at London's Heathrow Airport.

"Look at me Bob. I'm pathetic." She dabbed her eyes with a tissue and dragged him over to a coffee shop to find something to help settle her stomach. Bob eyed the sausage rolls longingly but put the idea to the back of his mind when Lexi said the smell would make her feel queasy again. While she grabbed a seat in a spot that could accommodate the two of them as well as the extra-large purple wheelie suitcase, he ordered a Frappuccino, some water and a small packet of cookies.

"We're here way too early," Lexi muttered, "And I'm boiling with all these layers on."

"Lucky with the traffic," Bob mused chopping at the ice in his drink with a reusable stainless-steel straw.

"Do you have to do that?" Lexi said, "It's really annoying."

"Well, yes. The ice is blocking it up."

Lexi bit her bottom lip. "Sorry. It's just I can't stand all this hanging around. It's making me feel even worse." She took a sip of water and broke a tiny corner off the cookie. "What flavor are these supposed to be?"

"Ginger. Look, it's got the Tr-AID-lib stamp on it. You've already done one good deed today!" Lexi shook her head. He went on, "Are they nice, anyway?"

"They are, actually." She gobbled up the lot and had another drink. "That's better."

"Look," Bob said, "The bag drop is open. Let's get rid of this monster, shall we? You'll be in the executive lounge having your massage before you know it."

The pre-flight spa treatment had been Ayesha's suggestion. She had been spending a lot of time with both of them since she had found Lexi unconscious on the hospital floor, right next to comatose Lars.

"It's a miracle she didn't have to stay in intensive care!" Ayesha had exclaimed that afternoon. "We're lucky she didn't crack her head open when she fainted. Can you imagine?!"

On returning from work, Bob had found Lexi immobile in an armchair, staring blankly into space, with a cold cup of tea on the table by her side. He was confused. She was not normally like that after Pilates. Ayesha was standing watch and had covered her with a blanket. When Ayesha explained what had happened, Bob thought some music might ease the tension and fiddled about trying to put on Queen and David Bowie's 'Under Pressure'.

As soon as she realized what he was doing, Ayesha snapped, "Will you just turn that nonsense off and give your partner some proper attention! Who knows how this will end if we don't do something?"

Every day for a week, Ayesha came round to keep an eye on Lexi while Bob was at work. To begin with, all Lexi wanted to do was sleep. Ayesha tiptoed around, filling the house with the enticing smell of home baking, bringing snacks to Lexi in bed and sitting with her when she wanted company.

"I can't stop asking myself if I would have actually killed him," Lexi kept saying.

"All that matters is that you didn't." Ayesha squeezed her hand. "Look at you! You don't have a murderous bone in your body. The subconscious is a wonderful thing, even if you wanted to kill that poor boy, you couldn't do it."

"But did I want to?"

"Of course not!"

Lexi would shake her head, and retreat under the covers.

After a few days of repeating the same hopeless conversation, Ayesha decided to put an end to the ritual and coaxed her friend out of bed for a walk. It was cut short when a torrential shower sent them scurrying home. The next day, with some better planning, they made it to the top of Telegraph Hill, where they could look out across London while drinking coffee from a flask and eating flapjacks they had made together. The Nordic Walkers passed by and gave them a wave. It was nice to see their friendly faces.

By the time the summer term started, Lexi was well enough to hold things together in the classroom, but at home she was still asking the same question, over and over again.

"Could I have killed Lars?"

But nobody could give her the right answer.

Even her old friend Alice, who lived on the other side of the world, was starting to lose patience when their phone calls were dominated by Lexi's fears. As a doctor, Alice found it hard to understand why Lexi was refusing to seek medical help. How could her getting therapy be such a risk when everything was enshrined in a code of ethics? When Lexi told her that The Corporation had been using people's confidential medical records to target them with advertising, Alice refused to believe it. She was convinced that her friend was developing paranoia on top of her anxiety.

"If you won't see a therapist over there, Lexi, why not come over to New Zealand?" Alice eventually suggested. Her psychotherapist had had a client disappear in the middle of a course of treatment, leaving a series of gaps. "And we can have a proper catch-up. Hang out together. We can make up for lost time on my last visit to London. All that stuff with Mum. It was hardly a picnic."

When Lexi floated the idea with Bob, he thought she should go. The problem was that he could not accompany her. Not even for a few weeks. He had used up the last of his holiday in the summer half term when, with time to brood at home, Lexi had another dip. There were only so many emergency dental appointments he could fake before the HR AI started to ask questions. Nobody at work could find out about Lexi's mental state. His security clearance would be compromised.

"I definitely think it's worth a shot," Bob agreed when Lexi told him about Alice's invitation. With the bonus he had received for his work on the BERK bikes, he had enough to cover the therapy fees and even pay for Lexi to upgrade to First Class. "Without me there to show you up," he had said, "You can travel in style. Have a cocktail. Book yourself a manicure and all that."

CRAP had supplied a tribe of service robots to look after the passengers in economy, but the airline had stopped short of putting them in First. With actual people looking after her, Bob thought there would be less chance of Lexi freaking out on the flight, than if a robot leant across to flip up her table.

"Let me know if Alice and Dolly like their presents, won't you?" Bob babbled on as they approached the entrance to the Security check zone. He had sent Faraday bags: Blue Oyster Cult for Alice, and a K-pop band all the eleven-year-old Kiwis were mad about for Dolly.

It was time for their goodbye hug. "You're going to have a brilliant time!"

"I wish you could come with me," Lexi squeaked, her face buried in his fleece, fighting back the tears and clinging to him tightly. He might not be perfect, but she always felt safe when she was with Bob.

"It's only for five weeks. I'm not going anywhere. Unless you count going round to Bryn and George's to meet their new cat."

He could feel her breathing deeply into his shoulder. Lexi had been practicing that a lot recently. When he gently kissed the top of her head, she relaxed a little and looked up.

"Right. Time to get moving. I don't know what it was that made me feel so sick. I've always loved going on planes, right?"

She did one last check of her documents.

"See you soon, then sweetie," she forced a grin. "I'm going to be fine." Another big breath and her shoulders dropped a little more.

"Of course you are. Go on. Don't forget to listen to the playlist I've done for you on the plane."

"Yep. Golden Years, right?"

"That's the one. Because when you get back, Lex, that's what lies ahead for you and me."

With one last kiss, Lexi turned and walked briskly towards the security gates. Bob watched until the metal doors had slid firmly shut behind her. He popped in his ear buds and turned on the playlist.

CHAPTER FORTY-FOUR

"I ALWAYS THOUGHT I'D RESIGN BEFORE you," Portia said, trying not to appear flustered. "But then I would need another job to go to. And who would want me?"

"You'd be surprised." Sonny smiled conspiratorially and inched nearer. They had not been so physically close since the evening at her flat.

Was he thinking the same thing as her? In a matter of weeks, they would no longer be constrained by the Brytely PUSSI policy. Sonny would delete the app on which they were obliged to self-report within 24 hours of intimate contact with a co-worker.

"So where are you going?" She tried to sound pleased for him. "It must be good to leave behind all this." She waved at the thrash metal band gazing down on them from the meeting room wall. Anthrax had recently been renamed Slayer, in a tribute to Lars, and the artwork swapped out. They all looked the same to Portia. It was just another group of sad white men in black clothing, pretending to be scary, sporting beards and guitars.

"I'm not supposed to tell anyone. Stella says there's going to be an announcement in *DUPE*."

Trust their boss to have a hotline to *Digital Uses for Persuasive Excellence,* her favorite trade rag.

"Saying she's sad to be losing you?"

"Gutted, obviously, but she's putting on a brave face."

"So you're not going to tell me who your lucky new employer is, then?"

"I'm not supposed to." He was reveling in his secret. "But I might be persuaded."

Portia was curious, but she was running out of patience with Sonny's games. She was resentful about the way he had been playing with her emotions since Easter weekend and annoyed that he still held any sway over her. It wasn't like his performance in the bedroom had been anything to write home about.

"What would it take for you to spill the beans? A blackmail threat, maybe? I could probably come up with a convincing one," Portia batted back.

Portia felt even more aware than usual of the gulf between her and Sonny's background. It did not seem fair that she had the most to lose and now of the three of them – herself, Lars and Sonny – she was the last person standing in the award-winning Endings campaign team.

With her mum out of work, Portia needed her job at Brytely more than ever, but longed for an alternative. Over recent weeks, she had covered for Sonny without asking any questions when it was obvious that he was going to job interviews. He could show a bit more gratitude for her loyalty, especially when he knew her out-of-work mother lived bang in the middle of the region where the

Endings were now being targeted at the unemployed over-35s under the Yuthie's levelling-up agenda.

"I'm sure you'll have Lars back soon to keep you company," Sonny speculated.

"What's second prize?"

"Anyway, I wanted to ask you something." He was still very close.

"Go on."

"Nan and Grandad have gone away on another one of their big holidays. They've asked me to look after the house for them. I was wondering whether you might like to come over. Return to the scene of our original, well, you know? Let me cook you dinner. We won't be working together anymore, so it would be fun to stay in touch, wouldn't it?"

She looked at him and thought: So that's why they call them 'come to bed' eyes. "When did you have in mind? You know how busy I am."

"As soon as I've left. Just to avoid any complications."

"I'm sure we can work something out," Portia said casually, "You have to tell me more about your new job, though. How did you get it, anyway?"

Sonny avoided looking at her.

"Oh, I met the head guy. It was ages ago. He sent me a text and it led on from there."

"Mason! I always thought The Corporation would come back for you." Portia had seen the way Mason looked at Sonny.

"No. It wasn't him. I wouldn't want to go back there, anyway. The environment was stifling."

"So, it's excitement you're after, then?"

Sonny raised his eyebrows and shrugged. "To be honest, I'd simply settle for a little more money in a job no less interesting than what we do here. My move promises to meet or exceed those criteria."

"Good for you." She did not want him to think that she never had any approaches. "I had a text once, you know, from someone influential. I never told you. You and me weren't getting on so brilliantly at the time."

"Us? Not getting on? When was that? I must have blinked and missed it!"

It was Portia's turn to shrug now. "Anyway, it's not important."

"Oh, come on. Who was it?" She could see he was racking his brains trying to work out who could possibly have been interested in her. "Tell me?"

"I just deleted it."

"Some grand fromage sent you a text and you didn't even reply? That's not how you play the game."

"I didn't want to get involved."

"Who was it?"

"Someone despicable."

Portia started counting in her head, determined not to speak again until Sonny told her who he was going to work for. She folded her arms and looked directly at him while he pushed his fingers through his hair and looked shiftily around the room. By the time he plucked up the courage to speak, she had guessed.

"I can understand it," she conceded, "I mean, Charles Manson isn't hiring."

Sonny appeared more uncomfortable than she had ever seen him. "You can see why I didn't want to tell you.

Please don't be like this."

"Actually, you've done me a favor, Sonny. In comparison my job suddenly seems like a walk in the park. And that's saying something!"

"Oh Porsh, I couldn't turn it down. I don't feel free here. You know my mum got me this job. Everybody knows. I need to show them I can do it on my own."

"Great. On the back of our combined achievements, you get promoted into working for Yuthentic. You're a complete shit."

"You could come with me…" She suspected as much. She would never tell Sonny it was Jasper's cheeky text she had deleted the night of the Yuthentic rally.

"Dear God! Then they came for the Scousers. But I said nothing because I was not a Scouser. That might work for you, Sonny, but what about me? They have targeted my mother. And you think I'd consider…"

Sonny's stance shifted to defensive. He stuck out his chin. "And anyway, I'm sorry, but I have to agree with a lot of what they stand for. Why shouldn't people who are ready to go have a choice to leave early and make things easier for those they leave behind. You know – 'freedom, choice…' "

"Shut the fuck up. You have no idea what most people's lives are like. What it means to be desperate or how being poor screws with the concept of choice. I can't decide whether you're incapable of imagining it, or you simply don't want to. You're talking like you've actually joined the party."

His face did not move.

"You've joined the party."

"If you work there you have to be in sympathy with their aims. Joining is just a fee that proves your commitment. Anyway, all the Yuthie policies are great for people like you and me. I don't see the problem."

"You know what, Sonny? I might have to work for the enemy for the time being, but I sure as hell ain't sleeping with them. With you out of the way and Lars under sedation I'm going to be making some changes around here. No one is ever going to target my mum with an assisted suicide campaign again. So think of me, when you are tucking into that dinner for one in that beautiful house. Think of me, when your grandparents cave into the propaganda, and you inherit your millions but there is nobody left to share it with. I may have indulged in the odd moment of following you about like a lovestruck puppy, but please, don't ever, ever, ever invite me anywhere again. Whatever this was – and I'm not sure it was ever anything at all – it's now well and truly over."

CHAPTER FORTY-FIVE

B OB HAD LEFT LEXI A handwritten note, propped up on the kettle. It was scrawled in his dreadful messy handwriting on a bit of cardboard he had salvaged from the recycling bin. It said:

1. I LOVE YOU

2. HAVE FUN AT SCHOOL

3. CHECK SPLUTTER – DON'T FORGET!

BOB XXX

Lexi sent him a quick text saying that she loved him too. She could not help wondering why he had been in such a peculiar, over-excited mood since she had flown back from New Zealand. He said he was just glad that she was back.

Still struggling with jet lag from the flight just a few days before, she decided to skip the pre-work swim she had planned, stay in bed a little longer, and treat herself to an auto to school. Her therapist would approve of her being kinder to herself. She would be able to tell her about it in a few days, when they had their next session, via an encrypted link.

Rather than getting the peace she had longed-for in the car, however, Lexi found herself glued to Splutter. As a broad smile spread across her face, she was grateful that Bob had tipped her off.

It seemed that Fakesy had paid another visit to Charlton Green.

Unlike the first time, however, when the apparition of Ziggy Stardust had appeared on the steel door to Bob's server room, on this occasion the artist had not been formally invited onto the premises.

Ardua was hiding in her office, wishing she could lock the door and pretend nothing had happened. Instead of standing at the gate to greet the children, which she usually did on the first day of term, she had dispatched the first teacher she could find to stand sentinel. It had crossed her mind to call a private security firm, but the optics would be terrible.

She had a feeling the art attack might have something to do with Lexi. After all, the woman had gone berserk when she found out that the school had sold off the Ziggy Stardust door. It was ridiculous for someone her age to be so sentimentally attached to a picture of a dead pop star. Ardua had told her in no uncertain terms that she did not have to ask the permission of a junior member of staff to do a little remodeling.

Mind you, Lexi had been right about Holly. Putting her on the board of governors had turned out to be a mistake. Of all the Yuthies they could have sent, Charlton Green had to get the one with body dysmorphia. Hardly role model material. You didn't want to be taking any chances with the Happiness Index. Someone with too long a memory even brought up the unpleasant business with May. She had to give Lexi some credit for helping them all recover from that. Empaths. If only they didn't have to get emotionally involved all the time.

The Corporation had rubber-stamped the sale. The stunt had served its purpose. When it was first installed, they had both got so much out of the publicity. And when they heard a Yuthie print would replace it, well, they were hardly going to complain, were they? Not long after she told them they were swapping it out, an agent based in Mayfair got in touch on behalf of an anonymous buyer. He offered an eyewatering amount for Ziggy and even paid for the replacement of the triple-bolted steel security door that served as its canvas.

Now, as if by magic, they had acquired a new Fakesy Bowie.

She would pretend to the staff that she knew it was going to happen and had been sworn to secrecy by the enigmatic artist. This one was more prominent, and instead of a glamorous 70s rocker, he had chosen a more sinister persona of the chameleon-like performer.

There, on the front door of the school, for all to see, was Fakesy's interpretation of the cover of David Bowie's Diamond Dogs, with a contemporary twist.

Being a woman with few cultural references, the subtleties of Fakesy's choice were lost on Ardua. Her heart skipped a beat after she turned to the internet for background and stumbled across a description of the original illustration. The first, uncensored version of the painting had been deemed by the record company too obscene to use. Breaking into a sweat she immediately checked the image she had seen online against Fakesy's latest gift. Thank goodness. The ghastly thing seemed inappropriate for children as it was, but she was thankful it had no genitals on show.

Fakesy's spokesperson had explained that the artwork represented the immortal creative spirit, adapting to survive in a world where people were constantly using technology to manipulate and destroy each other. They gloomily postulated that it was already too late to stop bad actors using the machines against 'the rest of us'. Individuals would have to consider hybridization to take back power.

Instead of Bowie's original half-man, half-animal crossbreed, Fakesy had given the Bowie-esque figure the powerful hindquarters of a robot dog. In the background, two distorted figures sported other cybernetic modifications.

A footnote mentioned George Orwell's *Nineteen Eighty-Four*, the novel that provided Bowie's inspiration for Diamond Dogs, universally recognized for its chilling exploration of life under a totalitarian regime. This mural, Fakesy claimed, was following in the same tradition.

Ardua doubted any of the children would understand what he was going on about. They had removed that depressing book from the school curriculum long ago.

PLAYLIST

IN ORDER OF APPEARANCE

Can't Get You Out of my Head
Kylie Minogue (2001)

You're Gonna Go Far, Kid
The Offspring (2008)

Wannabe
The Spice Girls (1996)

Ashes to Ashes
David Bowie (1980)

Pinball Wizard
The Who (1969)

Sweet Child O' Mine
Guns 'n' Roses (1987)

Glad to See You Go
The Ramones (1977)

Suzy is a Headbanger
The Ramones (1977)

Rockaway Beach
The Ramones (1977)

Drop Dead Gorgeous
Republica (1996)

Creep
Radiohead (1993)

Tainted Love
Soft Cell (1981)

Relax
Frankie Goes to Hollywood (1984)

Relight My Fire
Take That (1993)

Desperado
The Eagles (1973)

Are 'Friends' Electric?
Tubeway Army (1979)

God Knows I'm Good
David Bowie (1969)

Life on Mars?
David Bowie (1971)

Motherfucker
Robbie Williams (2016)

Angels
Robbie Williams (1997)

Queen Bitch
David Bowie (1971)

Heroes
David Bowie (1977)

Stairway to Heaven
Led Zeppelin (1971)

Sorted For E's and Wizz
Pulp (1995)

Respect
Aretha Franklin (1967)

Starman
David Bowie (1972)

Angel of Death
Slayer (1986)

Ziggy Stardust
David Bowie (1972)

Diamond Dogs
David Bowie (1974)

Get the Party Started
Pink (2001)

Instant Karma
John Lennon (1970)

Black Superman (Muhammed Ali)
Johnny Wakelin (1974)

Waterloo
Abba (1974)

The Bump
Kenny (1974)

If You Can't Give Me Love
Suzi Quatro (1978)

Rockin' All Over the World
Status Quo (1977)

Does Your Mother Know?
Abba (1979)

Imagine
John Lennon (1971)

Aladdin Sane
David Bowie (1973)

Let's Go To Bed
The Cure (1983)

Tomorrow Belongs To Me
Joel Gray, Cabaret (1972)

Riders on the Storm
The Doors (1971)

Singin' In The Rain
Gene Kelly (1952)

Trampled Underfoot
Led Zeppelin (1975)

Brain Damage
Pink Floyd (1973)

Brain Damage
Eminem (1999)

Dark Side of the Moon
Pink Floyd (1973)

Express Yourself
Madonna (1989)

Justify My Love
Madonna (1990)

Under Pressure
Queen and David Bowie (1981)

Golden Years
David Bowie (1976)

Available on Spotify at:
https://open.spotify.com/playlist/2HhX34mU
EmeRDOJKjNFNoh?si=e991c0e053ef4f3c

ACKNOWLEDGEMENTS

Knowing that the *Rockstar Ending* series has a future on TV has been a bit of a distraction from finishing *Rockaway*. But here we are.

It has been great fun reimagining Blackpool. I grew up in Southport, only a short drive away, and the annual pilgrimage to the Illuminations was a much-anticipated treat.

However, my trips to 'the lights', as we called them, were not like everyone else's.

I was taken there for my birthday by our family friend the former state executioner, Albert Pierrepoint, and his lovely wife Ann. Bob's blissful memories of dozing in the back of the warm car as the last illuminated frieze disappeared, mirror mine.

My mother, Peggy Rossi, and I spent many long afternoons at our local fairgrounds, in the days when the rollercoasters came without seatbelts. Screaming, we hung on for dear life, time and again. It was always more interesting than going down the pier, although that was not without its charms. And I was forever cadging a coin for a game of pinball.

The scenes set around Westminster are rooted in my shamefully distant past as an activist in the 1980s. I was rubbish when things got violent – as they did in Thatcher's Britain – and burst into tears at the merest hint of someone being manhandled. I was more comfortable making posters, lobbying politicians, and giving conference speeches.

Aspects of my former career, both as a lobbyist and in the corporate world, have informed the book and, I hope, have made it credible while being entirely fictitious.

Thank you to Tom and Louise Crawley for inviting me to a fabulous party on Tower Bridge some years ago. Using it as the location for the shindig in this story was a no-brainer.

David Walton and Barry Ryan at Free@LastTV have encouraged me from my very first steps into creating the Rockstar Ending world. I would never have been brave enough to start my first novel without them. Working together on the screen adaptation is a dream come true.

I have had a ton of support from family and friends. Among them my cousins, the Convent Coven, the Orwell Society, the Blackheath Divas and fellow travelers in the London writing community who have made me feel most welcome. Being invited to read an extract from Rockstar Ending at the Hilly Fields Fayre – where a few scenes in previous books have been set – was a highlight of my 2021.

I'm honored to hear from readers and friends from all over the world who have enjoyed the first two books and will keep trying to live up to your expectations.

Thanks as always to Tim Doyle for smashing it with yet another mind-blowing cover illustration. Geraldine Brennan, my editor, completely gets what I'm trying to do and pulls out all the stops so we can produce something to be proud of. Glendon Haddix at Streetlight Graphics ensures the finished books look great.

It is not a coincidence that this book was published on 8th January 2022, which would have been David Bowie's 75th birthday. I am forever indebted to him, and to George Orwell, for creative inspiration.

Simon, Amelia and Charlie. You are the biggest rockstars in my life. Thank you for everything.

If you are curious about the years preceding the Rockstar Ending series, you can download the FREE INTRODUCTORY NOVELLA

For Those About to Rock

at nicolarossi.com where you can also join my mailing lists to find out about news, releases and promotions

WOULD YOU WRITE A REVIEW?

If you have enjoyed *Rockaway* it would mean a lot to me if you could spend just five minutes leaving an honest review on Amazon.

As an independently published author, I don't have the resources to promote my books very widely, and reviews from people who have read my work can make a huge difference by bringing it to the attention of other readers.

ALSO BY N. A. ROSSI

For Those About to Rock

Introductory novella for the
Rockstar Ending series – FREE from nicolarossi.com

When Bowie-obsessed IT guy Bob leaves his job in a bank
to work in school surveillance he is expecting an easy life.
He could not be more wrong.

Rockstar Ending

The first book in the Rockstar Ending series

London, 2027. An ordinary woman discovers she is capable of extraordinary things. When Lexi finds out that
older people are being coerced into genocide by stealth,
she vows to take on the sinister corporation behind the
ultimate Rockstar Ending.

Rock On

The second book in the Rockstar Ending series

They came to kill her best friend's elderly mother. Now
Lexi can't rest until she has exposed the sinister corpora-

tion behind the hidden genocide. When she hits on a way to grab the headlines, she's in serious danger. If they find out what she has done, Lexi and her soulmate Bob will lose everything.

Join the mailing list to stay in touch with the author and be one of the first to know when the next book in the series will be available at nicolarossi.com.

ABOUT THE AUTHOR

N. A. (Nicola) Rossi has lived in London most of her life, moving there from the seaside town of Southport in the early '80s. After studying English Literature at UCL, she flirted briefly with journalism, and then began a 30-year career in communications management, eventually running international teams for big technology companies.

In 2017 she was awarded an MA in Digital Media from Goldsmiths University. That was when the trouble began. She started to write about surveillance, data ownership, consent and the potential for people to be manipulated without their knowledge.

Her debut novel, *Rockstar Ending*, started life as a short story, 'One Last Gift', which won a dystopian fiction award from the Orwell Society. The judges described it as 'highly original, macabre and very funny'. It was published in the *Journal of Orwell Studies*.

Nicola is a regular blogger on technology, society and the arts. She has lectured in universities on leadership, PR, ethics and corporate social responsibility and consults on communications management. She has appeared on *BBC Radio 4 Today*, BBC local radio, and written for a wide range of media outlets including *The Independent, Time Out, Louder Than War* and *Influence*.

She lives in south-east London with her husband and two adult children.

nicolarossi.com

Lightning Source UK Ltd.
Milton Keynes UK
UKHW012201211221
396039UK00001B/157